The Druid of Boston Common

E. N. McMAHON

DEDICATION

Once again, to Kevin.

ACKNOWLEDGMENTS

Thank you to Kevin, without whose encouragement and insight the book could not have been written. Thanks to Matt Smith for his great cover art. Thank you to Graeme Hurry for a keen eye and a willing spirit.

CHAPTER ONE

Halfway down the Atlantic seaboard, in a garret room overlooking Philadelphia's Rittenhouse Square, Ben Owen opened a geometry textbook. Geometry was not his favorite subject, or his best, although he did admire its rigid clarity. But a jobbing graduate student, if he hopes to pay his board and room, learns to teach what pays him.

Outside the dormer window, a cold wind rushed through the bare branches. The windowpanes rattled, and the roof creaked. With a high-pitched twitter, a bat wheeled by in the iron-colored sky - incongruous on this cold fall evening. Slightly uneasy, Ben glanced around him. His gaze rested a moment on a picture propped against his reading lamp: a photo of his father, in front of the Druid's Den.

The photo had been taken in a springtime long ago, when the walls were overgrown with ivy, the trees thick with foliage, and the daffodils fully in bloom. High in the distance, across the expanse of Boston Common, the golden dome of the State House gleamed in warm sunlight. His father stood in the doorway of the Den, dappled in the shadow of a mighty oak. His white hair was ruffled by a breeze, and his light-colored eyes were both piercing, and kindly. His hand was raised, as if issuing a mild directive.

Ben chuckled, for he was not alone in considering direction to be his father's customary mode. There were many people in Boston - and far tougher customers than he - who felt the same way. Like his father, Ben loved books and learning. He pursued literature, and thirsted for knowledge - but not the Druidical kind. For Ben yearned to walk the straight and narrow. Not for him the meandering and whimsical approaches his father so favored. He longed to strike out on his own, and live free from charms and spells and gangsters. He had become resolute in eschewing all things Welsh and Bostonian. He left Boston after a love affair went wrong. But his departure had nothing to do with Ellie, nothing at all. The break-up was meant to be. It was for the best. He had landed on his feet in Philadelphia. Without the distractions of a girl, he was able to focus fully. His mind was sharper, and he could tutor all kinds of subjects, even geometry.

With determined, slightly grim-faced zeal, Ben was about to turn back to his textbook, when he noticed a tall red light glimmering in the photograph. He turned the page, telling himself the light was merely a reflection from the streetlamps. But he was compelled to look at the photograph again.

And Ben could not help but notice this time that the streetlamp outside his window was white, and the light flickering inside the photograph was definitely red. Ben knew what it was, or was supposed to be: a "canyll corfe," a corpse candle, a light that wanders the land like tumbleweed of luminance, and stops wherever a death is imminent. Just superstition, Ben Owen had sniffed when his father first told him; and at the time Ben had been only nine years old. But inside his photograph of the Druid's Den, the light was still flickering: red as claret, and as tall as the picture frame allowed. *Red betokens the death of a man*, he remembered his father intoning, *and the older the man is, the taller the light will rise.*

Ben half-rose from his chair. The geometry text tumbled to the floor. A hollow bottomless ache was spreading through him. A stab of certainty pierced his heart. In that moment, he knew two things with more clarity than he had ever known any postulate of Euclid: Gryffth Owen had this day quit this earth, and Ben Owen was bound to return home.

CHAPTER TWO

The lights from the traffic along Park Street flickered in the dark windows of the Druid's Den. Through the Common, a wind was rising. The fir trees lining the path to the front door swayed, inky dark against the night sky. A branch knocked incessantly against the stained glass window above the Den's broad gleaming bar.

"And most of all," Ben went on, reading from the last stretch of the parchment scroll: "that this city finds peace. May peace, not marble nor the gilded monuments, be my legacy." His voice caught, and he was glad there was no more of the will to read. He had been named his father's heir, with sole charge of the Druid's Den. Was he now expected to keep peace among the gangs, as his father had, and to maintain the Den's overarching neutrality? The city's ley lines marked the boundaries of gang territories - and the Druid's Den was situated on the only point where the lines all converged. The Den acted as an anchor, fixing the ley lines in place. The power the Den held was mighty, and if any neighborhood were to seize it, the tenuous balance among the neighborhoods would be shattered.

Keeping the gangs in order had always been a juggling act. Roxbury's Coup DeGrace was at present allied in a speakeasy operation with King David in the West End,

4

though all that could change. The North End's Alphonse Costa headed up a bootlegging outfit that sparred increasingly with O'Connor in South Boston, who began in gunrunning, but had broader ambitions. And over them all, watching and waiting, were the Bluebloods, who ran the State House, the courts, most of the banks, and the Custom House Tower, with its massive clock. It was too daunting to think about. His brother Tim was better positioned to handle the Den and all its affairs. Tim knew the city better - he was a reporter for the *Transcript*, covering the events of Boston high society. Ben had his life in Philadelphia.

Ben put the parchment aside, and hunched over on his barstool.

The tall, lean-faced man standing at his side patted him on the shoulder. "Wife," he said, addressing the ancient and doll-like woman behind the bar. She stepped forward and refilled Ben's glass.

"Thanks, Maggie," Ben said. "And you, Allyn. It was good of you to stay."

"It's nights like this the drink was made for." Maggie patted Ben's hand. "Glad you're back with us."

Far down the bar, stationed in a pool of near darkness, Tim coughed.

"So that's the way Dad wanted it," Tim said. "Ben in charge. Even though you've been away for so long."

Tim's eyes were blandly blue, heavily fringed with lead-colored lashes, and full of empty light. Ben and Tim had never been especially close. They were too different in temperament. Ben had always been too much of a loner and an eccentric for Tim's tastes, and Tim too priggish and devoted to the ordinary for Ben's. They were even dissimilar in looks. Ben was lanky, thin, and a bundle of nervous gestures. He had a shock of thick black hair, dark hazel eyes, and a pink and cream complexion - features that would have been beautiful in a girl, but in him, hinted of brooding romanticism. Tim, by contrast, was intermediate in coloring, as in all else, slightly stocky, and as placid in mannerism as he was of opinion. Had their mother (long departed) not been the soul of virtue, unkind and treacherous tongues might have wagged.

This evening, the brothers had greeted each other with a stiff handshake, and immediately fallen into an embrace.

"I sure as heck didn't ask to run the Den," Ben said. "You know the city better than -" He flung his right hand out, and thumped Allyn in the chest. "Yikes - I'm sorry, Allyn."

Allyn laughed, and put up his lanky hands in surrender. "Got to staying fighting fit, I do, and see to a few repairs. The last thing your dear old dad said to me, he said: '*Allyn, the pipes have been chunnering.*'" And with a clank of his pliers, Allyn crouched down by the sink.

"How your da loved you, Ben," Maggie said. She polished a tumbler and held it to the light. "You too, Tim."

Ben tapped the parchment scroll. "He stipulated both of you stay on as caretakers."

"Well, this place could certainly use some caretaking," Tim said, glancing around. "And a lot of updating. It's 1924, for goodness sake, not the Middle ages." The room was low-ceilinged, and lined with dark oak planks. The fireplace was blackened with ash. In the corner, firewood was stacked. A small hatchet leaned against the logs and gleamed in the dark. The walls were rough whitewash, and decorated here and with the odd lambing tool - a wool comber, a hoof trimmer, a rusty shearer. They were from Gryffth Owen's childhood, long ago in the north of Wales.

"Dad was a creature of habit," Tim said. "Look at all this junk he held on to. Even that silly little harp." He pointed to the golden harp hung up behind the bar. "He never learned to play it that well."

"He was busy raising you boys," Allyn said, "all on his own, and taking care of the city, too."

"Dad was awful old school," Tim said.

6

"And a good school it is too." Allyn had stuck his head inside the sink cabinet, and his voice sounded hollow.

"President Lowell makes a marvelous distinction between tradition, and dogged backwardness." Tim fingered the rim of his glass. "We've gotten to know each other fairly well, the President and I. I've filled him in on all the gangs. He said he felt like an anthropologist taking field notes in deepest Borneo. He has such a turn of phrase! I've accompanied him to several Harvard functions, and he's always the wittiest one there."

"Don't say." Ben downed more of his drink.

"You could learn a lot from President Lowell," Tim said. "You don't know what you're in for, with the gang leaders tomorrow night, here, in my - our - home."

"It was what your dear father requested," Allyn said, straightening up. "After the first hoar frost, the augurs came fast and thick. A marble goblet crumbled in his hand. When he went to trim a pot of holly, the tendrils withered under his breath. And one dreary night, he saw a coach pass by, shrouded in black it was, and not a sound emerged from the carriage wheels or the horses's hooves." Allyn bowed his head. "He knew his demise was fast approaching. And so he put a paid notice in the *Globe*, a reception for his closest friends."

"Not in the *Transcript*," Tim said. "They probably wouldn't have wanted a notice like that anyway."

"And the lads responded, true to form." Allyn chuckled. "Coup DeGrace sent a letter on ivory linen stationery - such a beautiful copperplate, his hand. And so learned, with a reference to upheavals in the Turkish caliphate."

"Which your dad said he found remarkably apt," said Maggie. "His very words."

"Costa sent a messenger, as grandly turned out as a Renaissance ambassador." Allyn pointed to the front door with his pliers. "Stood there, and bowed deep in greeting."

Maggie laughed. "And recited a '*declaration of purpose*,' he did. Should have heard him go on and on."

"Before he bestowed a cask of Chianti upon us," Allyn added.

"As sour and thin as vinegar, no doubt," Tim said. "Too rustic for any discerning palate."

"And King David?" Ben asked.

"Oh, that one," Maggie replied with a snort. "He dashed off a note, bristling with all kinds of slang, and had it delivered inside a gift."

"Never seen the like," Allyn said. "A mechanical canary that flutters inside a gilded cage, modeled on the Taj Mahal. Up in your da's room now."

Ben smiled. "The kind of gizmo a young pasha would send."

"And intended to be taken as such," Tim said. "President Lowell has long maintained that the Asiatics have a lamentable weakness for ostentation."

"The canary was mute, your da did note," Allyn said. "An admirable trait, I'm sure."

"And O'Connor?"

"He penciled a terse response on the back of an old grocery list, saying he'd be there, and slipped it under the front door. A creature of fire and poetry he is not. But friends to our Owen, they were, and remain, each and every one."

"*Friends?*" Tim raised an eyebrow.

"And your da requested the meeting conclude with a dramatic reading. From *Henry V*," Allyn said. "The St Crispin Day speech. His last wish, and fondest hope."

"Still on that kick." Ben shook his head. Dad and his poetry - Owen had always believed a shared reading of that piece would foster fellow feeling among the gangs.

"He never stopped insisting Shakespeare was Welsh, either." Tim tsked. "President Lowell and I have shared many a chuckle over that bit of foolery. Well, I can't say I envy you, having to keep those barbarians in check. That's what the President calls them. He's being ironic, slightly.

Counterfeiters, gamblers, bootleggers, gunrunners - they're quite a crew. Not to mention that baffling array of primitive traditions they traffic in - voodoo, banshee, strega, kabbalah - they'll stop at nothing, Ben."

"Unlike that clean above-board Blueblood practice of compound interest," Allyn said.

Tim frowned. "It is legally sanctioned. Not merely tolerated, but a veritable bulwark of -"

"Only on account of the Bluebloods run the courts," Maggie said.

"Which are the legitimate sources of -"

"Poor Ben's got to keeps things steady," Allyn said.

"He's up to it," Maggie said. "His da had no doubt."

"I just have to see that things tick over smoothly." Ben swiped a hand through his hair. "Until I go home to Philadelphia, and hand the Den over to Tim."

Tim nodded. "Keeping the Den in the family is the best idea."

"Sounds like it," Ben said.

"You've been away from Boston for so long. And President Lowell has such an understanding of the world. Dad tried to keep up, but he got terribly old this last year. Fidgety, doddering - almost a second childhood."

"I didn't notice that," Allyn said. "Could be that I'm a dodderer myself."

"Only since the turn of the century," Maggie muttered.

"He developed a hankering for sweets," Tim said. "I brought him those little round tins of lemon candies he used to like, from France. And he smiled like a three-year old."

"I thought he liked the blackberry kind," Ben said.

"So he did!" Allyn said. "One of his favorite memories, at the clove of seasons, summer into autumn - the blackberries ripening on bramble bushes all along the River Wye."

"Nothing like a bowl of ripe blackberries," Maggie said. "Takes the sting out of the end of summer."

"And first flush Darjeeling tea," Tim said. "I brought him that too. In an elegant little caddy - black and gold cloisonné. I saw one in the Cabots's house - I was at a reception for the new library they funded - so I got a similar one for father." Tim sighed. "Last I saw, he was storing two-penny nails in it."

"Oh he did love his tea," Allyn said. "But nothing fancy - a strong Welsh brew, red as a brick."

"Kept a pot going all day long," Maggie declared.

"A workman's tastes," Tim murmured.

"Nothing wrong with that," Ben said.

"Not in a workman." Tim looked around the room. "Somebody who knows Boston the way I do could really do things with this Den. For the good of the city, I mean."

"And President Lowell thinks so, too, I'm sure," Ben said.

"As a matter of fact, he does."

"And I bet you're very proud of that." Ben looked down at his drink.

"You know, Ben," Tim said, "just because it didn't work out between you and Ellie Cabot-Lowell is no reason to hold it against all the Lowells. Ellie's barely a Lowell at all. Not really." Tim grinned and leaned forward on his elbows. "The man Ellie was engaged to last summer owns a lovely estate up in Gloucester, right by the water. She must be devastated now that the engagement's off. For all that she says she was the one who broke it. But girls always say that, don't they. And she's gotten fat. Even her ankles!" His face brightened. "It's sad."

"You're sure they have your best interests at heart, these Bluebloods?"

"Of course. They respect me. I can really bring this family along."

Ben looked down at his drink. "I didn't know we needed to be brought along."

"Gryffth Owen brought the world around him along," Maggie retorted. "If you don't mind my saying."

"Dad may have been hot stuff for the Druid circuit," Tim said, "but he never could have hacked it at it Harvard."

Ben scowled. "I bet you've told your new friends that, too."

Tim blinked his long, leaden-colored ashes, and nodded. If they'd been kids, Ben would have lunged for him, knocked him to the floor, and pummeled him. And then they could have gotten along, well enough, for at least another stretch. As it was, Ben felt a familiar surge of annoyance. He took another swig of his drink.

"Could I see the key?" Tim said. "Hold it, just for a little bit."

"Get used to the feel of it," Ben said.

Tim bit his lip.

Ben reached into his pockets, and took out the key to the Den. It lay in his palm, gold and glittering. He had seen this key so often, his father clutching it by the fire as he pondered matters into the night. It had an elaborate head, scrolled and heart-shaped, like a key in a fairy tale.

Tim put out his hand. "And just think, soon you'll be going back to Philadelphia."

"Getting there, these old pipes," Allyn said. "I'll have to take a look at the radiators, too." He gave Ben a knowing glance. "They don't drain themselves, you know."

"Guess not," Ben said. Ben looked back at Tim, and took a deep breath. He was about to drop the key into Tim's hand, when a rap at the front window sounded.

A man, short and almost perfectly spherical in build, was standing in a drift of snow. He waved to them all. The man was wearing a fedora hat too small for him. Under it, his round face was beaming. He pointed towards the front door with the exaggerated motions of a movie comedian.

"Oh dear," Tim murmured. "Frank Cremesi. Do you remember him, Ben? He's strongman to Alphonse Costa, the bootlegger."

Ben did remember, and more, that Cremesi, like his

boss Costa, had at his beck and call the powers of strega. He could cast a deadly illness with a glance if he chose.

"This is exactly the element President Lowell has striven to contain," Tim said.

Ben was just reaching the door when it opened, and Cremesi waddled in, accompanied by a gust of cold air.

He was halfway over the threshold when he was jostled aside by a grizzled old man with a flat cap jammed low over his eyes, and a majestic Airedale at his heels. Ben smiled. Hugh was looking worse for wear, but Eloise was as spry as ever, her coat glossy and well-kempt.

Ben raised his hand in greeting. Hugh nodded, and sat down at the bar, hands folded in front of him. Eloise curled up at his feet. "The usual," he said.

Cremesi gave Hugh a hard stare. "Door was unlocked," he said. "You fellas got to be more careful. Never know what bum might wander in." His bulk took up the width of the hallway. Allyn was still crouched up by the sink, dismantling a few nuts and bolts. Cremesi looked around the place, with a proprietary air, his hands in his pockets.

Eloise lowered her head and growled.

"Hold on to that fleabag mutt, huh? I ain't no Francis of Assisi."

"Dad never locked the door either," Tim said. "But he didn't have to."

"Now we - hey!" Cremesi raised his right foot, which was surprisingly small and neat for a man so rotund. A pair of pliers hit the floor with a clunk. He turned and looked down at Allyn. "Watch where you put things, okay, fella."

"Sorry, mister," Allyn said.

"Not used to interlopers hereabouts," Hugh said. He folded his hands and looked straight ahead.

"Better watch out for your pals, Ben," Cremesi said. "Might hurt themselves. Maybe find out they're sick, and ain't nobody can cure it."

"Well, I - Mr. Cremesi - I was just having a private get-together here with my brother, and my closest friends,"

Ben said. "What can I do for -"

"Your brother. That's nice. Wish I'd had a brother to look out for me. Only one thing's as important as family, and that's health. Kind of thing you don't appreciate until you don't got it no more. So I'll make this short. Nice place your old man had here. Nobody wants to see it fall into the wrong hands. So here's what you want to do. I say this as a friend, bearing the respect Al Costa had for Gryffth Owen."

"Go on," Ben said.

"A tribute is in order," Cremesi said. "As a mark of respect."

"A payment, you mean?"

Cremesi shrugged. "Insurance, maybe."

"Protection," Ben said.

"That's what they call it, all right," Hugh said.

Allyn reached for a crowbar. Behind the wall, a pipe clanked.

Cremesi's smile broadened. "A gesture of friendship and trust, to ensure the Druid's Den makes it through this transition." He took a step backwards, and Allyn's crowbar jabbed him in the fattest part of his calf.

Cremesi glowered. "I told you already, mister, I got a short fuse."

"No use upsetting the fellow, Allyn," Maggie said.

"Listen to grandma," Cremesi said. "She talks sense."

"And if I pay up?" Ben said. "What then?"

"If you choose to so honor our friendship," Cremesi said, "that'll cement the relationship real good. Oh - one last thing: Al Costa wants to do everybody a favor, and take over the joint himself."

Tim gasped.

"A final tribute," Cremesi went on, "to show how much you value your friendship to Mr. Costa."

"And my health," Ben said.

Cremesi grinned. "I always knew you was a quick study, kid. Not just an egghead like everybody says."

Ben gripped the key tight. The fob bit into his palm. "I'm not making any decisions right away."

"Ben doesn't like bullies," Hugh said.

"Kid, " Cremesi said. "You don't know what you're mixing with. What kind of a fix this town is in. You got the O'Connors and the Lowells lining up together. "

"Hardly together," Tim said. "The Irish are not on equal terms with the likes of the Lowell family, I can assure you."

"And DeGrace and King David have been buddying up too - the Cotton Club's only the beginning. All you got is us, the Costa crew, to keep the city in balance, like. The way your dad did, may he rest in peace." Cremesi took a step back in reverence, at the same moment that Allyn tossed a wrench aside. The wrench hit Cremesi in the side of his stomach, and ricocheted onto the floor.

Cremesi smiled. He lent down to the toolbox and picked up a flat iron. He looked down at Allyn, who was fiddling again with the plumbing.

"If Allyn were to apologize," Tim said, "Mr. Cremesi might withdraw some of his requests. Don't you think?"

"Apologize?" Ben said. He slipped the key back into his pocket.

Cremesi's smiled broadened.

Tim nodded. "President Lowell says -"

"Old man Lowell says all kinds of things," Cremesi said.

Tim pursed his lips. "He says that '*manners maketh the man.*' Or should it be: '*sayeth that.*' " He chortled, then regained his full seriousness. "Allyn did hit Mr. Cremesi."

The air stirred with the faint sound of chimes.

Allyn rose to his feet. "Trapped air. Makes a bit of a racquet." The radiator in the corner gave a mighty wet hiss.

"Or a breeze over the doorway," Ben said. "It always sets the chimes to running like that."

Cremesi raised the flat iron, and held it a few inches

from the back of Allyn's head.

"Allyn should say he's sorry," Tim said.

"Now just a minute there, Mr. Cremesi," Ben said. He stood up.

The chimes grew faster, lighter, higher.

"What about it?" Cremesi said.

Ben stepped forward, and stood between Cremesi and Allyn. He crossed his arms, and remembered to keep his chin steady.

"You're a nice kid," Cremesi said. "Don't get in over your head."

"It doesn't have to be like this," Tim said, from the shadows.

A cold wind rose through the room. The curtains rippled, and the old timbers groaned. Behind the bar, the strings of the harp sounded, as if plucked by an invisible hand.

"What's that?" Cremesi eyed the room warily. "One of you jokers turn on the radio?"

"No," Maggie said. "Not me, and I'm next to the fool contraption."

Ben slipped behind the bar.

"Planning some funny business, son?" Cremesi said.

Ben lifted the harp from its hook, and balanced it in the crook of his arm.

"The power of the bard is invincible," Allyn said.

"Yeah," Ben said, more uncertainly than he would have liked.

"Who can forget how your da," Allyn said, "armed with his knowledge and that same harp, made Al Costa himself take on the aspect of an old Negro woman, for just one day. "

"So that Costa became what he had so grievously disparaged," Hugh said.

"Long time ago, buddy," Cremesi said. But his smile was less broad.

"And didn't it lose your boss considerable respect, and

a number of assets, on his own turf," Allyn said, his voice a musical lilt.

"And that time Gryffth cast another charm." Hugh chuckled, "and transformed all the Costas's gold, their chains and trinkets, into a host of yellow daffodils."

"How I pitied those poor women," Maggie said, as she wiped down the bar. "Their finery gone to field flowers in the blink of an eye! Only for an afternoon mind, but still."

"Can it, grandma," Cremesi said. But he took a step back.

Ben gulped. He gave the harp a strum.

"A druid's magic is a fearsome thing," Allyn said, "transforming what it touches, deceiving the senses, causing shapes to shift. The mead and all such refreshments served here confound the police, for whenever put to the test, they turn out wondrously innocent of any alcohol. What charm might Gryffth's son cast now?"

"Ben has still greater learning than the father," Maggie said.

"If that be possible," said Hugh.

"All Ben ever studied was the Greeks and Romans. And the English Renaissance," Tim said. "Not a bit of Welsh."

"Thus the knowledge of all those worlds converge in Ben," Allyn said. "Imagine!"

Ben took another step forward, and plucked the shortest string of the harp. "*What'll I do*," was a popular tune that year. And Ben began to sing it, translating the words of Irving Berlin into ancient Greek. His voice was quavering, and thin, but it gradually gained strength, as he advanced step by step toward Cremesi.

Just as Ben entered onto the third lyric, Cremesi dropped the iron bar. It hit the floor with a clang.

"*Il capo gallese!*" Cremesi said, "*e l'arpa dell'oro!*" He backed away, threw the door open, and fled across the snowy pathway, his feet light and quick, his belly wobbling.

Candies and trinkets spilled from his pockets, and left a trail behind him that glittered in the dark.

" '*Capo!*' " Tim said. "Not for long, though. You've promised the place to me."

Ben went behind the bar, and slipped the harp back onto its hook.

"You are your father's son, Ben," Allyn said.

Maggie wiped her eyes. "We'll miss you when you're back in Philadelphia."

"I won't be leaving for a little while yet," Ben said.

"Oh?" Tim asked. "When exactly?"

"You're a young fella," Allyn remarked.

"You got your life elsewhere," Maggie said.

"I've got a bit of time here yet," Ben said. "To make sure dad's people are safe."

"How long?" Tim's voice was sharper than before.

"Can't have you sticking around to look after old folks like us," Allyn said.

"We've got Eloise to look after us, don't forget," Hugh declared.

"And I'm not going anywhere," Tim asserted.

"Oh, I'll get a move-on," Ben said. "Soon enough. Don't you worry."

But Ben reached into his pocket, and his fingers closed around the key. He looked at Allyn and remembered to smile. When the likes of Allyn Jones, and Maggie, and Hugh, and Eloise, were threatened, of course Ben had to step in. But it didn't mean he had to stay for long

CHAPTER THREE

A half hour later, alone in the Den, Ben finished his drink, and readied the place for the night. He locked the back door. He washed the glasses and put them away. He searched under the bar, and on the shelves for the key to the grandfather clock, but it was nowhere to be found. Seeing off Cremesi had been both exhilarating and scary. He tried to put thoughts of the encounter aside but all the while, his mind was sifting through those names he had not encountered since he left Boston - Costa, O'Connor, DeGrace, and King David. He had grown up calling them "Uncle" this and that - only A. Lowell Lawrence was never so dubbed, and as a child, Tim had dutifully lisped out "President," when addressing him.

Until he was around eight or nine, Ben thought all these men were simply family friends. They would arrive in the dead of night, sometimes singly and sometimes in groups, and stay, talking downstairs with his father until late. Only a few years later, when he began reading the newspaper, did he realize the world in which his father operated. Ben vowed it was a world he would never have any part of. Scholarly pursuits became his life. Well before the event was upon him, Ben had regarded the old man's funeral as the last obligation he would have in this city.

Tonight, all he wanted was a peaceful sleep; then he would make the rounds of the city of his youth, for the last time, and say a bittersweet farewell.

Ben checked the bolt on the side door was secure. He opened the door slightly, and as he yanked it back towards him, an arm reached in out of the darkness.

"Cremesi," Ben thought, though the arm wasn't fat. Ben glanced over to the bar, at the glittering harp, but it was too late. With a rush of cold air, the door was shoved open.

"Bensy, my boy," King David said. He grinned. His lips were as fat as a spoiled child's, surprising in a face so squarely masculine, eyes so coldly matter of fact, and a body almost negligently cruel in its strength. King David had not aged, Ben saw, so much as hardened into vulpine grace, from the long lines of his face, to the forceful lope of his movements. He released Ben's arm, made a fist, and bopped Ben on the shoulder. "Sorry to hear about your dad. Tough break."

"Thank you," Ben said. "But I thought tomorrow night was when -"

"Can't get too much of a good thing, can you," King David said, loosening the red silk scarf around his throat. He pulled out a chair, and sat down, splaying his feet out wide as could be, and set them to tapping. He looked at Ben intently.

Ben resented the inspection. He knew King David had inherited a peculiar ability (as had every eldest son in the family, for seventy generations): he could sniff out lies with a long hard stare. Under his concerted gaze, the Hebrew letters spelling out "liar" appeared before him. But Ben knew he was no cheat, and he thought King David should know that, too.

King David blinked, and gave a lazy smile. "We always got along, Benjy. Remember the time you played hooky, spent all afternoon in my theatre. Them dancing girls, you had an eyeful. I never said a word to your dad - not a peep."

"No, you didn't," Ben said. He had gone to David's Majestic Theatre to catch a Shakespearean actor, now down on his luck, reduced to playing vaudeville. Once King David had spotted him, Ben secretly hoped the story would go around how he had snuck into a girlie show - he hungered for notoriety - but no such luck.

"And I don't want you to get hurt now either," King David said. "That's how come I'm here. Going to fill you in on the facts of life in this burg. Have a seat yourself, why don't you."

Hesitating just enough to establish it was his own idea, Ben sat down.

"Here's the scoop. Now that your dad's out of the picture like, they'll all be making moves on this joint. Them that get the Den, gets the power. Tips the balance." King David looked around the Den, a hard gleam in his eyes. He cracked his glove-encased knuckles. "All this Scottish know-how -"

"Welsh," Ben said.

"Yeah," King David said. "O'Connor's making moves toward the Bluebloods. And that'll mean there's too much power between them. Costa's no peacemaker either. Got a loose cannon at his side - that fat goon of his goes ape at the drop of a hat. Can't have them hot-headed Sicilians running this town, can we, kid?"

"I guess not," Ben said.

"Now, who does that leave, Benjy? Me and Coup DeGrace, that's who. We've been working together. Set up a little musical establishment next to Coup's funeral parlor - the Cotton Club. Music. Girls. Hootch - it's the kind of thing you're dad wanted to see happen in this city, kid - people working together."

"Running a speakeasy?"

"If that's what it takes, kid. Fact is, Coup and me, we're the best hope this town's got. We got experience running a joint across neighborhood lines. Only ones doing that number, him and me. So how's about giving me - us - the Den. Sell it, I mean. Name your price. Best thing for you, and best thing for the city."

"And not so bad for you either, as it happens."

" *'As it happens'*! " King David lifted his pinky finger. "You always did sound so smart, Ben. Even as a kid wheeling around on your tricycle." The light in his eyes hardened. "But this time, act smart. The other boys'll be after you, too. Only they ain't so nice."

"I imagine not," Ben said.

"I'll give it you straight. If you don't give the Den to them, they'll do you. And if you don't give the joint to me and Coup, we'll do you." He smiled. "But I got a feeling I won't have to." He stood up and clamped a hand on Ben's shoulder. "Let me and Coup take them on. We got the chops for it."

Ben stood up.

"Ain't trying to scare you, kid."

"Of course not," Ben said. He opened the door. "Let's see how tomorrow night goes."

"Sure, kid. Go through the motions. But just remember who your friends are, okay?" And with a farewell punch to Ben's shoulder, King David disappeared into the night.

CHAPTER FOUR

Snug at last in the bed of his childhood, Ben looked around at his old room. The ceiling was lower, and the room smaller than he remembered, but everything was still in place. The twin beds were covered with ivory quilts embroidered in red and green with Welsh town names. His piggy bank, a ceramic Model T with a chipped left fender, was still on the bookshelf in front of the *Little Golden Encyclopedia* (volumes 3 and 12 gone missing). He closed his eyes, and was just drifting off, when a sharp knock startled him.

He opened his eyes. The window beside him was filled with a soft white glow from the streetlamps. Against that field of light, a crooked branch from the oak tree swayed to and fro. The branch knocked against the window with every gust.

Ben shut his eyes, turned over, and pulled the covers up.

The wind rose, and pounded all four sides of the building. The branch hit the window with a single thump, loud as a knock at the door. Ben opened his eyes. Still half-asleep, he leapt out of bed, and hotfooted down the stairs. He wrested the hatchet from the stack of firewood, and

ascended the stairs as quickly as he had gone down. He
opened the bedroom window wide. A gust of cold rushed
in. He leaned out, and with one hand, caught hold of the
errant branch. He hacked at the branch with the hatchet.
The branch was nearly severed. He hacked a second time,
and on the third strike, the branch fell with a crash to the
snowy ground.

Mollified, and strangely elated, Ben went back to bed.
A cool breeze came over him. As he slipped into sleep, he
heard chimes in the distance. They faded, and a pleasant
light took hold in back of his closed eyes: the Den
downstairs took shape there, as it had been earlier tonight.
But Hugh and Eloise, and Allyn and Maggie were cast in
shadow. Their faces dimmed, and went dark; and the light
came up on others who had not been there tonight: Costa,
O'Connor, and even Lowell, who was the soul of sobriety
and no gangster. His father was behind the bar. King
David's powerful form was stationed on the central stool,
and over to the side, Tim was perched upright. On the
stool next to Tim, Ben saw himself as he'd been a few
years ago, in the new suit he'd saved up for and bought at
Filene's Basement: the pearly gray jacket with a welted
waistline, the pants cut slim, with two-inch cuffs. He was
heading into fall of 1920 looking as if he owned it. A train
ticket for Philadelphia poked out of the lapel pocket. The
suit was just the thing for a university man - for that was
where Ben was headed the next day. At his feet was a
leather suitcase, a big red bow around the handle.

"How Ben always loved this city," Gryffth was saying.
"Forever roaming the streets."

"No kidding," King David said, the pointy toe of his
left foot tapping restlessly.

"I went for walks, too," Tim said.

"Went everywhere, Ben did. From one quarter that was
rank with the smell of dye and echoed with the pounding
of the shoemakers's hammers, to another, tangy with yeast,
from the breweries -"

"All out in the open then," Ben said. "Beer making."

"Now that's worth us talking about, Gryff." King David rapped the bar with a heavy fist. "Volstead Act's a gold mine, if it's handled right."

"For you and me both," O'Connor said.

"Make that three," Costa said.

"Oh yes, simpler days." Gryffth sighed. "The smell of bread baking on one street corner, and coffee roasting on the next, the beans rumbling in the vat as they turned - every street had its trade, and smells, and sounds. You'd go over to the seafront, Ben, and watch the ships set sail. The traveler even then, you were - smell the salt air and diesel and the sailcloth warmed in the sun. And you would come home and tell me all about it. The world was a wonder to you, Ben, and this city was your world."

"Well, I was a kid then," Ben said.

"And look at you now," King David said. "Ready to meet the world, decked out in style. Finest Moroccan leather, that case. No point getting what ain't the best. Like with this jacket." He smoothed the sleeve of his coat. "Silk and wool tweed mix. Imported. From Scotland."

"Clothes may make the man," Lowell said. "They do invariably proclaim the parvenu."

Tim giggled.

"Listen, bub," King David said. "I -"

"Did not Shakespeare write of this?" Gryffth said. "And it seems King David and Ben have taken to heart the lesson: '*Costly thy habit as thy purse can buy/ But not expressed in fancy - rich, not gaudy/ For the apparel oft proclaims the man.*'"

"Oh father," Tim said. "Really. President Lowell already told us as much - and more."

"I doubt he knows *Hamlet* as well as dad," Ben said.

Lowell's chair creaked as he leaned forward.

" '*And they in France of the best rank and station,*" he said. "*Are of a most select and generous chief in that.*' " He folded his hands.

Gryffth smiled.

Tim clapped his hands. "You recite it so perfectly, President. I wonder if that's true about the French."

"As a nation, they do strike me as kind of flitty," O'Connor said. "I will grant you."

"*Non virile*." Costa nodded.

"Nothing wrong with looking sharp, fellas," King David said.

"Shakespeare indeed does bring us together," Gryffth said.

O'Connor made a noise in his nose.

"Now I got a fine hat here myself," Costa said. He patted the chocolate-colored Borsalino laid out on the bar beside him. "Only because my wife's family are milliners. And for the rest - ." He shrugged. "I am a grown man. Not a woman. Not a youngster. Respectable is good enough."

"Not for this here college boy, it ain't," King David said. "Not for me neither."

"It is a nice suitcase, I guess," Timmy allowed. "But a bit showy. Those metal fixtures are terribly bright."

"It is a most generous gift," said Lowell. "I believe that is the salient factor."

"Yeah," King David said. "Now that the gang's all in, and we got the yak fest out of the way, how's about we get down to brass tacks. Volstead Act, and the moola we can spin from it." He cracked his knuckles.

With a glance at Lowell, O'Connor added, "Within the limits of the law, of course."

"A license to print money," Costa said, "for them that do not already print their own at home."

"Ha," King David said. "So if we here all -"

"Oh, but we're not all here," Gryffth said. "We await the pleasure of one other."

"If you could spare us unnecessary intrigue," Lowell said.

"Mr. Coup DeGrace," Gryffth said.

"DeGrace?" O'Connor said. "Isn't he -"

"That fancy *schwartze*," King David said.

Costa shook his head.

"Now wait a minute, Gryffth," O'Connor said. "It's one thing to ask me to shake hands with such like." With an outstretched hand, he indicated Costa and, after an infinitesimal pause, King David. "But this is -"

"A bridge too far," Lowell said. "Indeed."

"The DeGrace family is doing well for itself," Gryffth said. "A small empire in funeral homes that is ever-expanding. Coup DeGrace is already a leader among his people. He -"

"They're not like us," O'Connor said. "Their powers, and practices - the dead bodies they work with - it's not -"

"Kosher," King David said.

"There are differences among us all," Gryffth said. "Even here. Some grace their dinner tables with pasta, others potatoes. But that's no reason we cannot sit down together."

Costa shook his head. "*Animale.*"

"Their neighborhood is flourishing," Gryffth said. "That little corner of the South End is growing, by leaps and bounds. Work with them, or lose out, and lose altogether."

"I'll take my chances," O'Connor said.

"As you wish," Gryffth said. "But if you fail to meet with DeGrace, and secure some reasonable comity with him, rest assured someone else will win his favor, and get the piece of pie you rejected."

O'Connor hrrmped. But already he was stewing about that hypothetical foregone piece of pie. His brow lowered, and he crossed his arms.

"And it is aptly said, keep your friends close, and your enemies closer," Gryffth went on.

"The great Machiavell," Costa said.

"Sounds like him," Gryffth said. "But it's Chinese. Sun-tze."

"Fortunately, we have but few Asiatics in this city,"

Lowell said. "And will have fewer still in years to come. Such are the workings of a provident leadership."

"My point remains," Gryffth said. "As regards close enemies."

"The closest, and the best," King David said, and swatted O'Connor on the back.

"I hear DeGrace's haunt has developed a style in dress and music that's all the rage," Gryffth said. "A breath of fresh air in this staid city, it will keep us young at heart."

"Yeah!" King David snapped his fingers. "Heard that, too. I got to take a look-see myself."

"Such stylistic innovations are hardly a point in their favor," Lowell said.

"Indeed," Tim echoed.

"But in the terms of law," Gryffth said, "are they not equal citizens?"

"Laws can be changed, if needs be." Lowell's lips made a thin colorless line. "And there is an established, and dare I say, honorable tradition of separate but equal. One we do well to maintain in this circumstance."

"I am not asking you to invite Coup DeGrace into your own home," Gryffth said. "But to accept him here in mine, at this little get-together. I hope my friendship with each of you is solid enough to bear so simple a request."

"No commitment on my part?" Costa said.

"Not a bit."

"Or mine?" O'Connor said.

"Never that."

King David thumped the bar. "Copacetic, as far as I'm concerned."

"For this occasion, under another man's roof, I can hardly dissent," Lowell said.

"Good," Gryffth said. "A round of mead, please, Ben." Ben reached for the bottle, and filled the glasses.

"To old acquaintances and new," Gryffth said.

They toasted.

"Ain't gonna kill us," King David said, "to sit at table

with a colored for an hour."

"And what don't kill us, makes us stronger." O'Connor gave a mirthless chuckle.

"Maybe." Costa frowned.

There was a knock on the front door. Ben looked for his father's nod, then went and opened the door. Coup DeGrace stood, subdued and solid, his lanky dead-eyed valet at his side.

"Mr. DeGrace," Gryffth said. He came out from around the bar. "We are all glad to see you."

"I can imagine." A smile played at the corners of DeGrace's mouth. "I have felt the warmth of Boston hospitality all too often."

"I've prepared some pages for a recitation," Gryffth said, "that I thought we might all join in together."

"His idea of an ice-breaker, I believe," said Lowell.

"Let me guess," King David said. "St Crispy Day."

"Good night, nurse," O'Connor said.

"Crispin Day," Ben corrected.

King David laughed. "College boy." He wrapped an elbow around Ben's neck, and rapped him on the head.

In the corner of the room, the grandfather clock gave a click and a whir, and began to chime.

"10:47," Gryffth said. His clock had always been set to its own time, for Gryffth hated time to be designated on the hour or "sharp." ("Is time a knife?" he once asked. "A musical note? A twist of lemon, or a slice of cheddar?" Gryffth maintained that the moment betwixt and between held all promise, and set his own clock accordingly.) "And never, my friends, has there been a better moment to recite this poetry, from the greatest of all Welsh bards." He ruffled a sheaf of papers. "I have a copy for each of you."

"You say that every time," O'Connor said. "It's always the best moment."

"And so it is," Gryffth said. The clock still chiming, he settled into his great chair by the fireplace. He turned, and addressed Ben - no longer Ben in the dream, but Ben lying in bed dreaming. Ben was conscious of stirring in his sleep.

"Dear son," Gryffth said, "you remember this long ago day, don't you? When you went off to college, and left Boston, forever, it seemed."

And in the moment that his father had turned and spoken to Ben's sleeping self, the others in Ben's dream had frozen in place. In one hand, King David had his drink hoisted in mid-air. The other hand was poised halfway to slapping DeGrace on the back. They had gone motionless, like in a photograph, each of them. The clock was still chiming.

"I have words to tell you, my son, before you leave this city again."

"Yes," Ben said, miserably. He was trying not to listen. But already he knew the effort was futile.

"Heed me well. Evil doings are afoot. I have written what and how, and stowed the missive in your bedroom closet. There you will find the last thoughts I had on this earth. It is up to you to make good on them, my son."

And with that, his father's face softened and widened into a luminous cloud. His features dissolved. The cloud of light shrunk to a pinpoint, sped outwards to the far edges of the dark behind Ben's eyes, and disappeared.

Ben sat up, stricken by a wave of exhaustion. He knew he was awake, and in bed. The broken tree branch cast its shadow across the ceiling, swaying back and forth in the wind. The clock downstairs was chiming. Ben rubbed his eyes, and got up. The soles of his feet shriveled on the hard cold floor.

CHAPTER FIVE

Ben rummaged through the bedroom closet, half-hoping he would find no missive. The closet smelled of camphor and mint. He pushed a rack of old winter clothes to one side, and several items tumbled off the back shelf: a baseball mitt, a crystal pentagon, and a folder stuffed with clippings and notes that came open and scattered. Ben sat down on the floor, and sifted through them.

His father's letter was near the top, an ivory scrap of parchment, in flowing, familiar script:

My son, our friends King David and Coup DeGrace are at grave risk. A trap has been laid against them, on New Year's Eve, the Blueblood civil authorities in strange and singular concert with our friend O'Connor. The balance and order of the city is in jeopardy unless ...

Ben read the missive. When he had finished, he rubbed his eyes. He had been dreaming, he was sure of it. But the missive was here, in the closet. He picked up another odd scrap and read through it.

The honorable O'Connor is a creature of eccentricity. He sequesters himself in his garage, in the driver's seat of a fancy little roadster - lemon yellow with a robin's egg blue interior. He cannot drive, but he managed to secure the car at a knockdown price, and the man never could resist a bargain. The car's the only place he can get a bit of peace from the call of the banshee, and the demands of his family. He's rigged the garage door so that the more the lock is turned this way and that, the tighter it gets. The trick is to turn it just once, to the left, and then to the right, but only a quarter of the way. A little birdie told me, as the saying goes. This birdie is called Hollie and she is the form the banshee - .

Ben read on and shook his head at this quaint and curious lore. He skipped ahead.

A dapper gent, Coup DeGrace's cousin Andre Pierre always sports white kidskin gloves. The hands they cover are commonly called "iron fists," but are in fact formed from brass, a church bell melted down, and ...

What had this to do with him - with anything - with "the price of potatoes in Russia" as his father used to say? He tidied the clippings together. He stopped once more, and began reading.

The captain of the Mayflower was born in Wales.

Mount Everest was named after a Welshman.

Up to half the signatories of the Declaration of Independence had Welsh ancestry - including Thomas Jefferson! Let not the Saxons claim primacy in all matters of Democracy!

St Patrick was Welsh by birth, being from Banwen, Wales.

A Welsh-American invented the automobile. A Welshman invented the equal sign. And golf's Stableford scoring system was invented in Wales - as was that for lawn tennis!

Ben put his head in his hands. He did two things he had not done since he'd received the news of his father. He wept, loudly and openly, in a way he would have been ashamed to do in front of another, even his brother. And then, through his tears, as he began to gather up the clippings, he was laughing. For he had here before him his father in spirit, in these, the anarchist papers of Gryffth Owen: friend, Welshman, citizen, Druid.

Ben scanned the floor. One last scrap remained. It was a short handwritten note.

You will want to start draining the radiators on a regular basis, every week at least, in winter. All part of being a homeowner, my son - stewardship.

CHAPTER SIX

Red-rimmed around the eyes, Jackie Francis O'Connor planted his elbows on the bar, and leaned forward. Ben handed him a drink. His own first measure barely touched, Coup DeGrace sat upright, in a somber suit, a broad maroon silk tie, and a black armband. Costa bowed his head. His hands had been trembling during the first toast, Ben noticed. At the far corner of the L-shaped bar, King David sprawled out over several spaces. He reached over his drink, and knocked Costa on the shoulder.

"Sorry, pal." King David's voice was a little rough, and his face more hangdog than last night. These men would miss his father, Ben could tell, criminal though they were.

"You look a little worse for wear, kid," King David said.

"Understandable," O'Connor said.

"I had kind of an odd dream," Ben said.

King David tipped back his glass. "Like drinking a beeswax candle." He winked.

"And the dream wasn't the only thing," Ben said. "An unexpected visitor came by, too."

King David's face jolted upward. He gave Ben a glare. Ben could feel the coldness of the look, but Ben's own gaze was trained on Costa. Costa betrayed nothing, not a flicker of eyelid, or a twitch of his mouth. So it was possible Cremesi had acted on his own, even likely - a "loose cannon," hadn't King David called him? Still Ben had to be cautious. There were histories and tensions at work among these men, subterranean alliances and half-forgotten grievances lurking, and no doubt soon to emerge. Ben was the heir to the Druid's Den, but he was now largely an outsider. The wind rose, and whipped the outside walls of the den. A stray gust rushed down the chimney, and the fire raged up and cast ragged shadows around the room.

Ben sipped his mead. The grandfather clock was set to strike soon, in the manner his father had designated long ago, at odd increments, never on hour or half hour. Owen had left instructions that this gathering was to run until 11:37 - twenty minutes to go.

"Of course, as I was saying, what with the wail of the banshee, it was I what knew the sad news first," O'Connor said. "The day dear Owen passed, the wail rose and echoed from one end of Gustin Street to other, then the whole of the city, clamoring off every brick and brownstone, from Beacon Hill to Roxbury. I thought it was the death of the Mayor Curley's little girl, young Dorothea, but instead -" He shook his head. "It's practically cousins we are, you and me, Ben. Celts akimbo."

Costa's jaw tightened. "I too felt the chill of the grave that day, my friends. In a single moment, every mirror in my house fell to the floor, and shattered. It was as if some great and unseen wind had passed through."

"That day, not a single echo sounded in my house," DeGrace said. "And shadows were strangely absent - sure signs someone was slipping from this earth. The radio went dead, then sputtered back to life, playing the '*Black Ribbon Blues*.' Most unsettling."

"Yeah, now that you mention it, my nose was kinda out of joint too." King David put down his glass. "Down in the basement, where it was packed away, Pop's old ram horn blew - all by itself. Let's say it weren't the kind of toot-toot-tootsie that gets your feet tapping." He laughed, then his face went serious. "I lost my old man a couple of years back myself. My sympathies, kid."

"Thank you," Ben said.

"To the memory of a great man," O'Connor said.

"May we preserve his legacy," DeGrace said. "I have suffered a recent loss as well. Last spring, my cousin Andre Pierre was cruelly cut down. And the courts showed blatant disre-'"

"I heard he'd run amok." King David shrugged. "Broke into a truck loaded up with guns or hootch or some such."

O'Connor's lips pursed into a smirk. "And here was I thinking it was your funny money poor Andre was after, King."

"No mischief on his part was ever demonstrated," DeGrace replied. "And a prank such as you suggest hardly warrants the injustice our -'"

" '*Mischief*' ? '*Prank*'? " Al Costa slammed his fist on the bar. "To deprive a man of his livelihood?" He turned and stared at O'Connor. "Do not imagine I am ignorant of who's behind this. Stealing the fruits of my labor - or spoiling them, with mists, fogs, and gusts of heat. The powers of the bog are -'"

"Livelihood? Let us speak instead of depriving a man of his very life." DeGrace's face was stern and emotionless. "Cut down in cold blood, and from the courts, no justice was -'"

"Aw, take it easy, Coup," King David said, "the palooka was already dead, weren't he? More or less?" He took a sip, grimaced, and gave DeGrace a cool, considering gaze. "Icing him through and through ain't half as stinky as, I dunno, cooking the books, say, and shortchanging a partner."

Behind his large wire-rimmed spectacles, DeGrace blinked. "I don't know wha -'"

"My beancounter's squawking there's been some irregularities, like. But Rhinegold don't know you like I do. Or thought I did."

"You want to talk about death, fellas?" O'Connor said. A cold light settled in his eyes as he turned and looked at Costa. "The Curley girl was struck down last week - in the North End, by St Leonard's - your parish. She caught a fever no one can cure. And now she's on death's door."

"Not of my doing." Costa's right hand made a fist. "I have sworn to it! And still you take vengeance on my livelihood and -"

"Poor kid," King David said. "And before that, Hizzoner's twins, weren't it?"

"Yes," O'Connor said. "The little babies. Johnny and Jimmy, God rest their souls."

"On my mother's grave, I have swo-"

Ben tapped his fingers against his glass and looked up. "Could we remember why we're here tonight?"

"Kid's got a point," King David said. "Let's put away our beefs, chumfoos, and show some respect."

Costa cleared his throat, straightened his tie and sat up to his full height. DeGrace and O'Connor exchanged glances.

"A great man's passing is a momentous occasion," Costa declared, slowly, so that every syllable could be justly pondered. "An occasion of mourning. Of remembering. Of reckoning. Of -"

"One thing's for sure," King David said. "We got to hang together."

"Us island peoples." O'Connor winked at Ben.

"Haiti's an island," DeGrace said. "Wales most certainly is not."

"Hang together," Ben echoed. "Or we will surely hang apart."

"Ben Franklin," DeGrace said.

"Celts - we're like blood brothers, was what I'm meaning, Ben," O'Connor said. "I can't help but think the most peaceable transition, for the city, for all of us, would be from your father to -"

"As you first pointed out, my Hibernian friend," Costa said, "now is not the time to further one's own ambitions. Or to dwell on one's grievances. Such as the destruction of the fruits of a man's long labor. The turning of good wine into vinegar - some wayward mist or blast of heat - forty-eight vats."

"Go toss a salad," O'Connor said.

DeGrace coughed softly. "There's a theory I ran across."

"Ran across?" O'Connor said. "And I had you pegged as a more a *'perusing'* kind of fella."

" - a theory," DeGrace went on, "that far from being Celts, and related to the Welsh, the Irish have a different tribal affiliation altogether."

"The race of Cain perhaps," Costa said, and glowered once again at O'Connor.

"The Irish," DeGrace said "may be a lost tribe of Israel."

King David laughed. "This I got to hear."

"All ears me-self." O'Connor smiled, showing just the tips of his tiny pearly teeth, which made him look genteelly menacing.

"J. H. Allen advanced the notion," DeGrace said. "In *Judah's Scepter and Joseph's Birthright*, that the prophet Jeremiah went to Ireland, and set up shop, so to speak. To this day, many place names and customs between the two peoples correlate."

"Crackpot theory," King David said.

"Is not the harp the ancient symbol of Ireland?" DeGrace said.

"Yes," O'Connor said. "And associated with the great and good Gryffth Owen himself, so it was. And there again Ben we see -"

"And was not the harp the favored instrument of King David?" DeGrace said.

"I'd never presume to name a man's favored instrument," O'Connor said. His little cupid bow lips twitched. His skin was fine, nearly poreless, and he flushed as readily in heat as in cold, or in the delicately delicious task of needling an acquaintance. He was a sly one, Ben remembered, with a melancholy, cool undertone to his merriment. O'Connor was famously tight with a buck - but he did not love money, Gryffth once pointed out, so much as loathe the thought of someone else getting hold of it.

King David chuckled. "Hey, Coup, lighten up."

DeGrace pursed his lips. "Ribald innuendo is distasteful."

"Oh yeah? That Baron Samedi of yours sure hucks it up like nobody's business," King David said. "He ain't no schoolboy. No offense, Ben."

"Raillery belongs to Baron Samedi alone," Coup DeGrace said. "To serve the loa, and is never proper for mere entertainment."

"I read your letter in the *South End Gazette* last week," Costa said.

DeGrace nodded. "On the infelicities of modern negro music." He fiddled with his glass and quoted himself, still pleased with his wording. " '*With the popularity of gutter music, local 'jazz' acts have infiltrated society with sexually devious lyrics, and are the craze among the young and gullible.*' "

O'Connor slapped himself on the side of the head. "And you in the business!"

"My livelihood is not my philosophy," DeGrace said.

"More's the pity." O'Connor crossed his arms.

"Coup may come up with some quack theories, but at least he ain't trying to muscle in." King David gave O'Connor a look. "Which seems to be the stunt some people got in mind."

Outside, in the distance, the wind rose, howling and fierce. The branch knocked sharply against the stained glass window.

"Another go and that window's gonna break," King

David said.

"A timely reminder," Costa said, his voice gaining an orator's depth and volume. "Something has already shattered. This world is not the same without Owen." He held one hand upright and pumped the air. "Gryffth Owen was fortunate to have two children, both equally of the masculine persuasion."

"Say, where is your brother tonight?" O'Connor asked.

"Maybe he's a little steamed." King David shrugged. "Last wills and testaments can do that."

"He'll be by," Ben said. "He had to work."

"Gossip pages," King David said.

"Society reporter," O'Connor said.

Costa cleared his throat. "No, the world is not the same," he began again. "Nor are we. And now we must look ahead."

"Al's got a point," King David agreed. "We got to make some plans, Arrangements. Settle things."

"But our Anglo friends are strangely missing," DeGrace said.

"Maybe they're still in mourning for one of their own," O'Connor said. "That senator, barely a month ago - oh, that was a keening to beat the band. But a far second to your da's."

"Henry Cabot Lodge," DeGrace said.

Costa withdrew into the shadows.

"Senator Lodge, I should say." DeGrace smoothed his tie. "Even in death they carry the title."

"Where it does them all kind of good." King David snorted.

"Depends on where they're headed," O'Connor said.

King David grinned. "I think I can guess."

O'Connor leaned forward. "Correct me if I'm wrong, but 'twas was never determined exactly what caused the good Senator's demise. Was it -"

"Gallbladder," Costa cut in.

"Wasn't it Lodge - Senator Lodge - who supported that

bill?" O'Connor said. "A few years back. An anti-immigration act. The first one."

"Oh yeah," King David said. "If not reada' the English, no letta in."

O'Connor looked at Costa. "Only one of us here would've had a major league gripe with that."

"Better make that two, Jackie-boy," King David said. "Ruskies and polacks weren't top of his dance card either. And these days, them Blueblood banks are looking cross-eyed at my money."

"Imagine that." O'Connor shook his head. "And now another political family has been struck down. This time a child."

"People get sick," Ben said. "For all kinds of reasons. Let's leave it -"

"And even when a crime is proven," DeGrace said, "no justice is given. The beasts who slaughtered my cousin - the two monsters, named Prescott Ames and Nicolas Prega - both walked free."

"Nothing worse than losing a child, as our good Mayor already knows," O'Conner picked up his glass. "He held fire, the last time. But this time - who can say? A man has his limits."

"*Diabolico!*" Costa rose to his feet. "Again you dare to -"

"Remember, you are in my father's house," Ben said.

Costa's glance shifted from O'Connor, to Ben - and then before his eyes could flicker back to O'Connor, a sliver of light beamed over Costa's face. With the creak of the door and a rush of cold air, the sliver of light widened. Framed in the opened front door, under the falling snow, a streetlight glowed, and cast its beams far inside the Druid's Den. Under the streetlight, a tall, substantially built man, with a tight-lipped gray face, adjusted the black armband he wore over the sleeve of his Ulster coat. Then he glided soundlessly over the threshold. Costa sat back down.

"Mr. Lowell," Ben said.

"President Lowell," a voice corrected. A figure

distinctly less imposing slipped out from behind Lowell's shoulder.

"Tim," Ben said. "Glad you could join us."

"I came as soon I could." Tim sidled in behind Lowell. "I was at an anniversary dinner for one of the Lowell cousins. Ellie Cabot-Lowell was there - you remember her, don't you, Ben."

"That was a long time ago," Ben said. "Another drink, Coup?"

DeGrace shook his head.

"It seems the man Ellie was seeing has gone and married somebody else," Tim said. "A Peabody, I believe."

Lowell took several noiseless steps into the room. "I've stopped by to pay my condolences. Governor Cox requests that I send his as well."

"Thank you," Ben said.

"Of course," Lowell said. "We all wish for the most peaceable transition possible. Whatever I can do to make that possible -"

"Let me guess - for the good of city, right?" King David said.

"I won't be making any decisions right away." Ben swiped his hand through the air.

"Of course, take your time, young man," Lowell said. "I did, however, wish to let you know that a professorship in English will be opening up this semester. At the University of Philadelphia -"

"Ain't that swell," King David said.

"I thought perhaps you might be interested. I daresay, with my recommendation, and your background in -"

"I'll be going back to Philadelphia all right," Ben said. "But on my own steam."

"Be that as it may," Lowell said, with a dismissive sweep of his long pale fingers. "The Governor wishes you to know he considered your father to be a fine man, and a force for good in this city."

"And he was a force for justice as well," DeGrace said.

"Not all justice is found in a courtroom, and sometimes not an iota."

"And so was your Senator Henry Cabot Lodge a fine man, Dean Lowell," O'Connor said.

"President," Tim corrected.

"Such a pity he's left us," O'Connor went on. "A native English speaker, same as you. And for that matter, me own good self."

"Don't forget DeGrace," King David said.

"Surely the good senator limited his esteem to -" O'Connor said, and passed his hand over the pale oval of his face.

"Goes without saying," DeGrace said.

"Too many things do," O'Connor said.

"In my experience, not enough of them do," Lowell said. "Especially when the ladies are involved."

Tim Owen laughed, first, loudest, and longest.

O'Connor waited for the laughter to subside. "President Lowell, you and I have got to chat, so we do. There's no doubt the city needs a peaceable transition. Together you and I can guarantee that. Peace is up to the forces of authority, like it always is."

"Indeed," Lowell said, making a tent with his fingers.

"Ben's unfamiliar with how the city works," Tim said. "He's promised me to -"

"I'll be staying here as long as it takes," Ben said, "to ensure peace and -"

From the corner a faint whirring sounded, and a bell chimed. The grandfather clock was striking the half hour, several minutes late - 11:37 exactly, as his father had instructed. "The iron tongue of midnight has told 11:37" - the English had mis-transcribed Shakespeare, his father long contended.

Ben took a breath, and felt it go cleansing and deep inside him. He had done his duty by his father. He had a better idea now of the tensions among these gangs. Each of these men had only its own interest at heart - not the good of the city. Ben would not allow such a situation to be his father's ultimate legacy.

"Gentlemen, we will speak again, I promise. But the chime has sounded, and this gathering is adjourned, in accordance with my father's wishes." Ben stood up, and the gang leaders did the same. Ben went to the front door and opened it. All but clicking his heels, he said goodnight.

"I'll close up," Tim said.

"That's all right," Ben said.

"I may as well get used to it."

"Don't get too used to it, pal," King David said. He looked at Lawrence Lowell who strode past him, head high, and expressionless. Ben watched as one by one, the men disappeared into the dark cold night, and went their separate ways.

CHAPTER SEVEN

Governor Channing Cox leaned forward in his straight-backed chair, and leafed through the sheaf of papers in front of him. The State House meeting had gone as well as could be expected. Now safely repaired to the oak-paneled confines of his office, Cox permitted himself to relax a bit, going so far as to undo the top button of his suit jacket. A new governor was due to be inaugurated in January, and these were Channing Cox's last few weeks in office. He had been determined to make his mark on history, a desire that had sharpened over these past few months. And the death of Gryffth Owen afforded an unparalleled opportunity.

What endless paperwork this last legislative session had spawned, and what interminable committee meetings! Worst of all, the make-up of the legislature had grown increasingly alarming - hordes of Irish, Italians, and worse, were getting voted into office. It was the price of democracy, Cox had heard it said over and over in the State House. And for quite some time now, Cox's unspoken answer had been: then the price is altogether too high. Just last month, he had been presented with a bill to establish a park - in South Boston, of all places, a project dear to Mayor Curley's heart, of course. When Cox's men pointed out that no funds were available for such a scheme, Curley proposed a bill to raise the funds by putting the Public Garden up for sale. How Cox's men writhed in agony, and submitted one committee report after another to document the illegality of such a proposal. And all the while, Cox was sure, Curley was chuckling to himself in that hideous manse of his on the Jamaicaway. Curley had got his park (funds were found from elsewhere), proving him to be a formidable foe.

Cox pushed the stack of papers aside. He had at least escaped having to attend the Welshman's gathering tonight. The older son had returned to Boston, but he was just a schoolteacher, settled somewhere in the south, and would no doubt soon return there. And once Cox had located the handwritten original of Owen's will, he would effect a most magnificent transformation. In these, the last days of his governorship, anyone he chose would be installed in the Druid's Den. He would broach the topic with Lowell tonight. Had the Owen son made any mention of the will and its whereabouts? Lowell would hold nothing back. The man exasperated Cox with his well-meaning stolidity, although that had been the very quality that led Cox to install him as deputy in the first place.

Cox turned to the modest matter at hand. He opened his desk drawer, and drew out a single sheet of paper - handwritten, in a spidery fragile script, and faintly smelling of violets and stale talcum powder. He peered down at it - a codicil that his great aunt Mrs. Charles Amsley Pierce III had scribbled out, a behest to a shelter for unwed mothers in Dorchester. To any civic-minded person - and Cox considered himself that - it was obvious the monies could be far better spent elsewhere. Why abet a rabble that evidently could not control themselves in the first place? In her dotage, it appeared, his great aunt had developed certain peculiar and regrettable sympathies. Cox had in mind a far more worthy beneficiary - the Boston Public Library. At $50, the behest was so meager that Cox had no qualms about performing a transformation here in the State House, rather than within the safer precincts of the offices of Grimley and Graybody.

Cox reached into the depths of the desk drawer, and extracted a velvet box. It was narrow and rectangular like a necklace case from a fine jeweler's. He opened the lid, and gazed a moment at the quill pen inside. Its majesty never ceased to humble him, for this was the Quill of Justice. He removed it from the case, cradled it in his fingers, and gave it a barely perceptible flourish. The quill feather was silver-white edged with black, and it glistened in the lamplight. The metal nib was platinum, and sharper than a serpent's tooth.

The existence of this quill and its workings were shadowy to those outside its direct stewardship. With this quill, Governor John Endicott had signed the death warrant of the Quaker Mary Dyer in 1660: she was duly hung from an oak tree in the center of Boston Common.

In more recent decades, the quill had fallen into near disuse. Any extensive use exhausted its power, and the quill required time, and the energy of civic vengeance, to be replenished. Typewriting, print and publishing had encroached upon the scope of transformation: handwritten documents had grown increasingly rare in this age of clamorous, print-ridden democracy. The transformation of any document dangerously diminished the Bluebloods's power in their other sectors, as when a sudden demand for electricity in one quarter leads to a brownout everywhere else.

But this matter at hand was paltry stuff, and presented no such difficulty, Cox was confident. Cox passed the point of the pen over the words his great aunt had written, line by line. As the pen passed over them, the words were swept off the page, one by one, and whisked into the pen's feathered end. There, they swirled, in a plume-shaped maelstrom, like the flakes inside a shaken snow globe.

When the page was rendered entirely blank, Cox took a

deep breath. He steeled himself, and concentrated anew. He positioned the quill at the top of the page again, and exhaling, passed the quill over the page, as he had just done, line by line - only this time, words emerged from the point of the quill. One by one, they appeared across the page, and line by the line, the page was filled. Cox regarded the finished document with satisfaction: here now was the handwritten behest, from Mrs. Charles D. Pierce III, for $50, this time to the fines and fees collection office of the Boston Public Library. Cox sat back, exhausted and pleased.

Oh to perform a similar operation on the will of Gryffth Owen! Such an operation carried dangers, to be sure, but if he could get his hands on that will, Cox would wreak a fundamental transformation of this city. Musing still, endeavoring valiantly to keep his enthusiasm in judicious check, Cox opened the newspaper. He scanned a few pages. At the classifieds section, a chill went through his heart.

Under "Legal Notices," the first item read:

Being the last will and testament of Gryffth Owen, of the Druid's Den, Boston Common...

Wily to the last, somehow sensing a possible danger, the Welshman had consigned his last will and testament to print. By locking the will into black and white, and promulgating it to the vulgate of typeface, the Druid had rendered his will all but immune from Blueblood transformation by quill.

"Drat!" Cox said, into the empty room. He bowed his head, and folded his hands, ashamed of his outburst. He was due at the Harvard Club within the half hour. He collected himself, and considered. He did not utter a sound, or move a muscle. He was deep in thought - for without a doubt, the death of Gryffth Owen still provided an unmatched opportunity. He was sure of it. Exactly how it did so was the conundrum Cox vowed he would crack posthaste.

CHAPTER EIGHT

"A close call, of sorts," the fine-featured young man said. He grinned, and glanced around the smoky, dimly lit café. It was almost empty at this hour of night. "But then, they're the most delicious kind." He leaned forward, took a sip from his teacup, and shivered with delight. "Earl Grey never had quite this kick, believe me, Comrade Prole."

"Citizen Vanguard, I do," his companion replied.

It was delightful, the nicknames they'd given each other, a small secret among the larger ones they were already sharing, a badge of intimacy, and a token, Citizen Vanguard hoped, of more intimacy to come. He was swarthy, Comrade Prole, almost grubby, like a grisette in a comic opera - thin to the point of malnourishment. His head was bullet-shaped. His eyes were hollow, but the cold light in them pierced the gloom. Even after all they had been through recently, Comrade Prole was still circumspect, not hot-blooded the way his people were supposed to be - at least not yet.

"I knew they couldn't pin anything on us," Vanguard went on. "We'd hardly done any harm, after all. A boyish prank, like taking wings off a fly. Judge Chauncey had to conclude in our favor." He sighed, put his head to one side, and laid his slender ivory hands across the table. "The whole affair has been exhilarating, hasn't it? We're reprobates, together." With a small toss of his head, he shook his floppy blond bangs out of his eyes. "And what plans we have."

Comrade Prole nodded without smiling, and raised his right hand. A bedraggled ribbon dangled from his scrawny wrist. With weary certainty, Citizen Vanguard knew from the gesture a quote, or pronouncement of some sort, was in the offing. Comrade Prole was always so solemn. "When our turn comes," Comrade Prole said, in his careful precise English, "we shall not make excuses for the terror. The royal terrorists, the terrorists by the grace of God and the law, are the most brutal."

"Aren't they just?" Citizen Vanguard fiddled with his cuff. "The Red Terror's suddenly old hat. I'm unleashing the Crimson Terror - one in the eye for my dear old alma mater." He snickered. "I conceived of it one afternoon as I was crossing Dunster Street, the last day I was -" He frowned, and took another soothing sip.

The vodka was rough but pleasantly so. His nerves, agitated at the memory of the impudence dealt him, began to calm. "The chemistry between us will be remarkable - I dare say, explosive." He laughed, squeezed Comrade Prole's wrist, and called for the bill.

CHAPTER NINE

Al Costa turned down Hanover Street. It was a busy road lined on both sides with four-story brick tenements. Small grocery shops, cafes, and bakeries operated on the ground floors. He glanced up to the windows of his apartment. They glowed faintly. But he was on business. He went past the building, continued for a block, and turned onto Battery Street. He entered the first building on the left, and trudged up three flights of stairs, a dark narrow hallway with cracked plaster walls. The door at the top of the stairs had a red ribbon affixed to the lintel. The ribbon was starting to unravel, but was still potent enough to ward off the evil eye. Costa knocked twice, then once. The door opened a sliver.

"My place," Costa said. "Ten minutes. Sharp." And then he turned and went home.

At his kitchen table, a glass of Chianti at his elbow, the waxy-sweet taste of mead at last beginning to wash away, Al Costa reviewed the night's events at the Den. As expected, O'Connor was making common cause with the *inglese*, or attempting to. The *capigliatura rossa* (a hair color Costa did not consider proper in a man) would not get far, Costa surmised. The Bluebloods held everyone in contempt, and would never accept a bog-trotting *irlandese* as an equal. But there was no doubt that unless he took action against any renegade use of strega magic, Costa would find himself under threat. Had someone in his neighborhood passed an evil eye over the Curley daughter? Had they also done in Curley's infant twins two years ago? Costa did not know, but he was taking the first step to finding out.

With a starchy rustle of her dress, made from some stiff shiny dark material, and a rattle of silverware, his wife set a dish of roasted peppers before him. He took one pepper, to avoid the interrogation he knew would ensue if he did not.

"I got some prosciutto, too," Concittia said. Costa shook his head. Even at this hour, she was smartly dressed, with a touch of lipstick, as if she were about to go out. Concittia came from an illustrious line of strega: from as far back as the tenth century AD, the first born daughter of every other generation possessed an evil eye of surpassing potency. Everyone in the neighborhood knew of Concittia's lineage, and that knowledge itself was insurance so powerful that Costa seldom had to call upon it. Concittia had goldish auburn hair, and greenish gold eyes the color of rum-soaked blond raisins. Many Sicilians suspected her of Lombard blood on those grounds alone, but no word was ever spoken. Concittia neatened the tablecloth under the plate of peppers, and raised her knuckled hands to her lacquered pompadour, pushing a single errant strand back into place.

Costa sipped his red wine. The waxy flavor of mead still lingered. He considered a swill of whiskey, but decided he had more than enough of the northern countries for one evening. How *sinistro* the north was - misty fogs, ugly skies the color of phlegm, the ground soggy and squelching underfoot. It was the landscape of a nightmare.

A knock sounded at the back door. Concittia went and opened it, and after a mumbled greeting, Cremesi entered the kitchen and sat down at Costa's table. The chair squeaked under him. Soft-shouldered, and his face as round as a custard pie, he smiled, sunny and good-natured. He would know, or could flush out, any strega activity that might have affected Dorothea Curley. Cremesi's smile seldom deserted him, even when "extreme measures" were called for: Cremesi collected from every storefront in the area, offering the establishments protection from robberies, fire, and the like. He seldom even had to mention strega to make his point.

"So, boss," he said, "anything big happen tonight?" His eyes shifted right to left, all the while his smile broadened, so Costa knew Cremesi was on edge about why Costa had called him over. "The Owen kid's a bright-eyed little punk, ain't he?"

"Our friends were all there, panthering around like beasts in a cage," Costa said. "O'Connor buddies up to the Bluebloods - the *irlandese* got a bee in their bonnet on account of the Curley girl. And Lowell sat looking at me with his cold fishy eyes."

"Good thing he don't got *malocchio*!" Cremesi said. "We'd all be in the soup!" He reached over, took a slice of bread, and considered. "Looks like some joker's overstepping their bounds. Renegade strega, we got more a beef with than anybody."

Costa nodded.

"Henry Cabbage Lodge was one thing," Cremesi went on. "But the girl, that's bad business." An attack on a civilian, particularly a child, was never advisable. It played right into the Bluebloods's hands and gave them an excuse for a crackdown. He helped himself to the peppers. "Ain't ate for a couple of hours."

Light quick footsteps sounded on the staircase. The hallway door creaked open, and a small head of russet curls poked out.

"Hi, Paulie," Cremesi said.

"Whatcha' doing?" Paulie asked.

Cremesi reached out and playfully dragged Paulie forward by his pajama collar.

"Getting ready for Santa Claus." Cremesi grinned. He put his hand to the boy's ear and plucked out a silver dollar. "Hey, Mr. Moneybags."

"Thanks!" Paulie snatched the coin from Cremesi's hand.

"His daddy's boy," Cremesi said.

"You know what day Christmas is," Paulie said.

"December 18th, ain't it?" Cremesi shrugged. "Only this year it came on July 23rd. I must've missed it."

"Christmas is my birthday."

"A Christmas baby, huh," Cremesi said.

"I'm not a baby." Paulie stamped his feet.

"How old you gonna be," Cremesi said. "Let me guess, thirty-one, or -"

"Five." Paulie held up his hand with all his fingers extended.

Cremesi smiled at the boy, and catching eyes with Costa, managed to keep the smile going. Both Lucia, Costa's oldest child, and Paulie, the youngest of his four, had been born on Christmas Eve at the stroke of midnight. This was potentially a grace, or a major mishap. As Costa and Cremesi both knew, being born midnight Christmas Eve had consequences. A girl so marked would likely grow up to be a witch; a boy, to develop into a werewolf. Or fortune could play out more generously, and such children would find the opposite - that they were equipped to cure anyone who had been gazed on by the evil eye. They were too young, Costa's children, to be put to the test. And Costa hoped never to do so, and that they would never be drawn into the family business. He nursed ambitions that Paulie would become a lawyer or a doctor; the girls, maybe a teacher, briefly, before marrying.

"I know a four-year old that ought to be in bed," Costa said.

"Yeah?" Paulie said. He ducked his head before his

father could swat him. "Where'd you find him?" Then he slammed the door, and went scurrying up the stairs.

Cremesi turned his attention back to the bread and peppers. Costa sat and regarded him. Cremesi was destined to be forever an underling because he lacked self-control. Restraint and measure had long ago commended itself to Costa. Where the *angelese* got it wrong was this: they had not so much held their passions in check, as never had them in the first place. Lawrence Lowell was a case in point: the man had no children, and he did not even live with his wife. He preferred instead to lodge among his similarly gray-faced cronies at the Harvard Club. Costa regarded this arrangement as dubious and unnatural.

"So," Cremesi said, wiping his lips. "You want me to track down the renegade strega operator. And make an example of him."

Costa nodded.

"I got a good kid working for me," Cremesi said. "Been using him for my street ops. Nicky Prega."

Costa remembered him: Prega was the weedy street punk who'd had a recent brush with the law - the incident with Andre Pierre and the DeGrace outfit. But nothing much had come of it. Nor was Costa afraid of any serious retaliation from DeGrace: the *melazana* had no sense of family and honor, and that lack had weakened them from within. In truth, Costa felt distaste for Prega, ferret-faced and needle-chinned, a furtive look to his eyes. But his distaste was of no consequence, because apparently, Prega would be useful.

CHAPTER TEN

"Your port, Dean Lowell." The butler deposited the heavy-bottomed crystal decanter on the mahogany side table, and glided out of the study as soundlessly as he had entered.

Lowell poured a glass, and offered it to the figure sitting across from him. "Governor Cox," he said, then poured a glass for himself. "Let's pity those for whom prohibition was necessary, and hope it improves their lot."

Cox grunted. They clinked glasses.

"Our club steward thought to overstock the wine cellar just before the noble experiment began," Lowell said.

Cox frowned. "Would that we were as provident in larger matters." He gave his snifter a swirl. "The State House finance committee dragged on interminably. Be fruitful and multiply, I pointed out, refers more profitably to cash reserves, than to human progeny - a truth all too many of our recent arrivals sadly neglect. And to our cost more than theirs." Cox's merriment at his witticism was so deep it made no sound. "I shall be almost glad to relinquish office next month, and return to the practice of law."

"Ah yes, our new governor," Lowell said. "The motor

car salesman." He shook his head. "Mr. Fuller is no doubt a fine man, but he hardly has the background to be a governor. He did not attend Harvard. He did not attend Yale. He didn't even attend Dart-" He stopped himself.

Cox looked at him.

"He has not the education of a gentleman," Lowell continued. "From John Winthrop onwards, the Governor of the Commonwealth has been made an honorary partner in Grimely and Graybody."

"An honor indeed."

"This new one has no legal background whatsoever, and that lack concerns me."

"The alternative was considerably more dismaying." Cox sighed.

"James Michael Curley," Lowell said. "Running for governor while still serving as mayor. Having him in City Hall has been distressing enough."

Cox nodded, took a sip of port, and savored it briefly. "To move on from the pleasantries, the Owen gathering - what transpired?"

"Early days, of course," Lowell said. "The meeting disbanded less than an hour ago, but I would say, without wishing to get ahead of myself, that it is fairly probable Timothy Owen will take over the Druid's Den. Ben Owen, it seems, has a life elsewhere."

"Where?"

"Philadelphia."

"Goodness," Cox said, so softly it was scarcely more an exhaled breath.

"Timothy Owen, however, is well known to us."

"Timothy?" Cox said. "The paper boy?"

"He calls himself a reporter."

"He commits journalism, does he?"

They chuckled.

"Very nearly," Lowell said. "Timothy Owen writes for the *Transcript*."

"And Timothy Owen....aspires to be of our party?"

Cox said.

"I believe so." Lowell smiled sadly. Tim Owen was terribly eager to be accepted. In a way, it distressed Lowell, the futility of the project, when non-Saxons attempted to pass. Still, it was an attempt to progress - commendable and strangely moving, for all that it was doomed. Lowell believed in progress. That was why the voodoo of Roxbury had to be suppressed, the North End strega uprooted, the occult power of Hebrew letters shattered, and the bog-trotting hag-ridden magic of the Irish crushed once and for all. It was for the good of civilization – more than that, it *was* civilization.

"And if Timothy Owen were to oversee the Druid's Den," Lowell said, "it would be almost as though we were established there ourselves."

"We'd be in a reasonably propitious position, certainly," Cox said. "But let's not get ahead of ourselves."

"Indeed," Lowell said. "At the moment, tensions are brewing among the neighborhoods, and against us. Mr. DeGrace is not satisfied with the justice our courts dispensed in the case of his cousin. Both Mr. Costa and Jerome David decry our efforts to keep this country American. Mr. O'Connor is making overtures to us, under the guise of maintaining civil order. Mr. Costa claims his livelihood is being ruined by the O'Connors. And it appears the O'Connors have their own animus against the Costas, on account of the illness in the Curley family. "

"Curley," Cox murmured. His fingers tensed up as if they'd been burnt. "I have learned from our banking sources that Curley has inquired into refinancing that outrageous house of his, as a means of funding his next campaign."

"Shameless," Lowell said.

"But best to keep still on that front for the moment," Cox said. "First things first. We have to consider our arrangement with the police force, many of them of Curley's persuasion, in relation to the Cotton Club."

"New Year's Eve, just two weeks away," Lowell said.

"Do you believe O'Connor can be trusted on this occasion?"

"I do."

"We shall let the O'Connors '*do our dirty work,*' I believe is the expression. Our Hibernian friends, so to speak, may prove useful to us, for a time. Our enemy's enemy is our friend - allow me a cliché if you will."

"A sordid boon," Lowell said. "We have our own animus against strega. Senator Lodge has been gone scarcely a month." He shook his head. "Alas poor Cabot."

"I knew him well," Cox said.

They raised their chins in muted and momentary mirth.

"And just as Senator Lodge strove to contain the undesirables in this great nation, you have labored mightily to quell the alarming Hebraic quotient in your own bailiwick," Cox said.

Lowell bowed his head slightly, accepting the compliment.

"Would that the Senator had limited immigration more stringently, and earlier," Cox said. "He might still be alive today."

Lowell considered his glass of port. "His work lives on, Governor. The legislation enacted this past spring is a most worthy legacy. Immigration of Asiatic peoples has been effectively banned, and of southern Europeans, severely curtailed."

"A mercy on us all," Cox said.

"Perhaps, in time, certain immigrant peoples might be educated sufficiently to enter civilization," Lowell said. "I would be the first to invite them to share in our prosperity – provided, first, they share in our ideals. But far too many cling to their origins, and refuse to embrace America."

"So we are agreed, as regards the recalcitrants," Cox said. "Divide and conquer."

"At this juncture, yes."

They toasted, and took a long slow sup.

"How is your sister these days?" Cox asked.

"Busy with her poetry."

"And smoking her cigars?"

"The same as always. Dear Amy."

"Still unmarried, I presume."

"Yes." Lowell sighed. "She used to be a fairly attractive woman. But lately she's let herself go." He regarded his fingertips. "It seems there is always one member of a family who must march to the beat of a different drummer."

"Sometimes more than one," Cox said. "Your bloodline is graced with not merely the poetess Amy, Boston's very own Sappho - I refer to her poetic gifts alone, of course - but also that distant cousin. The free-thinker, on Marlborough Street. A Unitarian Universalist, I believe. He went to...Bowdoin College, wasn't it?"

"Yes."

"He plays the recorder," Cox commented.

"Robert Cabot-Lowell," Lowell murmured. "Thankfully our paths seldom cross."

Cox took another sip of port, and then cleared his throat. "Speaking of such matters, a certain affair within my own family has come to my attention. It is of surpassing delicacy. A nephew of mine - a former student of yours - is pursuing certain unsuitable affiliations."

Lowell almost raised an eyebrow.

"Prescott Ames."

"Prescott." Lowell gave his glass of port a twirl. "Had a brush with various authorities. Ah, well. Youth is often -"

"I was referring to certain unnatural tendencies."

"Oh?" Lowell said. "I thought that was all in the past."

"The boy's my flesh and blood, I am ashamed but bound to admit. I had nursed hopes that time would cure him of his peculiarities. But it would seem not."

"The University suffered an infestation of such in the past," Lowell said. "Prescott was but one abscess among many, and he was hardly the most festering."

"I am pleased," Cox said.

"I took all necessary steps," Lowell continued, "and the disease was purged from the body *universitas* and I dared hope, *civitas*." He looked up and shook his head. "I was sorry to have to expel him, Governor. But there was an issue of fairness. I had already expelled so many like him."

"Of course," Cox said. "We all hoped the shock of expulsion would purge him of his deviancies. It seems, however, that he's taken to haunting certain establishments. The Gaslight Club, for one - a demimonde establishment at the foot of Beacon Hill, akin to the theatre in its extravagances and perversion."

Lowell joined his hands together, fingertip to fingertip, and frowned.

"Prescott has also been spotted in Green Shutters," Cox said. "A *'tearoom,'* so called - in a gross befouling of a fine and genteel tradition - on Cedar Lane Way. Cocktails are served in porcelain teacups. Psychoanalysis is the rage - discussions of a largely sexual nature, and almost without exception Jewish in origin. And the most radical of political talk flourishes like bay trees. Neither Sacco nor Vanzetti could be more incendiary."

Lowell's mouth made a thin tight line in his long colorless face. "Who knew such a narrow brick-lined alley could host such iniquity?"

"My thought exactly," Cox said. He sipped his port. "Further, these establishments are spawning legions of Bohemians. They crowd our streets, sporting shiny black suits, broad brimmed felt hats, wide Basque-country belts, and" - he hesitated and lowered his voice - "van dyke beards."

At mention of the last, Lowell shuddered.

"The anarchist and the degenerate," Cox said. "In such redoubts, they join together so very readily."

"Indeed," Lowell said.

"I must ask that you exercise your full prerogative as my deputy, in connection with Prescott. And that you bend your thoughts towards what chastisement is most appropriate. Take care, devote time, and be thorough and exacting."

Lowell knew he was being directed to do what needed to be done in the best interests of the boy's family, his people, and his city. Adjudicating on another's fate, determining the degree of fault, and bestowing appropriate blame - such was the task that chastened Lowell's heart, and made him glow from within. "Certainly," Lowell said. "May our fair city, like the University, be forever free of such taint."

Lowell allowed himself to settle further into his chair. Even with the conflicts at hand, how congenial Lowell found his existence in this gentlemen's club. The grand estate in Brookline, with its acres of gardens and clipped hedges and vast green lawns, only succeeded in making Lowell feel trapped. It became positively claustrophobic whenever Anna opened her mouth. His wife's voice seemed to track him down, and rattle him loose from whatever comfortable corner he ever managed to find for himself. How much more companionable this - the Harvard Club, with its quiet order, sense of right in the offing, tacit understandings among men, lack of fuss, and project of eternal progress.

President Lowell and Governor Cox took the last of their port in silence, and watched the fire burn down to a suitably decorous gray ash.

CHAPTER ELEVEN

As Ben stood by the sink, and finished the last of his morning coffee, the clock struck 9:22. He was already bundled into his overcoat, a well-worn copy of *Julius Caesar* from last semester still stowed deep inside the right-hand pocket. Last night he'd been about his father's business. This morning, he was preparing to confront his own. Today, he would walk by the townhouse on Marlborough Street. If he saw her, he would speak to her.

He hoped he wouldn't see her.

The back door rattled. A creature was scratching at it, and whining.

"Eloise, no," a voice said.

Ben opened the door. Head down, cap low over his eyes, Hugh trundled in. His boots squeaked faintly.

"Those shot glasses could do with restocking," Hugh said. He settled into his bar stool, and folded his hands. "I noticed that the other night." Eloise sat at his side.

"How about an eye-opener?" Ben said.

"A gentleman never drinks until noon," Hugh said. He twiddled his thumbs.

As he slipped on his gloves, Ben looked through the window into the Den's back yard. It was a miniature grove

- three maple trees, a copper beech, two elms, and closest to the den, the mighty oak. Not a single branch was broken. There was no doubt - that whole incident in which, goaded beyond all patience, he'd grabbed the wood axe and hacked off a branch, had been a dream. How grief wreaks havoc with men's minds, he thought.

To assure himself that the branch was absolutely intact, Ben moved closer to the window. He rested his forehead and palms against the cold glass. A ladder was propped up against the outside wall of the Den, the long spare figure of Allyn Jones balanced on the top rung.

Allyn was leaning forward, and binding the drainpipe with a silvery repair tape. His lips were moving - talking to himself, the way old men do. Ben tapped on the windowpane. Allyn looked down and gave Ben a quick nod.

Ben opened the window an inch. "Allyn, come in and warm up. And have a cup of coffee," he said, and shut the window.

*   *   *

"Saw that drainpipe, just as I was passing by," Allyn said. His frame was now wedged onto the end barstool. "It cried out to me, like a wounded creature." He took a sip of coffee. "Whenever your father's place needs tending, I am at the ready."

"There's always a place for you here," Ben said. "Whoever takes over."

"A blow to us all, your da's passing." Allyn looked down at his hands. He fiddled a bit with his signet ring, which was gold, and emblazoned with a dragon. Then he looked up, grinning. "Maybe it's just seeing you back on your old stomping grounds. But somehow, it doesn't feel like he's left us at all. Not entire, like. You know what I mean?"

"I do," Ben said.

"While you're still rattling around town, I wonder if you'll be looking up - oh she was pretty - Ellie Cabot Lo -"

Ben put down his coffee cup. "I'm just making sure the Den is in order, and then I'm going back. To Philadelphia." There, no one had a claim on him. He was left to his books and his solitude. Boston was fraught with complications. Here, the streets were cramped and noisy. His deceased father hovered over him - the eternal guardian of the draining of the radiators. And Miss Ellie Cabot-Lowell, the girl who had one eye blue and the other one green, still breathed and walked.

"Sure," Allyn said, with the hint of a smile. "Before you go back. To Philadelphia." He drank the last of his coffee, and stood up. "A couple of roof tiles could use patching up, you don't mind me saying." He loped out the front door. The bells over the lintel rattled in his wake.

Ben stood up, and tightened his scarf.

"I'll mind the fort," Hugh said, staring straight ahead. "Eloise at the ready."

"Good," Ben said. "I was hoping for that." Eloise flopped over on her side, and snored. Ben went out the door, and with a mixture of joy and trepidation, rejoined the city of his youth.

The air was crisp, and the sky was blue. Ben's footsteps rang out on the ice-slicked path across the Common, and the wind sliced through him. The pale winter sun glanced off the expanse of Charles Street. At the curb, Ben stopped and waited for the traffic to clear. He stamped his feet. Passersby buffeted him from both sides. A boxer dog strained forward on its leash, breath steamy in the cold. A burly codger of a man, hands in his coats, his hat brim flopping down to his nose, and his face deep in shadow, brushed by him, and drew to a stop on his right. On his left, a tall, spindly-shouldered Negro man swooped in. He was stiffly buttoned into a church-going black overcoat, and had a red bow tie at his throat. A car pulled up to the curb, directly in front of Ben. It was a hearse.

The skinny man in the bow tie lurched forward and pulled the door open.

"Get inside," the man ordered. His voice was not only faintly muffled, but curiously flat in tone.

Ben braced himself, about to flee, when the man in the bow tie and the man in the floppy hat both stepped squarely into him, and pushed him forward into the hearse. One man slammed the door shut; the other rapped sharply on the roof, at which point the hearse immediately sped forward.

Ben was wedged up sideways on the coffin platform, his knees jutting into his chest, and his head bumping against the car roof. "Where are you taking me?" he asked, but he was pretty sure he knew.

The driver said nothing. The car accelerated, and veered around the corner onto Tremont Street.

"A hearse," Ben said. "How convenient." He laughed.

The driver looked into the rear view mirror. The eyes staring back at Ben were lusterless.

Now Ben knew for certain where he was going

CHAPTER TWELVE

DeGrace's establishment was the end row house on a block of three-story brownstones, set apart from the street by a narrow stretch of yard, and a wrought iron fence. A large black sign, with self-important gold lettering: "DeGrace's Home of Eternal Rest," was affixed to the gate.

The hearse drove past the gate, turned down a side alley, and drew to a stop. A guard was pacing back and forth by a shadowy doorway. He had a stiff-legged mechanical gait, and when he turned and approached the car, his eyes were like the driver's: vacant and intense. He opened the back door of the hearse, clamped a heavy, unwarm hand on Ben's arm, and drew him from the car. The guard retained his grip on Ben's arm as he led the way to a side door of the house. He kicked the door twice, paused, then kicked it once more.

The side door creaked open, revealing a sliver of dark hallway. What light there was glinted off Coup DeGrace's wire-rimmed spectacles, and the broad white of his shirt under a dark suit.

"Nigel, let go, and return to patrol," DeGrace commanded.

The guard released his grip, and lumbered a few steps away.

"Andre would have known better," DeGrace said. "Don't mind Nigel. He's new to it all."

"Join the club," Ben said.

DeGrace remembered to smile, then his face fell back into its customary grave, almost lugubrious, expression as he ushered Ben inside. "I am pleased you came here, Ben."

"I had a choice?"

"You did not fight my invitation. I choose to see that as an auspicious sign."

DeGrace led the way through the elegant townhouse. It was thick with silence and blue shadows. They went down a carpeted corridor, and turned left, past the funeral home parlor with its heavy curtains, then past the embalming room, tiled in light green, and smelling of disinfectant. The hallways throughout were decorated with paintings in thick gilded frames. Under one of them, a child's crayon drawing had been affixed in place. It depicted a man sitting at a piano. The title scrawled under the image, in bright purple, read: "Nigel as Was."

"My youngest, Amelia," DeGrace said, with a chuckle. "A budding artist." He led Ben down a short staircase, and into a drawing room. The room was slightly sunken, and furnished in lush, gray upholstery.

King David was lounging in the plushest, deepest armchair, his two-tone brogues splayed out in opposite directions like they'd had a quarrel. He raised his tumbler of scotch in greeting.

"Your father was a far-sighted individual," DeGrace said, offering Ben a chair. "Untainted by the prejudice so many unfortunately bear, he invited me into the Den. It seems you carry on in his great tradition, meeting with a colored man."

"I'm just doing what needs to be done," Ben said, sitting down. "And then of course I'll be going home."

DeGrace sat back in his armchair.

Ben was not sure if he'd heard a creak of a chair, or a snicker from one of the men, so he clarified: "To Philadelphia."

"Sure, kid." King David sat up and smoothed his tie. It was chartreuse silk adorned with crimson horseshoes and electric blue diamonds.

DeGrace reached over to a sideboard, and pulled the stopper from a bottle of rye. He poured a measure, and offered the glass to Ben, who shook his head. DeGrace poured the rye back, not spilling a drop.

Overhead a bell chimed, sweet and silvery.

"The postman," DeGrace said.

The bell stirred the recesses of Ben's memory, deeper than his consciousness, and spurred his sense of duty and honor. He found himself blurting out: "I have a warning for you. This New Year's Eve, don't open the Cotton Club."

"New Year's?" DeGrace sat back. "That is our most profitable night."

"A real shindig," King David said, grinning. "Rake in the big clams and the sweet tomatoes both, you get my drift."

"The police are planning a raid on the premises," Ben said. "They'll make it look like a standard speakeasy bust. But what they're after is a total clamp-down on your operations."

DeGrace pushed his spectacles up.

"They know you're vulnerable, Mr. DeGrace. When you lost Andre, you lost your top bodyguard. Unique, wasn't he?"

"Perhaps he was," DeGrace said.

"Because you grafted iron fists onto him, though actually they were made of brass," Ben said. "Melted down from a church bell."

DeGrace drew back slightly.

"You hid them," Ben went on, "under those white kid gloves he always wore."

King David snorted. "Got to hand it to you, kid, you're in town - what, a coupla days, and you're telling us what's what."

"Not many know about the hands," DeGrace said. "I have to ask myself how you do."

"I am my father's son."

"I am beginning to see that," DeGrace said. He did not smile.

"Ok, kid," King David said. "So what's with this New Year's Eve scam?"

"A platoon of party girls will show up at the club," Ben said.

King David smacked his lips. "Okay by me."

"White ones," Ben said. "And younger than is legal. To cause maximum outrage when the Vice Squad sweeps in and word gets out."

"Who's behind it?" DeGrace said. "The rank and file?"

"Or the mucky-muck commissioner?" King David said.

"They're in it together."

"O'Connor and Lowell," King David cracked his knuckles. "I knew it!"

"And together, they've got the firepower," Ben said. "The Bluebloods deliver the police headquarters. And the State House."

"The courts." DeGrace frowned.

"The banks," King David said.

"The power plant," Ben continued. "And Harvard University."

"O'Connor delivers the mayor's office," DeGrace said.

"The cops on the beat," King David said.

"As well they hear the forewarning of deaths soon to be, and control the vagaries of wind and mist," DeGrace said. "Who can stand against such cold?"

"Who indeed?" Ben agreed. The question echoed the one his father had asked him in that dream.

" *'What is peace, son?'* " his father had said. Ben, exhausted in that dim hour of dawn, and in the midst of re-arranging the blanket, had been stumped. He covered his ignorance by landing a solid punch to the pillow. "Not the absence of tension," his father had gone on, "for that is the peace dreamed of by fools. Practical peace is this: the judicious distribution of tension."

And Ben heard himself say: "You two could stand against the cold. Form an alliance, just as they have."

King David slapped his forehead. He winked at DeGrace, who pursed his lips in response. "Now that's using your noodle, ain't it, Coup?"

"We have a veritable Metternich is in our midst."

King David looked at DeGrace and shrugged. "Didn't catch that one, Coupster."

"A diplomat," DeGrace said. "He championed the notion that a balance of powers among nations is the surest means of securing peace."

"No kidding," King David said. He rubbed his nose with the flat of his palm.

"Ben, this establishment is already testament to the spirit of concord that exists between King David and myself."

"Wasn't I telling you the other night, kid?" King David said. "Coup's saying we both got a stake in this joint. We get along simpatico."

"Right," Ben said.

"For the most part," DeGrace said.

"So what if a few of my dollars here and there go missing?" King David shrugged. "I don't get my drawers in an uproar. All for the good of the city, Bensy - that's what I got on the bean."

DeGrace raised an eyebrow. "Still, this club is but one small establishment. And my foot soldiers, I fear, are not as obedient and industrious as in previous generations."

"Kids today huh!" King David glanced at DeGrace, reached forward, and swatted Ben on the arm. "Look at me - since my own dad kicked the bucket, there ain't been a whole lot of strong-arm magic-power from my neck of the woods."

"So while your proposition is sound in concept, Ben," DeGrace said, "it is lacking in scope."

"Your idea's pretty swell, he means," King David said. "Only it don't go far enough."

"Correct," DeGrace said.

"How's about Coup and I buy you out of the Den," King David said.

"And without any of that so-called '*funny paper*' that's been circulating in certain quarters," DeGrace said. He gave King David a sideways look.

King David pantomimed bewilderment. He turned to Ben. "You got it on the nose, kid. The only way this burg'll have peace is if me and Coup take over the Druid's Den. Together, like."

"That's not what I was getting at," Ben said.

"King David and I hardly constitute the threat to order that the O'Connor-Lowell alliance does," DeGrace said. He gave a sad, knowing chuckle. "The northern races still conspire to control the world, excluding both the African and the Semite, at every turn. If they combine, unopposed, they will inevitably take over the Druid's Den itself."

"Oh no," Ben said. "I -"

"But if the Druid's Den were to fall under our management at this juncture," DeGrace said.

"From the get-go," King David said.

"A proper order is maintained."

"Balance things out," King David said. He sat forward. "Like you said -"

"I've made another arrangement," Ben said. "It will keep the city at peace, and -"

"What arrangement is that?" DeGrace said.

"My brother Tim."

"The scribbler." DeGrace pursed his lips.

"Knows all the hot gossip, that's for sure," King David conceded. "Choice bits that don't get no choicer. Got them inky fingers to prove it. Doubt he can ever get them clean."

"I'm aware Lowell has been cultivating Timothy," DeGrace said. "But I doubt he will for much longer."

"Tim's my father's son, too," Ben said. "His loyalty isn't in question."

"Sure of that, kid?" King David said.

"Forgive me, but your brother does seem rather enraptured with our bow-tied brethren," DeGrace said.

"Sucks up to the Lowells," King David said, with a wink. "Get it?"

"I got it," Ben said.

From the gloom of the hallway, a maidservant, slim and specter-like, emerged. She passed a note to DeGrace, and with a faint clicking of her almost fleshless joints, retreated back into the hall.

DeGrace read the note and slipped it into his pocket. "The dead are always with us. Thankfully." He straightened his cuffs. "I am grateful to you for giving us word about New Year's. But I ask that you think about our proposal. The future of this great city depends on it. Comity is an excellent suggestion. It only needs to be followed to its logical conclusion, the running of the Den itself." DeGrace stood up. "Could I offer you a lift home, Ben, or -?"

"No, thanks." Ben got up to leave. He glanced at King David, who remained seated.

"Coup and me, we got some biz to attend to," King David said, and downed the last of his scotch

CHAPTER THIRTEEN

Ben lumbered over the snowdrifts along Tremont Street for several blocks, and turned onto Berkeley Street. The traffic was busy, and the slush was dirty. The spray from a passing laundry van spattered over him. But he was not dispirited. He had delivered his father's warning, and he was still intent on his mission of this morning. His feelings for Ellie Cabot-Lowell had to be declared, or laid to rest - and possibly both.

He had planned on going through the Common, then into the Back Bay. But the road and sidewalk ahead were blocked with heavy bollards and a couple of police wagons.

A bright-eyed young policeman emerged from the shadows, his badge glinting in the winter sun. "Roadworks, mister," he said. He pointed to a sign marked Detour. "Just take it all the way along, and you'll wind up on Boylston Street, good as new."

The detour took Ben along the edge of a Chinese enclave. The signs were mostly in Chinese. The street smelled of roasting meat and unfamiliar herbs. The men had close-cropped black hair, and hurried along, hands in their pockets. They were bundled into dark shapeless clothing, navy, black, and gray; and there were no women or children among them. The wind was rising. It whistled through the narrow spaces between the tenement buildings, and sent the trash cans at the curb crashing to the pavement, where they rolled, rumbling, across the street.

Ben put his head down, and struggled into the brutal wind. The sky went black. A hard rain began to pour, fierce and unremitting. In an instant, Ben's hair was sopping wet, and the driving rain pelted through his overcoat into his shirt. A cold clamminess seeped across his chest. He could not see where he was going. He persevered for a several blocks, and came to a stop. Shop fronts, traffic, and passersby had been swallowed up in the dark.

Summoning his strength, Ben turned the corner. The sky lightened a bit. The street ahead was deserted, and lined on both sides with hulking three-deckers. Somehow he'd landed in Southie, it looked like, though Ben remembered Southie as further away. Was he that disorientated? A tin can rattled down the street. The sea wind blew, carrying a whiff of salt and spray and diesel, and high above, a seagull called.

Up ahead, on his left, a pink and green neon sign began to flicker. It read: Mahoney's Diner. The glass front of the diner shimmered with rivulets of pink and green light, and Ben rushed towards it. Gratefully he pushed the heavy door open. Inside, the cafe was warm, and almost deserted. It smelled of coffee and bacon.

A bleary-eyed young man was wiping down the counter. A cigarette dangled from the center of his mouth. He looked at Ben. "Cats and dogs, fella?"

"Oh yes," Ben said. He stamped his feet on the mat, and hunkered into the first booth. "Coffee, please."

"You got it," the young man said. He poured water into a pot, and lit a burner. The phone beside the cash register rang. The young man jimmied the cigarette to the side of his mouth and answered. "Who?" He looked up. "You Ben Owen?"

Ben nodded.

"Somebody's looking for you," the man said. "Be my guest." He slung the disk cloth over his shoulder, and, whistling, turned back to making coffee.

Ben went to the telephone and picked up the receiver. "Hello?"

CHAPTER FOURTEEN

"Hello yourself," O'Connor answered. He drew his kitchen door shut. Rosalie was in the front parlor, reading a book, and humming softly. "Your friend from Southie here." The phone line crackled, and O'Connor went on. "Heard you've been stepping out, Ben. The old soft shoe, all the way to the Roxbury line. So I felt it was incumbent upon my own sweet self to show you some hospitality, O'Connor style. Heard it was raining in your neck of the woods, so I did." Whenever O'Connor tried to pour on bonhomie, the effort took a toll on him. A little pinch settled at the back of his eyeballs, and it tightened with every syllable of cheer he uttered.

Down the stairs, in O'Connor's basement, Hollie began to warble and beat her wings against her silver cage. Built like a hummingbird, but with a miniature woman's face atop her feathered neck, Hollie had been key to O'Connor's ascent to the head of all Southie's underworld: her wail had proven to be not merely the portent of death, but also a self-fulfilling prophecy, a virtual guarantee a given hit would be successful. Everyone knew he had the power of the banshee, but the form the banshee took was, so far as he was aware, a secret known only to himself and his wife. Hollie was a tremendous weapon in his arsenal - but she was still an A-1 pain in the neck. For now, she could wait.

"A squall came up," Ben said. "Out of nowhere, now that you mention it, and led me astray. What do you want?"

"Can't one good friend call another?" O'Connor said. Arranging the wind, the rain, and the detail cop had gone off without a hitch - lots easier than when Gyrffth Owen had been minding the shop. O'Connor even had plenty of time left this morning to cut a deal with Garrity on that consignment of munitions. They'd agreed a price - O'Connor getting every penny he demanded, and then some; and they'd cut Sniper Healy out of the picture. That felt good. Healy had only one eye, but what eye he had was cold and gimlet-like, and Healy had been getting too big for his boots of late. All that was left was for O'Connor to get the munitions to Charlestown by tomorrow. "Just wanting to hear that you are well, so I was. Have you ordered lunch yet, Ben?"

"Hey, how did you even know where I -"

"Get the lamb stew. It's the best in the city."

Hollie's wings fluttered more insistently against the bars of her cage. "A cupcake would be most delightful," she twittered. She had reached the far edge of cheerful, and was on the border of cranky. O'Connor was feeling the same. He got to the point.

"It would be a pity, a shame, so it would," O'Connor went on, "if your fellow Celts were to feel excluded from your favor. Like depriving us of the sun itself. You surely can't be planning to turn the Den over to that pair."

"I'm not," Ben said. "I'm only ensuring the peace is kept, and -"

"Leave it to those of us who live here, Ben, to keep our own peace," O'Connor said.

"Cupcake, please. Now!" Hollie shrieked

"And the corned beef hash," O'Connor said. "Every

mouthful is a poem." He hung up.

"Chocolate frosting," Hollie trilled.

"Take it easy," O'Connor said. He went to the breadbox, took out a chocolate cupcake with pink sprinkles, and plodded down the basement stairs.

Hollie took one look at the plate, and rushed at the bars of her cage. "Only one, dear?"

"Finish this one first." O'Connor was already looking over the contraption on the floor. It had a square base of glass and wood, with an earphone attached to the side, a "sound amplification machine." He pushed aside a few old paint cans, and opened up the large cardboard box behind them. The inside of the box was black with Tommy guns. From the shelf overhead, he took down a large bag of bows and Christmas tree ornaments, and emptied it over the guns.

"Another one, please," Hollie chirped.

"Keep your shirt on," O'Connor said. He took a pen from his pocket, and a roll of tape from the shelf.

"I don't wear a shirt, dear," Hollie said. "I don't need to. It's called plumage."

O'Connor scrawled "XMAS Decos" across the top of the carton. He taped the box shut. Between that, and the oddball contraption next to it, O'Connor was sure he'd provided a fine decoy for the contraband.

"Chocolate, and marshmallow," Hollie trilled. "And purple sprinkles. It would be most delightful."

"Whatever shuts you up," O'Connor said.

"I don't think rudeness is a good idea, dear. Ever. Do you?"

O'Connor called up the stairs. "Rosie?" From the glass in the back door, a rectangle of winter sunlight slanted in across the kitchen floor.

"Yes, my love," Rosalie called back.

"Could you be bringing me down another cupcake?"

"More than just one," Hollie said.

A rap sounded at the kitchen door.

"I thought you'd be better prepared," Hollie cheeped.

Rosalie appeared on the threshold, holding a plate of cupcakes. A shadow blotted out the rectangle of sunlight.

"It's Healy," Rosalie said in a low tone. "On his own. I think."

O'Connor reached behind the cans of paint, and extracted a gun.

"I'll see to Hollie, why don't I?" Rosalie said.

"That might be best," O'Connor said as he checked the gun was loaded.

"You take care of boy's business, dear," Hollie warbled.

Rosalie descended the staircase. O'Connor passed her, on his way up.

"Cupcakes are for girls," Hollie sang. Her wings began to beat faster. A wail rose from her tiny body, and gaining in volume, resounded against the walls of the house.

O'Connor smiled. Matters with Healy were about to be settled, for good.

CHAPTER FIFTEEN

Down in the shadowy depths of the tenement, the revolutionary took up his pen, and smoothed out the blank page in front of him. At his elbow was a parcel of thinly sliced cold cuts, wrapped in a bit of old newspaper. He was about to reach for a slice, when he glanced down at the grimy newsprint. He could not avoid reading:

Mayor's Daughter Fading

With the point of his pen, the revolutionary stabbed the notepaper straight through. It was not his intention. But he had inadvertently caused the serious illness of one of a particular age. He could not deny it. The revolutionary is committed to truth in all things.

The horror of that fact came over him now and again, and covered his mind in a darkness it took days to shake. He pushed the parcel of cold cuts aside, and with a determinedly firm wrist and in a steady script, he wrote:

Bourgeois sentimentality is a lingering disease, at first debilitating and finally fatal.

The Curley girl had never been his target; nor even

Curley himself, for all that the Curley was part of the ruling class. Curley's endless battle cry, that the Irish were the oppressed, was blatant false consciousness, a distraction from the fundamental and manifest class injustice. Those who held office or maintained the law were part of the apparatus of oppression - the revolutionary knew that in his marrow. But now, when he heard the cry of a sick child, a cloud of despair descended over him. His hands tightened into fists and his heart turned to stone.

The revolutionary had meant to inflict illness, but not on the mayor's daughter. His target had been a certain policeman - a red-haired, blue-eyed lug, who had repeatedly bullied him, whistled at him, called him a "pretty boy."

It was on a misty, wind-swept day in October. The streets had been slick with rain, and yellow with fallen leaves. The revolutionary stationed himself on a street corner with a direct view of the policeman. The Curley girl was on her way home from school. As she went by the policeman, she slipped on the wet leaves, and dropped her school satchel. The contents spilled every which way: pencils, crayons, and papers. The policeman stepped forward. He leant down, took hold of the girl's satchel, and helped gather up her belongings. The revolutionary fixed his gaze resolutely on the uniformed tool of the state; but the girl, scrambling after her belongings, depositing them into the satchel, kept bobbing in and out of view. How the revolutionary had longed to hear the watchman for bourgeois capitalism collapse in a coughing fit. But the girl, as it emerged, had received the force of his gaze.

He tried to take no interest in her fate. He took to humming, tapping his foot, and adopting a vacant look in his eye whenever her name was mentioned. But the papers and the radio carried so many reports that he could not avoid learning of the girl's condition.

For all these efforts that had gone wrong, the revolutionary was morbidly contrite. He assuaged himself the only way he knew. He picked up a pen, and began writing.

Let the ruling classes tremble at a communist revolution. The proletarians have nothing to lose but our chains. We have a world to win. Hindrances feed our fervor as surely as dry wood feeds a fire.

CHAPTER SIXTEEN

Baron Samedi, the loa of the dead, might prove reluctant to make an appearance. DeGrace uncorked the flask of rum that was set out on the altar, alongside a Cuban cigar and an ebony cigarette lighter. Perhaps he should have purchased a new top hat, black silk with a bright purple lining - Baron Samedi had the dandy's weakness for all such finery. Or perhaps DeGrace should have set the altar up in a more impressive room than this little alcove off the garage. Still, Henriette had given them that fine midday feast, with roasted hen, capon and rooster all on offer; and the altar was as nicely appointed as many he had attended.

Perhaps after this ceremony, he could sleep soundly again. Ever since the verdict on Andre's murderers had been pronounced, and the killers set free, DeGrace had felt a perpetual weight on his chest. Several times, heavy pots had been dashed against the floor, unaided by any visible hand; and every night, just as he was hovering on the precipice of sleep, every door in the house slammed, and jolted him back to wakefulness. Neither DeGrace's home nor his person had been at peace since the vermin who had murdered Andre Pierre had been released. DeGrace turned now to the loa to counsel him.

"An offering for Erzulie Freda," Marie Beniste, said. She stepped forward, her ankles wobbling in her high heels. She had a prim twist to her lips. She snapped open her oversized pocketbook, and took out a bottle of perfume. "The scent is Evening in Paris," she informed DeGrace, as though that fact were of the utmost significance.

Erzulie Freda was the spirit of love, and Marie was Henriette's niece, and though now well over thirty, had no suitor, nor prospect of one. Out of consideration for his wife, DeGrace feigned surprise at this circumstance. Henriette had insisted DeGrace include Marie in the next ceremony. And DeGrace knew a show-off loa like Baron Samedi would never stir himself for an audience of just one. Joseph Napoleon, the youngest nephew of DeGrace's attorney, stood apart from them, his hands in pockets. He was a tall, slightly built, almost fragile-looking man. His pinstriped banker's suit was loose, as though he had shrunk inside of it, and from its folds, a sickly sweet smell rose. His eyes were heavy-lidded, dolorous, and bloodshot. Joseph had been married six years and still had no children. Baron Samedi would have something to say about that.

DeGrace fed a twig into the fire. The fire crackled, and sent up trails of smoke.

Joseph turned around, with a look in his eye that was not entirely his own. He sashayed up to the altar, a cakewalking strut, and in a voice that was uncharacteristically deep, rough with scotch, cigars and raucous laughter, he announced, "Gonna have me some of that!" He scratched his crotch, and turned and burped in DeGrace's face.

"Baron Samedi?" DeGrace said.

"You got that right," Joseph/Baron Samedi said.

"You have come up from the world of the dead,

and -"

Joseph/Baron Samedi hooted. "Must be why you are the bokar, you know so much," he said, with a taunting grin.

"What has happened to the soul of Andre DeGrace?" DeGrace inquired. "Is he at peace?"

"Well," Joseph/Baron Samedi said, "let's see." He lit the cigar, took a puff, and blew the smoke into DeGrace's face. "There are them that go over the other side, and he can't rest a wink - in torment, like they rubbed his privates with a fresh-cut chili pepper. And he'll go wandering, and look to inflict such misery as he can. On them that didn't look out for him, body or soul. Them that let him get smashed *splat* like a rotten egg. Them that got no justice on poor little him's account neither."

"I can only strike once," DeGrace said. "And there are two of them."

Joseph/Baron Samedi's hips twitched. "There be one that's roaming the earth free as you please. Gets his picture in the paper like a movie star, and him's a nasty creature. Eyes like stone, and teeth like a rat. A girl rat! Got himself a pretty little girlfriend - blonde as can be. What they do get up to!" Joseph/Baron Samedi took another long slow swill of rum. He shook the flask, and from the glug DeGrace knew the flask was almost empty. "Burns fierce, this stuff. Like a dose of clap I got once - not off you, sister, I don't think."

Marie backed away.

"How'd you get so bow-legged, honey?" And Joseph, calling his own name, began twisting up, twitching this way and that, like a fish on a hook. The voice that was not Joseph's own alternated with a voice that was, and his body was pulled hither and thither with every call and response. "Ain't got no spawn, huh, Joseph? Shooting blanks. Remember that time you went to New Orleans.... *Tout seul* I was, Baron.... Only you weren't *seul* for long, Joseph. If you had been, would've only gone blind or got hair on your hands like a *loup garou*. But uh-uh - more gals than you could shake a stick at and by golly you did shake that stick of yours..... You can heal my affliction, Baron, you .... Joseph, I can do all kinds of things. Lots! Keep a person alive by not digging the grave, drive all women to distraction, and cure what ails you - you want me to, Joseph? ... I surely do!....Then you better get more rum next time, Joseph. And tobacco. I mean the good stuff. I know you got it. A peaceful sleep soon as I'm feeling good. Get me that good stuff huh, Joseph? ... Oh, sure thing, sir. I will do. I -"

And Joseph/Baron Samedi whirled, and slumped down, in a heap in the corner, exhausted, smelling of rum, and something sweeter and smokier.

DeGrace was already dashing up the stairs. He nimbly avoided stepping on one of Amelia's stray crayons, only to find another one crushed under his heel. But he had discovered what he needed. The ritual left him feeling both pure, and exhausted. It was as if he had recovered from an illness that had some beneficial purging effect. And he was braced for action. He knew himself to have drunk of a knowledge deeper than any other.

CHAPTER SEVENTEEN

"As a judge of character," Hugh was saying. "Eloise is always right. Did I tell you that, Ben?"

"I think you might have," Ben said. He was struggling to button the cuff of a fresh shirt. After the soaking at the hands of O'Connor, it was good be dry and warm again.

"Any board meeting," Hugh said, "if Eloise took against a fellow - tensed up, or drew back - I knew not to trust him. The one time I failed to heed her advice, I came a cropper." He leaned down and gave Eloise a scratch behind her ears. "The front windows could use a wash," he said, straightening up. He folded his hands, twiddled his thumbs, and looked ahead at nothing. "And there wasn't a drop of rain here."

"Well, Hugh," Ben said as he slipped on his coat. "I've got to be go -"

The phone rang. Ben reached his hand through his coat sleeve and answered on the first ring. "Hello."

"This is Mister De -"

"Coup," Ben said. "Have you and King David been talking things over?"

"Your call for peace has indeed resonated with me," DeGrace said. "I have taken it to heart. I am calling

87

because I wonder if you might arrange a meeting for me."

Ben clutched the phone tighter. "The Druid's Den is neutral ground." He hoped DeGrace would read the squeak in his voice as a fault on the line.

"Like an edifice designed to weather many storms, peace needs a firm foundation. I am indeed asking you to set up a meeting, but at this juncture, I would prefer to provide the location. And the person I require to see is Nicolas Prega."

"Prega?" Ben said.

"Before I can make a lasting alliance with anyone, I require tranquility in my heart. I need first to make peace with that Prega boy, and as expeditiously as possible."

"You're sure it's peace you want to make with him?"

"The only way I know how," DeGrace said. "The tensions are such at present I can hardly approach Costa on my own. It's up to you, Ben, to be the ambassador of peace."

"That's what I wanted to be, all right," Ben said. "I'll have to think about this."

"As you wish," DeGrace said. "But remember, peace and the chances for it are ever perishable." He hung up.

Ben slammed the receiver back in place. The last thing the city needed was another revenge hit.

And Ben still had plans of his own that day: the encounter he most dreaded, and most longed for.

CHAPTER EIGHTEEN

Ellie Cabot-Lowell was a thin shy girl with an upper lip that quivered when she was happy, and when she was sad, and sometimes for no good reason at all. Her right eye was azure blue, and the left one, a deep sea green. This feature had always amused Ben, for in his father's tradition, a creature with two different colored eyes had the power of seeing ghosts; moreover, the blue eye was empowered to see only good, and the green eye, only evil. Ben of course had advanced beyond such notions himself. But it was a fact that Ellie had a habit of holding her head to one side or the other. She seldom looked at people straight on, a tick Ben ascribed to shyness, and decided to find charming.

Ben and Ellie had first encountered each other one windy wet September afternoon at the Boston Athenaeum, at a lecture entitled: "Your Bark is as Good as Mine: Canine Companions in the *Song of Roland*, and *Tristan and Isolde*." From the audience, at question time, Ben had pointed out that in the Bible by contrast, not a single dog is even named. The lecturer, a retired professor at Boston University, and also Ellie's father, chuckled, and said that he considered that a sad lack to both Christianity and

Judaism. He was hardly a religious hothead, being genteelly Unitarian. Ellie was bringing a glass of water up to the lectern, and on her way back to her seat, she smiled at Ben, nearly tripped, and brushed an unruly strand of hair from her eyes.

The next day, as Ben was walking through the Common, ruminating over his latest monograph (Milton's apparent tri-theism in the *Aeropegietica*), a golden retriever came bounding down the hill, and collided into him. "Hey there fella," Ben said. The dog sat down, and nuzzled Ben. A cobalt blue enamel locket, shaped like a dog biscuit, dangled from his collar. Ben was about to snap it open, and find who the dog belonged to, when from the other side of the hill, a despairing cry was raised: "Brutus!" Over the hill came Ellie herself, pulled ahead by another galloping retriever, this one black, and on a leash.

The affair between Ben and Ellie progressed through the fall into the New Year, with laughs, small misunderstandings, and scenes of reconciliation. Then it ran aground, on the demands of family. Her father, a distinctly lesser Lowell, was well removed from the doings of his distant cousin Lawrence Lowell and Harvard University. Moreover, he disapproved of the world to which both Lowell and Ben's family were rumored to belong, and while he did not hold the son accountable for the failings of the father, still he had no wish for his daughter to enter such a world. (Ben did not help matters by asking, conversationally enough he thought, over a slice of dry fruitcake and a pot of lukewarm tea, if one could both be a Unitarian and also practice a real religion. When Ben thought back, the sound of the mother's teaspoon clicking more and more rapidly against her teacup signaled the beginning of the end of the courtship.)

Despite Ben's avowals that he was no part of his family's business, the misunderstandings between him and Ellie grew less small, and the scenes of reconciliation more strained, until one warm spring afternoon, just as the lilacs were coming into bloom, they walked home from the Old Corner bookshop. Ben had attempted to smooth things over by concluding in an easy-going jocular fashion that at least the Unitarians had yet to cause a war, as evidently some theologies were not worth fighting for. At the corner of Marlborough and Exeter Streets, Ellie turned to him, her upper lip no longer trembling, and told him she thought it best they stop seeing each other.

In the years since, a curiosity overcame him now and again - what was Ellie doing, who she was with, what had become of her. In all his time in Philadelphia, he had never met anyone who compared to her - her odd silences, and that curious two-toned gaze. The gaze unsettled him. It was like that moment in a dream, of walking down a steep staircase, and with the last step finding that he was stepping into an unknown space. The sensation was unsettling, but not entirely unpleasant.

And once Tim had told him of Ellie's recent woes, Ben was determined to seek her out. He wanted to assure himself that her state was not so dire. And he wanted her to know he was still her friend. He would be willing to stand aside, if it came to it, although he could not help wishing she would see him stand aside, so she would know how tender an affection he bore for her. Perhaps he could stand by her window, in the rain, under a dripping tree, and the spectacle would be impressed forever in her heart. Failing that, he would like to know she at least remembered him.

The cold air filled his lungs. He was exhilarated. He felt light-hearted and clear-headed, as if he had breathed in a patch of sky. Buoyant and nervous, he made a quick-step passage across the Common, through the Public Garden, and into the Back Bay. He prepared several likely scenarios that would ensue from his knock on her door: Ellie would rush into his arms and weep, regretting the mistake they'd made three years earlier. Or she had reconciled herself to their history, and would greet him with a cool distant politeness. Or more likely, Mrs. Cabot-Lowell would answer the door, and with a pained expression, close the door in his face.

The Cabot-Lowells lived in a townhouse on Marlborough Street, a narrow, once stately five-story townhouse that had fallen into a pleasant state of mild decay. It was as though the modern age had surveyed the house from on high, and, unimpressed, declined to make any further demands. The house was red brick, and surrounded by a tall, wrought-iron fence. Each fence post ended in a fleur-de-lis, although over the decades, several had gone missing, never to be replaced. The gate swung on rusty hinges that squeaked piteously in the slightest breeze, and opened onto a thorny, stamp-sized thicket of rose bushes. Every summer, that garden yielded just a single perfect bloom: coral pink, or butter yellow, or deep crimson tinged with black.

In the back, the house had a copper-roofed cupola, gone to verdigris, where several dozen potted African violets, and a neglected and cantankerous Venus fly trap, held court. In this room, Mr. Cabot-Lowell hosted early chamber music sessions, featuring himself on the recorder. Three piebald cats, the two retrievers Brutus and Marc Antony, and an elderly golden cocker spaniel called Cicero, who doddered around the kitchen in hopes of scraps, also had run of the place. Marc Anthony by rights should have been named differently, Ben and Ellie agreed early in their courtship. The retriever Marc Antony was lean, sullen, and unimplusive - a canine Cassius if ever there was one. Brutus, by contrast, was ebullient, brash, and loyal. Stout in both chest and heart, and reckless in pursuit of that which he loved, this Brutus had never been accused of undue caution.

Ben approached the house. The gate banged in the wind. At the other end of the pathway, the front door swept open, and revealed Ellie, Brutus rushing around her in circles, barking. Ellie was looking at Brutus, and commanding him to stay, all the while she was progressing down the path. Still looking back at Brutus, she put her hand on the gate - only to find that Ben had laid his hand on it first.

"Oh!" she said. They each let go of the gate at the same time, and caught in a fresh gust, it was about to clang into them. With a flip of her voluminous skirts, Ellie leapt onto the sidewalk beside Ben. For a girl with a progressive father, she was decidedly old-fashioned: a Gibson girl adrift in the middle of the flapper era, her long hair pulled up, an emphatically nipped-in waist, and dresses halfway down her calves. And Tim was wrong: her ankles hadn't gotten fat at all.

"I was so sorry to hear about your father," Ellie said. She brushed a stray lock of hair out of her eyes. She hung her head to one side. The azure eye regarded him.

"We all were," Ben said.

"But somehow it's like he hasn't left. Not really - not forever."

"I know what you mean," Ben said.

"It's the strangest thing. I could swear I've seen him - just yesterday. I was out walking Brutus and Marc Antony. We were approaching that rise in the Common -"

"Where we met." Ben looked down and fingered a loose thread on his cuff.

"And there he was - plain as day, or someone who looked so like him. Almost plain, I should say." Ellie giggled nervously. "Didn't see him right away, he only came into focus when that oak tree was square in view." She pointed, her head still listing heavily to the right. "He was examining the bark on it - running his hands over where it had suffered a knock. I was a little afraid, because well - but - and I was about to call out to him, when Brutus tore off in another direction, chasing a squirrel, and by the time I turned back, the man - he did look so much like your father - had disappeared. The cut in the tree was healed though."

"Maybe it was somebody who looked like him," Ben said. "And works as an itinerant free-lance arborist."

"Or a trick of imagination," Ellie said. "I hadn't had breakfast that day. An empty stomach is usually at the root of strange sightings."

"Ellie!" a voice called from inside the house.

"Oh, almost always," Ben said. "I expect a Unitarian mystic made that discovery."

A wind rose, and a few stray twigs tumbled across the pathway. Ellie crossed her arms. "I'd invite you in, but my father's hosting a get-together. He's invited -" she lowered her voice, "the Presbyterians. Maybe next week, we could -"

"Well, I'll be back in Philadelphia by then," Ben said. He regretted it soon as he'd spoken. He sounded prim and smug and stuck-up.

"Well," Ellie said. "So long then. I guess."

"But maybe we -"

"Ellie!" The voice called, louder and more insistently. A tallish figure was hovering now inside the threshold.

"Yes, mother," Ellie said. She reached up, and before Ben knew what was happening, Ellie kissed him. With a swirl of her unfashionably long skirts, she swept back up the path, into the house. The door closed behind her so sharply that a mound of snow fell from the eaves to the bare rose bushes with a soft wet thump.

Ben walked two blocks down Marlborough Street. He was elated to have seen Ellie, and disconsolate because he did not know if he would ever see her again. He turned onto Arlington Street, and began walking faster. "She's one of us despite herself, that Ellie," he remembered his father saying. Ben must have said the phrase out loud because a red-faced man roasting chestnuts on the curb looked up at him.

"Sure she is, buddy," the man said. He gave a short unfriendly laugh. "Bet that's what the fella in the white coat tells you too."

Ben hurried past him, and crossed Arlington Street. He had just entered the Public Garden when a solid tip-tap of somebody else's footsteps echoed behind him, along with another sharp, smaller tap joining in. Ben glanced back, wondering what that third tap was, and caught a glimpse of a heavy gold tip of an umbrella. Not the weather for an umbrella, he thought, and he was just picking up his pace, when a warm, heavy hand landed on his shoulder, and clamped down.

Ben stopped and turned. King David stood, almost to nose to nose with him, resplendent in a cognac-colored, wide-lapelled overcoat. The gold-tipped umbrella was his - superfluous, but its paisley cloth matched his coat to a fare-thee-well.

"Kid!" King David said. He poked Ben's shin with the tip of the umbrella. "How about that! I was just heading your way. Follow up on our chat. You saw how well I work with DeGrace. I work with all kinds of people. Same as your dad did."

"I've got a few things on my mind just now," Ben said. "If you don't mind."

"Bet she's a living doll, too." King David gave a grin as he tightened his grip. "Let's us guys have ourselves a stroll and a chit-chat." He took his hand off Ben's shoulder, put it on Ben's elbow, and propelled him forwards. Ben found himself pushed into the path of an oncoming baby carriage. He veered away as best he could. Her face averted, the governess tsked as the wheels of the carriage rolled by on the icy pavement, nearly clipping Ben on the ankle.

They proceeded along. King David was humming to himself, stepping in time to the tune. The branches overhead were bare and frozen and in a steady gust they made a clicking sound, like loose bones. A tin Lizzie rattled by, blaring its horn. It was answered by a higher pitched toot-toot of a rusted turquoise roadster. In response, the first car issued a longer, louder blare.

"You know what, kid?" King David said. He punched Ben on the sleeve.

"Wh-"

"I'm like you. On the outside of things. Like your dad was. Jewish, Scottish -" he waved his broad hand, indicating a rough equivalence.

"My father was Welsh. He -"

"And an outsider's what's best for this city. Only type who can take over the Druid's Den and handle it proper. Keep the wolves at bay."

"I don't believe any one neighborhood or faction should take over," Ben said. "It's -"

"And you've seen how I got what they call experience, running a club," King David said. "The Cotton Club's become a rip-roaring success since I got involved. On account of my acumen." He snapped his fingers at the last word. "Oh don't get me wrong, Coup's no slouch, but the bebop, let's just say that don't come from him. Between you, me and the fencepost." King David steered Ben past the statue of George Washington, mounded high with snow. Ben's foot slipped on a patch of ice, but King David's grip was firm enough to keep him upright and moving forward.

"Wonder when we'll see a statue of somebody that ain't a Bluebood," King David said. "Like your dad, how about? That would be something. What I'm going to do, kid, soon as I'm set up in the Den is -"

"My father never wanted any statue of himself," Ben said. "He wanted a peaceful thriving city."

"Great, kid," King David said. "Now -"

Ben felt a tug at on his left sleeve. He turned.

"Out and about on my daily rounds," O'Connor said. "And who do I happen to run into? You wouldn't be trying to give another Celt the slip -"

"No," Ben said.

"I was kidding you, for sure," O'Connor said.

"O'Connor's a real kidder," King David said, not

smiling. The three of them walked together, King David with a firm hand on Ben's elbow, and O'Connor on the outside. The two of them glanced at each other warily. A crowd was milling by the newsstand in from of the State House. Above them, the paper boy's cry rose:

"Extra! Extra! Mayor's -"

The cry was drowned out by the siren of three passing fire trucks.

O'Connor ran forward, and disappeared into the crowd.

"Fire in the North End!" the newsboy roared. "Raging inferno fed by high winds! Read all about it!"

"North End?" King David said. He whacked Ben on the arm. "Those sons of bitches! O'Connor and his crew have gone and done it. No wonder he dusted! See, kid, this is why you - hey!"

But Ben had already escaped King David's good-natured vise, and was hurrying toward the newsstand himself.

CHAPTER NINETEEN

"I so want our dear Lowell to feel he's accomplishing something. As you suggested, I intimated to him that you have been frequenting certain deviant haunts - communist, and worse. I directed him to keep an eye on you, and devote his energies to what proper chastisement is due you."

"His hobby and vocation both," Ames said, examining his fingernails.

"I trust you can abide attending such places, for the duration. That they are not too distasteful to you."

Ames looked up. But Cox was not being sly. "I believe I can see my way through. Well enough, uncle."

"Hardly a pleasant task," Cox said. "Though you did propose the idea yourself. I trust you find no temptations therein."

"My youthful indiscretions were just that."

"A phase of experimentation that many a young man passes through," Cox said. "Your expulsion was uncalled for. An intemperate response on Lowell's part."

"Oh I don't mind so very much." Ames clenched his fist before he remembered to relax it. "I'm still listed in the Year Book. Harvard doesn't make mistakes. When people ask me what year I graduated, it doesn't bother me. Not a bit. My particular history gives me a certain distinction in some circles."

"Not circles I frequent, to be sure. Lowell will receive his comeuppance, have no doubt. He is a little too earnest for my liking."

"Or his own good."

"Indeed," Cox concurred. "Once distracted with thoughts of your demerits, he will hardly notice what I have underway - heightening tensions, creating divisions among our newer citizens - the real stuff of statesmanship. And you of course are my man in the North End. By now, you must have much to tell me."

"I'm gaining an education like no other," Ames said. "Come Sunday, I do believe I'll have something to tell you."

"Sunday? How mysterious you can be, Ames. Criminal arrest, I am told, binds men together, inclining them to share confidences. What has that Prega boy passed along exactly?"

"So far, nothing we didn't already know," Ames said. "But I am working on it. They are so terribly secretive, those people."

"And as quick with a knife as with a smile. Now that the Welshman's gone, the prospects for infighting are unparalleled. We might wake up one morning, and find the Negros have been attacked, and in such a way as to cast suspicion on Jerome David, perhaps."

"A time for rejoicing," Ames said.

"I have long noted, with considerable dismay," Cox said, "the unfortunate confluence between the Negro and the Jew. The relationship initially centers around the manufacture and procurement of flashy cheap clothing, and disreputable music. Lowell believes many such peoples can ultimately be assimilated into our great republic - if not, however, into our better summer hotels."

"One has to draw a line somewhere," Ames said.

"I remain unconvinced, and am hardly desirous either."

"Idealists are so very tiresome. " Ames pantomimed a yawn. "Usually."

The secretary hovered on the threshold. "Governor, Mr. Grimley is on the telephone." He lowered his voice. "In regards to your pending tax legislation."

"I'll speak to him," Cox said.

The secretary disappeared. Cox rested his hand on the telephone, and looked at Ames, who had already rolled to his feet. "That Prega creature must know what Costa has planned next. Find out."

"Uncle," Ames said. With a careless salute, he sauntered out of the oak-paneled gloom of the Governor's inner office into the ivory marble and gilt of the State House rotunda. It was like stepping from earth to sky. The sudden light pierced his eyes, and blinking, he heading down the steep marble stairs into the winter's day.

Ames had already given much attention to Nicolas Prega. Thoughts of the boy had of late come unbidden, but hardly unexpected. He had such a tang of the streets about him, sweet Nicky. Though Ames lived only half a mile away, Prega's neighborhood was a world apart. It was tough and raucous, riddled with traffic, convulsed with petty commerce, and stank to the heavens of garlic and dirt and sweat. It was most intoxicating.

Nick was a true exotic. To be sure, the Green Shutters set had its share of the willful eccentrics - Missy Davenport, with her aubergine hair and the cockatiel she kept perched inside the hood of her sealskin cape as she downed another bourbon and held forth on the dangers of suppressed desire; and Beckman Gray, who wore fifty-odd platinum rings on his fingers, clicking and clanking, as he poured the "tea," because he could not stand anyone to see his bare *doights*, as he termed them: the sight of them would be positively indecent. Amusing to a point, these threadbare aristocrats that ruled the cafés, but no doubt they every last one of them had a trust fund or two stashed away. Nicky, however, was like no one else in Ames's experience.

Ames had first encountered Prega early one morning on Commonwealth Avenue, inside the stretch of trees and grassland that ran block after block from the Back Bay into the Fenway. The Ames family owned a massive five-story house on Commonwealth Avenue, around the corner from the Public Library. In the summer after his expulsion, Ames had taken to waking before dawn, dressing in the dark, and slipping out the back door. Aching and lonely and wild, Ames roamed block after block of the mall, the dew still rising from the deep green grass. The loitering figures stood out in sharp relief in the early morning light. Ames developed the habit of fixing his attentions and desires on a series of anonymous figures: a well-dressed older man hovering by a park bench one day, or, on the next, a vagrant furtively glancing this way and that as Ames approached. Ames was half-desperate to make an encounter, and half-desperate not to.

Early one warm May morning, the smell of lilacs already heavy in the air, Ames picked out from a distance a waifish, woebegone figure loitering by the corner of Commonwealth Avenue and Exeter Street. The boy slowed down as Ames gained on him. Then he stopped and turned. His features were of a reasonably even Mediterranean style. His front teeth were snaggled, and that imperfection tore at Ames's heart and delighted him. As the boy drew a matchbook from his pocket, his cuff rode up, revealing a red ribbon tied loosely around his skinny arm. The ribbon was some sort of primitive Italian charm, Ames had gathered. The boy noticed Ames watching him, and he smiled, a cunning smile with much calculation to it, fully aware of its own effect, and to Ames, no less charming for that. Ames smiled back, and nearly fainted.

Lost in this pleasant recollection, Ames headed down Beacon Street. His heels rang out reassuringly against the icy cobblestones. His communism had indeed been a phase, a youthful *cri de coeur* against injustice, and he regarded it with indulgent affection. "The other" interest, as Cox had put it was not a passing phase - unless being alive itself could be termed a phase. Both interests, it turned out, could be shared with young Prega. Prega had shown himself an avid reader of the books Ames passed to him, although, somewhat disappointingly, Prega had clearly been more taken with John Reed's *Ten Days that Shook the World* than Havelock Ellis's *Sexual Inversion*. And Prega was shy in some ways, like a virgin almost, holding back at key moments in their courtship, an eternal dive and feint. His conduct was piquant, intoxicating, and exasperating. The incident with that hellish Negroid creature - Amos? Anton? - had been a thrill. Ames considered that he and Nicky became one person in the commission of that deed, not murder exactly but its kissing cousin. And it was exhilarating. Still, Ames could not help longing for an encounter even more intense.

Ames took a side path through the Common, the frozen gravel crunching underfoot. Up ahead, at the corner of Park Street and Tremont, a crowd was gathering.

"Extra! Read all about it!" the newsboy cried.

One passerby had the paper open in front of his face, and Prescott read the headlines:

MAYOR'S DAUGHTER HANGING BY A THREAD NORTH END RAZED BY FIRE

Ames pushed his way through the crowd, and grabbed a newspaper.

"Hey mister, it ain't free," the vendor said. "We ain't in Russia, you know?"

Ames fished a nickel from his pocket and tossed it on the counter. He walked away in a daze, almost stumbling as he read. It was not supposed to be like this. He and Prega had planned the scheme so carefully. Sunday, when no one would be present to be hurt, a small bomb was to go off in the law office of Popeo and Gremoli, the North End practice that catered to Italian immigrants, and had thereby earned Lowell's public condemnation. Only a file cabinet or a desk would be destroyed, Ames was certain. The bombing would both allow him to share a frisson of the revolution, and poke a well-deserved thumb in Lowell's eye. Ames had greatly enjoyed the intensity of planning the scheme with Prega, poring over diagrams, hauling out his old chemistry textbook and putting it to a use he had never imagined at university - and sharing something secret with Prega that soon the whole city would know about. But had he miscalculated? Well, Nicky was terribly distracting.

Ames's heart skipped a beat, a reaction which surprised him. He broke into a run, and his chest felt so empty it hurt: what had become of Nicky?

CHAPTER TWENTY

Ben rushed down Washington Street, his scarf flying out behind him, dodging the onlookers beginning to crowd the sidewalk.

A fire truck roared by. The blare of sirens was unceasing. Ben pressed on. He smelled smoke. It tickled the inside of his throat. An ashy mist hung over the waterfront. As Ben entered Prince Street, stray bits of ash were floating down, slow and large, like snowflakes in a dreamscape. A scorched scrap of paper tumbled along the sidewalk, and wrapped itself around Ben's ankle. Ben leaned down and removed it. The scrap was a sheet from a children's handwriting book, Palmer Method, capital S's. The cold bore down, and the wind was piercing. But Ben hurried on. He had to see what had happened in his - well, his father's - city.

Across the street from the blackened storefront, Al Costa and Cremesi stood on the sidewalk, surveying the damage. The fire had struck a four-story building. The worst damage was on the top floors, where the bricks had been blackened to char. The roof had caved in, and smoke and ash were rising in waves into the winter sky. Glittery stars, and some construction paper snowflakes, were still plastered to the third floor window. The sign for Tammbassio's Dry Goods remained in place, as well as the counter inside, but the front windows had been blown out. Glass shards crunched under the firemen's feet as they hosed water into the smoldering wreck. The street echoed with their shouts, and the rumble of collapsing masonry and woodwork. The smell of burning and of wet wool filled Ben's nostrils. At Ben's approach, Cremesi took a step back. His perpetually jovial features were for once downcast, angry, and vaguely fearful.

"So there don't look to be anybody hurt, boss," Cremesi said. "At least there's that."

"So far as we can tell," Costa said. He looked at Ben, and pointed at the squat building that adjoined the burned office. "My son attends that school. By the intercession of the blessed saints, the children were all in the church. Singing Christmas carols."

"Thank the good St Francis," Cremesi said. He blessed himself with his right hand. His left one cradled an open sack of popcorn. His molars crunched down, pulverizing a kernel. "But we know what this means. And who. The *Irlandese*." He spat a kernel onto the snow.

"I'm not so sure," Ben said. "The firemen, they're mostly O'Connor's domain. They came right away, didn't they? And look at them, still here, struggling to -"

"A good story, kid," Cremesi said. "Only we ain't falling for it. This fire's got little green shamrocks all over it."

"Nobody knows, not for certain who -" Ben said.

"You are so young, my friend," Costa said, cold contempt in his eyes. "So innocent. Go back to your books, your studies, your - Philadelphia."

"If you'd taken the offer like a good boy," Cremesi said, "none of this would have happened."

"Offer?" Costa said.

"It might have happened sooner," Ben said. "And it might have happened worse."

"Don't bet the rent," Cremesi muttered, and turned to Costa. "Ain't heard from Prega yet, boss," he said. "But he did tell me he was closing in on who was doing the business over in freckles-ville." He stared at the blackened shop front. "Not like it matters much now."

"You don't think Prega was in there?" Costa gestured towards the burned out building. "Tammbassio never paid up on time."

"Naw," Cremesi said. "Kid's out doing some legwork." He looked at Ben and glowered. "Beat it, pal."

Ben stepped backward several long paces. He nearly reached the street corner, turned, and was about to bolt - when he found he was treading on the broad soft toes of a policeman.

"Now if it isn't Gryffth Owen's boy," the policeman said. He had a fat low belly, but a skinny neck, and just above his shirt collar, his little white Adam's apple bobbed up and down.

"Sorry, Officer," Ben said.

"Officer Greely, in case you're wondering," the policeman said. Another policeman rounded the corner, and took his place shoulder to shoulder with Greely. This one was short, solidly rotund, and had a bounce in his step. The two of them stood there, looking at Ben, each one swinging his bully club into his gloved hand.

"The lad's been here, how long - a week?" Greely said.

"Three days," Ben said

"Officer Mulvaney, I must draw your attention to what transpires so soon after the boy's return to our fair metropolis."

"The situation does merit consideration," Mulvaney said, bouncing on the back of his heels.

"When my father died," Ben said, "it was natural both that I return, and that tensions also ensue."

" *Tensions ensue!* " Mulvaney said. "Listen to the lad."

"Not exactly got the common touch," Greeley said. "More's the pity."

"If you'll excuse me," Ben said.

"I'd like to, but I don't believe I can," Greeley said. "What's your esteemed judgment, Mulvaney?"

"I for one have been enjoying our little symposium."

"He's a well-read personage," Greely allowed.

"On that we can agree," Mulvaney said.

"And further, I have concerns as to the lad's well-being," Greeley said. "No telling what a hot-blooded Sicilian might pull on these streets."

"And they've only gotten hotter, since the fire," Mulvaney said.

"That's a rare jest." Greely looked at Ben. He swung the billy club a little slower, and with greater deliberation.

"I'm okay, thank you. Just going home, in fact." Ben prepared to leave, stepping to the left, by the curb, but from across the street, another policeman materialized, and blocked his exit. Three officers stood around him now, in a semi-circle. They each smiled at Ben in turn.

"What conclusions have we reached, boys?" Greely said.

"His father was a great man, make no mistake," the third policeman said. He had a low colorless voice, and no discernable chin.

"I speak in regard to his progeny before us," Greely said.

"Him? This one need's taking in!" Mulvaney said, and he bounced so emphatically on his heels he went from the curb to the street.

"But I haven't done anything," Ben protested.

"We'll see about that, mister," Greely said. Before Ben could protest, a police van swung around the corner, and stopped beside Mulvaney. The officer with the colorless voice shoved Ben inside. Mulvaney slammed the van door. Greely stepped forward, and waved, grinning, as the van sped away, through the fading winter day.

CHAPTER TWENTY-ONE

From the small round window set high in the wall of the little cell, Ben saw that the dark had settled in. The traffic rumbled overhead. He had been here almost two hours. Around the corner, a guard sat at a desk, doing a crossword puzzle.

"Hey, college boy," the guard called out, in a raspy wheeze of a voice. "I got a poser for you. Eight letters. Ends is 's-h'. '*A short-lived, inconclusive battle or conflict*'."

"Skirmish," Ben responded.

The guard blew his nose. "Looks good."

Ben flipped through his battered copy of *Julius Caesar*. There were things Ben was determined to do, before he went back to Philadelphia.

He would go by Ellie's house, just as before. But this time:

-He would be indomitable.

-He would declare his interests.

-He would not insult Unitarians.

In fact, he wondered if he might find out beforehand about some great Unitarians in history and, ever so casually, drop their names into the conversation. And he would have to get in touch with Tim. Spell out when he could inherit, and the transfer take place. That would be as soon as the city settled down - and it would settle down. It had to. Ben suspected the fire had an entirely natural origin, unrelated to the O'Connors or anybody else. The dry goods man might have been smoking a cigar, for instance, and accidentally let a stray spark fly into a bolt of cotton. When O'Connor showed his face again, and Ben hoped it would be soon, they'd have to find a way to quell the Costa rage.

"Yawzer! Now here's a doozy, Mr. Smarty-pants," the guard said. "Ten letters. A 'g' in the middle. And an 'l' at the end. " 'A cre - ' hold the phone, mister, looks like we got visitors."

Ben heard the heavy front door creak open, and then swing shut. Footsteps rang out along the hallway. They were coming towards him.

Ben stood up. He hoped it would be Ellie. In fact, he pictured Ellie rushing in, falling into his arms. She would want to go with him to Philadelphia. But the footsteps were not Ellie's skittish, uneven quickstep. They were heavier, and deliberate. It must be Tim, he thought, and the thought did not please him. He went to the bars, and looked into the dim short stretch of hallway. A dapper figure swung into view, elegant but somber, almost theatrical but nothing cartoonish to his presentation.

"Mayor Curley!" Ben said.

"Myself and in the flesh," Curley said, brandishing a key. He let himself into the cell, closed the door, and sat down on Ben's bunk. He took off his hat, glanced about him, and pointed to the copy of *Julius Caesar*. He looked at Ben, put his head to one side, and began declaiming:

" '*Nor stony tower, nor walls of beaten brass, Nor airless dungeon, nor strong links of iron, Can be retentive to the strength of spirit.*' " His elocution was precise and resonant, his voice rich and lilting. Almost musical, it rolled easily and expansively from baritone to tenor and back again. To him who processed it and to those who heeded it, it was a thing of beauty, and a source of strength.

Curley folded his hands, and almost smiled. "Not bad, for an Englishman, I'll admit. But there's no doubt to them that study the matter, Shakespeare was a staunch Catholic. As for yourself?" Curley made an open-palmed shrug, suggesting that Ben's evident lack of Catholicism was a regret Curley could accept, just. "I've come to see you, Ben, in your hour of need, to -"

"A need that you and your police created," Ben said.

"And me here as a friend to you, and to all the city!"

"A friend? That fire will -"

"O'Connor neither set this fire, nor fanned its flames. Nor did I, nor any of my tribe. You know that yourself. You pointed out that the fire trucks arrived with not a moment's hesitation, and at risk of their own lives. the men struggled long and hard in the bitter cold to subdue the blaze."

"How did you even know I'd said -" Ben began. But of course - the North End had been crawling with policemen. He sighed and sat down next to Curley.

"Not that I wouldn't like to have set it, mind," Curley said. "I have my reasons. Two of them, and now a third."

"Dorothea," Ben said. "How is she?"

Curley looked at his hands before he spoke. "With us still, but barely. You know, your own dear pa thought the world of her, Ben. She never could stand to see anyone left out of things. Just last July it was, a little girl came to our house, visiting with her mother. Dorothea took the girl to the Common, with a gaggle of chums, but she had to wear an eye patch, this little girl, and she stood off by herself, all but hiding under that mighty oak."

"I know the one," Ben said.

"Dorothea broke away from her pals, and sat down next to her, under the oak, and set up playtime right there. Made the one who felt herself the outcast the center of it all. Your dear old father saw it, too. God rest his soul, and told me. Oh, and she's a daredevil too, Dorothea is. Nothing scares her, not big dogs, or heights. Even now, she's not a bit -" Mayor Curley's voice clenched up.

Ben looked away.

"So you see, Ben," Curley went on. "It's up to you."

"What, exactly?"

"To find out who's doing this to my little girl. And who's responsible for the fire."

"But how I am supposed to -"

"That's your look-out, son." Curley stood up. "I've got a city to run. You've got a peace to secure and maintain. It's well we both recall: '*The peace of heaven is theirs that lift their swords, in such a just and charitable war.*' "

"Shakespeare again," Ben said.

Curley nodded.

"*King John*," Ben said, "Not a lot of people have read that one."

"There's a lot we have in common, Ben," Curley said. "I've been a worthy denizen of this fine establishment myself - not as worthy as you to be sure, but I knew they'd treat you fair and square here. The Charles Street Jail has an illustrious clientele. It's held the likes of me and you, and Sacco and Vanzetti. Anyone, in fact, our Blueblood friends decide they can't much abide."

"The Bluebloods didn't throw me in here, Mayor. It was some other friends of mine."

Curley chuckled. "Your father's son and no doubt about it. Jim'll be by any minute, to let you go, official like, free and clear. Fingers crossed, he may have finished that infernal crossword puzzle." Curley put on his hat, shut the cell door with a small decisive clang, and was off.

CHAPTER TWENTY-TWO

Just after six o'clock in the afternoon, and already the afternoon had thickened into evening. Ames was feeling sentimental. He put his arm around his companion. Sam, his name was. Or Sal, or -? Well, it hardly mattered.

"Hey," Ames said. He nuzzled the man's neck. He could smell his own breath, and it was heavy with scotch.

After learning of the conflagration, Ames had had a drink, and then another. He'd ventured towards the North End, in search of Nicky, but the crowds and the ash and his own turmoil overcame him. In the end, he'd gotten no further than School Street. A drink seemed a good idea, for openers. An hour or so later, not quite staggering, for a gentleman knows how to hold his liquor, Ames ventured up to Loudin's. On a cold dark afternoon, a Turkish bath was just the ticket. Loudin's was stashed away in an alley across from the Common, and it stayed open all night. Hot steam and willing boys - Ames knew of no better restorative. This fellow with him now - Jim? - had been idling at the edge of the pool, no more than a towel around him. There had been a leggy blond lounging there as well, gloriously refined in profile. By contrast, this redhead was a bit crude both in accent and in features, and

Ames had always gone in for a bit of rough.

The companion drew away from him.

Ames swayed towards him. "We're friends, aren't we?"

The companion responded with a square punch to Ames's nose, and another one to his stomach.

"I ain't friends with fags," the man said.

Ames crumpled up.

From somewhere in the dark near distance, a voice called out. "Hello?"

The man stuck his hand into Ames's coat, and yanked out his wallet. With a thump, Ames fell on his knees into the snow.

"See you around, twinkle toes," the man said. He gave Ames a kick in the side, and ran, his footsteps swift, and muffled by the snow.

"Hello," the voice called again. This time it was right beside him. Ames looked up. "You okay, mister?"

"Tolerably," Ames said.

"You know, it's a cold night," the stranger said. "I'm sure there's a charity or someplace you could -"

"Thank you," Ames said. He sat upright as he best he could and offered his hand. "I'm Prescott Ames. We Ameses fund the charities around here. We don't make use of them."

"I'm Ben Owen." Ben leaned down so they could shake hands. "You look a little worse for wear."

"Owen? Your father was -" Ames said.

"Wasn't he though?" Ben reached into his pocket and took out a handkerchief.

Ames accepted it, and nodded his thanks. "We're in your father's neck of the woods, so to speak. The miscreant punched me and made off with my wallet."

"There's a police station right around the corner - I've got an in with them, you might say. You'll want to file a report."

"I have an '*in*' there myself, so to speak." Ames grinned with a wince, as he pressed the handkerchief to his nose. "I cannot agree to reporting this unfortunate misadventure. My family abhors fuss and publicity of all varieties. We've had rather more than our share of late."

"So I've heard," Ben said. "But whoever did this to you could do it to somebody - anybody - else. There's enough disruption in this town as it is, without amateurs."

Ames thought a moment. He looked up at Ben. "I won't report it. I agree there's enough stress in this city as is. But I will tell you what happened. Look here, Ben, you seem to me to be made of the right stuff, if you don't mind my saying. I want you to know what happened, Ben. For the good of the city."

"Lately, all kinds of people seem to have the good of the city on their minds," Ben said.

Ames sat upright. "They were two Negros. Arrived out of nowhere and ganged up on me, which is how I came to get the worst of it. One of them had a bullet-shaped head."

"Did they say anything?"

"One of them did. He unleashed some fast-paced urchin slang - gutter language, I warrant. It was the very devil to follow."

"Were his eyes - ?"

"Hollow. And they glowed."

"Glowed?" Ben said. "Not cold and dead like stone?"

"They were - well, both. Glowed like fire, and when he turned, the eyes went dull as a rock."

"Oh," Ben said.

"And he had the most ungainly, slightly mechanical movement to him. But he did pack a punch all the same." Ames rubbed his nose with the flat of his hand, and looked at Ben. "I do so hate to stir the pot of racial strife, but facts are facts. It was Coup DeGrace's crew."

"Sounds like it," Ben said.

"We've not had this kind of strife between us before. They offend all decent sensibilities to be sure, with their music and their superstitions and their outlandish get-ups that no decent person would be caught dead in. And there was that unpleasantness, a misunderstanding really, that landed me in court. But it doesn't do to bear grudges. I find the toll on oneself is altogether too great." Ames got to his feet, and dusted the snow off his chest.

"Well, as a matter of fact, Coup DeGrace has been looking for your cohort," Ben said. "Do you know where Nicolas Prega is?"

"As a matter of fact, I don't."

"DeGrace says he wants to make peace with Prega. You better get word to Prega what's happened. Because I'd say tonight was just a warning shot."

"I certainly shall try my best," Ames said. "DeGrace seems intent on vengeance. We must all do our best to defuse it. The white man's burden, so to speak." He put his head to one side, half-smiling through his bruises. "I can't say meeting you was an unalloyed pleasure. But I do appreciate your assistance. Goodnight, Ben. My good Samaritan." They shook hands. As Ben set off, Ames stifled a giggle. He had set the cat among the pigeons.

CHAPTER TWENTY-THREE

"No, momma," Prega called up the cellar stairs. "I told you, I'm not hungry."

"Why you not eat?" his mother said. She shuffled away from the cellar door, a pot of soup in her hands. "Why you not go out with friends, meet a nice girl?"

All afternoon, ever since he heard the blast and witnessed how badly wrong the scheme had gone, Prega had holed up in the cellar pantry, amidst his secret bunker of books and pamphlets. He reached into the back of the shelf, rummaged around the off-cuts of bacon rinds his mother saved for soups, and extracted what he was looking for: a composition book, entitled *Cellar Notebooks*. He sat down at his makeshift desk fashioned out of lettuce crates. An unshaded light bulb hung over him.

The bomb had been Ames's idea from beginning to end. Prega should have known not to trust the son of privilege. Ames played with revolution, but never bore its brunt - well, not yet he hadn't, but that was subject to change. True to form, Ames had insisted on targeting a working-class neighborhood. All the while they'd been building the bomb, Ames assured Prega he knew how to time the explosion, and how to limit the strength of the blast. He'd studied chemistry at Harvard, Ames remarked several times. Prega had argued that the target should be a police station, in the Back Bay or Beacon Hill - but Ames said no, that was too obvious, and in the aftermath of Sacco and Vanzetti, altogether too easy to trace back to an Italian anarchist. Ames insisted the target be the law office popular with Italian immigrants. He'd been delighted with his own cleverness in coming up with the idea. Lawrence Lowell was on record repeatedly criticizing Popeo and Gremoli. Everyone, Ames chortled, would blame Lowell, for inciting the deed and worsening relations throughout the city.

Prega picked up a pen, opened his notebook to the first blank page, and began writing. His rage began to cool. His purpose became clear. He would put Ames on trial in the revolutionary tribunal of the *Cellar Notebooks*, and expiate any complicity of his own.

What is genuine is proved in the fire, Engels tells us: what is false we shall not miss in our ranks. Conversely, did not the fire today prove that one among us is a traitor? History is the judge; the proletariat, the executioner.

Writing always helped him make sense of his world. Self-conscious about his accent, which had been so pronounced his teachers concluded he was a slow learner, Prega in his early teens had turned to Marxist and anarchist squibs. Their call to violence and unrest calmed him. Only when caught up in the sweep of their argumentation did Prega feel he was not alone. Marxism captured his anger, and transformed it. And today his anger was greater than ever.

He went on:

The last capitalist we hang shall be the one who sold us the rope. Why not the first one as well? The rope, in this case, was a bomb...

As of this afternoon, he had put his mother under instructions to deny all knowledge of his whereabouts, and she would sooner break her own neck than go against his wishes. He was all she had, a widow with an only child. Prega twisted the red ribbon around his wrist. He'd worn it first as a protection against strega, at his mother's bidding, but as his studies had progressed, more as a Marxist emblem, a badge of discontent.

His politics had led him to cultivate a relationship with Ames in the first place. Since his early teens, Prega knew where his desires inclined. His own neighborhood was too close-knit to allow him to pursue such proclivities, even clandestinely. Not ashamed, but secretive by nature, and prudent, he looked further afield. And Prega saw in his predilection an opportunity for Marxist praxis.

Prega staked out the Commonwealth Avenue mall, the green stretch of grass and trees that ran block after block from the Back Bay to Fenway. The men who trolled there were often Bluebloods from the surrounding mansions. The money and information they supplied could be useful to him. And too, the ire he would take against their easy privilege would no doubt feed his fervor. Prega more than tolerated Ames's caresses, but he did not hunger for them. And the longer he was involved with Ames, the more Prega found Ames's longing - need even - for such contact, repugnant. It did nothing to further the revolution - it impeded it. Prega took a deep breath, and wrote:

The mark of the revolutionary is the pleasure he denies himself.

Around the same time he began cultivating Ames, Prega had taken to hanging around the Costa crew. In short order, he'd made an impression on Cremesi. He'd proved himself a quick study, and close-mouthed. And he could write a letter as good as any lawyer's. He made himself useful to them. Prega found them useful, too. One, membership in the Costa gang provided a living that did not directly feed the capitalist machine. Two, it would ensure he received due respect on the streets of the North End. Three, it provided a good cover. A member of a bootlegging gang was not likely to be suspected of radical politics. And finally, Prega had developed a theory of his own, that gang activity was part of the revolution, an as yet unremarked stage in the dialectic between peasant and proletariat, an interval that would soon be recognized by the Marxist imperative. (He had liked the sound of that without being sure entirely what it meant, and had duly recorded the phrase in his *Notebooks*).

"I need some olive oil," his mother called down. "Leave a bottle on the top step for me." And she lumbered away.

With the carelessness allowed only to the rich, Ames had misled him into doing violence against his own, unrelated to the socialist cause and serving only Ames's purposes. Ames had it in for this man Lowell, more than he ever did for Governor Cox. Prega realized this all too late. One time at Green Shutters, that little saloon stashed away on Cedar Lane Way, a young man clearly in his cups slapped Ames on the back and asked him, with a hiccup, what year Ames had graduated (that it was from Harvard University was understood). Ames went silent, and his lips turned white. He was sullen the rest of the evening. Ames played at revolution, but his sense of outrage, it turned out, went no further than such bourgeois slights. Ames would always go back to his rich quiet house, his do-gooder banker father, and his vast carelessness. Such was not allowed to the likes of Prega - nor sought by him either.

A heavy tread resounded overhead. The light bulb jittered. "Nicky!" his mother called down. "I need -"

Prega rose from his chair and plucked a bottle of olive oil from the shelf. Reaching upwards, he put it on the second to top step, and sat back down at his desk. He added a few more sentences:

This is a true account of how a corrupt son of privilege misled a working son of Sicily. It is an indictment of the false revolutionary. I have no compassion, and I ask no compassion from you.

Prega would see Ames one more time. He was sure Ames would be eager for an encounter. In one stroke, Prega would wipe away all his previous errors. Strega he hereby renounced as reactionary. It was the way of the peasant, and not the urban proletariat. He wrote that down, and chin in hands, collected his thoughts once more.

The revolution properly belonged to the proletariat, and Prega would now reclaim it. His heart was calm and steady. He would avenge himself against Prescott Ames, and Ames's class. As a point of honor - he was a true Sicilian, he thought, with a swell of pride - he would do so on his own, without recourse to Costa or his gang.

Prega tore a blank sheet out, and wrote a short note. Then he rolled his notebook up and slipped it inside his shirt. It was his truest companion, that notebook. It told no lies. Its truth was the stoutest armor against the cold winds about to blast him. Wherever he fled, it would go with him.

Strega had proven unreliable as an instrument of the revolution. So had bombs. But a gun would surely do the trick.

CHAPTER TWENTY-FOUR

Officer Mulvaney pulled the car onto Salem Street, and parked at the back of the police station. A little past seven p.m., and the rubberneckers had finally drifted away. As he maneuvered his round, compact belly out of the car, Mulvaney moved slowly, confidently. An officer of the law would never be a target of any North End shenanigans.

Mulvaney sighed as he went around to the trunk. It was just like O'Connor to call him - a policeman on duty - and ask a favor. Not even a favor, but more a command to a servant. O'Connor had directed him to pick up two items from the garage in Southie, and stow them in the police station's backroom: a carton, large enough to hold an icebox, taped up, with a grease-pen scrawl across it: "XMAS Decos" - an unexpected touch of holiday cheer from the tightfisted grump, it had to be said, and then this: an oddball contraption that looked like the megaphone from a gigantic Victrola grafted onto a rat's maze. O'Connor feigned aggrieved surprise when Mulvaney asked what in holy hell the thing was. "Your ignorance takes me aback, Officer Mulvaney, so it does. What you see before is a *conclavis reborare*. Amplifies and directs sound

- of singing, say - the Christmas concert in St Francis church will go resounding throughout the city. Echo off the bricks and clapboard and back again." And O'Connor said it in that wheedling voice of his, so clever-clever. "Thus Dorothea Curley, as she's lying sick abed, will hear the joyous singing that may yet restore her."

Mulvaney had lived around the block from O'Connor for five years now, but O'Connor could never be called a regular guy. O'Connor was so cheap he squeaked. His tightfistedness was legendary. He was forever "forgetting" his wallet - "pick up this one, could you," was the customary sign-off to a bite out with O'Connor. And one warm summer afternoon, when a few of the officers had arrived at his house for a powwow, O'Connor had asked, and a surprise it was, "How about I get us a beer, fellas?" They nodded, and agreed, all smiles. Within a minute, O'Connor came back, carrying a tray with five glasses and precisely one small bottle of beer. He split it five ways, exact to the drop. There was nothing like him in all of Southie. The only thing the man held onto tighter than a dime was a grudge.

There was no excuse for him. His family was okay - a brother was a priest over in Charlestown, denouncing crime and magic in his Sunday sermons, and hearing confessions of the same all week long, with admirably short penances. Another brother sold insurance and made a pretty penny at it, but not too pretty. He also had three sisters, each one the salt of the earth, good as gold, and practically indistinguishable from each other. No one got ahead of themselves. It was the way a family ought to be, and a neighborhood. But O'Connor was different, a real cold fish.

In his darkest moods, Mulvaney suspected O'Connor of putting on airs. O'Connor didn't drink much. He didn't follow sports. And he was always reading books by fellas with oddball names - slashes of accents, and double dots erupting over every other vowel. Just looking at those oddball names caused an ire to brew inside Mulvaney. He was certain O'Connor was high-hatting him. And the topics - *Principles of Audio Technology* - did grown men read such things as a hobby? Plus, O'Connor had an interest in birdwatching, of all things. When Mulvaney found that out (he'd come over to return a roasting pan his wife had borrowed, and through the screen door, he spotted O'Connor leafing through an *Audubon Annual*), Mulvaney had wanted to laugh, tell the other guys, and rib O'Connor about it. But O'Connor was not a guy you could rib. So Mulvaney bit his tongue, and put the matter to one side, and willed himself to silence. The silence made him sour, disconsolate, and snappish. It was as if he had eaten a bit of old beef that lodged in his belly, leaden and indigestible. Mayor Curley was more his speed, there was no two ways about it.

The carton had been no trouble to hoist inside, but this contraption was proving the devil - not too heavy, not for him, but it was difficult to balance. Taking a deep breath, Mulvaney hauled it another foot further out of the trunk, and hoisted the square base on top of his left shoulder. He swung his right arm around to steady it. As he took his first steps toward the station, he noticed a woman across the street. She was staring at him. She was dressed all in black, and had on a hat as wide as a manhole cover. A gust of wind rose up, and blew the brim back, revealing a brief flash of golden hair. A strawberry blonde huh? She seemed to like the look of him, that was for sure. And who could blame her? The dame had taste. Mulvaney stuck his chest out and sucked his stomach in. He went towards the back door of the station, taking his time. No doubt the lady was enjoying the view.

The door swung open. Greely stood in the threshold, the wind blasting into him. "What are you waiting for?" Greely bellowed. "An engraved invitation?"

Mulvaney started whistling, to give the continued appearance of being relaxed and casual, though he did pick up his pace. He glanced back.

The lady, whoever she was, was still looking at him.

*   *   *

"Sure, Jackie," Greely was saying to the phone. "Mulvaney brought them things over. About fifteen minutes ago. Went back out on his beat - shift runs another hour. "

"Find him," O'Connor said. "And as soon as you do, call me. I'm hearing something I don't like the sound of." O'Connor hung up.

No gift of the gab at all, Greely thought. He got to his feet, pulled on his coat, and stepped out into the bustle of Hanover Street. At the corner, in front of Umberto's Haberdashery, he caught sight of Officer Houlihan, hands folded behind his back, looking into the shop window.

"Hey, Fedora-boy," Greely said, "If you see Mulvaney, tell him O'Connor wants to talk to him."

"Okay," Houlihan said, straightening up. "Will do."

Outside the police station, a Ford Model T police car was just drawing in. Gliding through a small puddle of slush, it came to a smooth stop. Under the streetlight, the car's gleaming fittings stood out against the grimy snow. The police commissioner must be paying a visit. Greely straightened his hat, and hurried towards the station.

*   *   *

Costa sat down at the kitchen table next to his wife. He patted her hand, and she smiled. She looked both exhausted, and exultant, like an athlete who has called on some last, great reserve of power, and achieved victory.

Costa raised his glass. She raised hers, and they toasted.

Four stories below their kitchen window, three boys were playing kickball in the street. The smallest gave the ball such a mighty punt that it sailed over the bank of snow on the side of the street, into an alleyway several doors beyond. "I got it," the boy called out, as he scurried after it. He clambered over the fence. And in a moment, he clambered right back, empty-handed, and leaden-faced.

From across the street, Office Houlihan spotted him. "Ball go AWOL, sonny? I'll track it down." He strode across the street, and unlatched the alleyway gate.

Mulvaney was leaned up against the fence.

"O'Connor's looking for you," Houlihan said.

Mulvaney did not respond.

Houlihan moved in. "Come on, you got to -" Then he cried out. Mulvaney's face was covered with fresh pox marks, almost encrusted with them. His skin was blue, as if his blood had caught fire inside of him, and scorched his outsides.

He was dead.

CHAPTER TWENTY-FIVE

Ames sat at the dining table reading the paper, a china teacup at his elbow. Already it was clear no one had been killed in the blaze, and his early fears had been misplaced. He could be such a flibbertigibbet sometimes. Nicky was having that effect on him.

"Elbows off the table, son," his mother said.

The servant poured him a cup of coffee.

"Thank you," Ames said, and went on reading.

The news stories were everything he hoped for. Already the papers were blaming Lowell for the fire - not for setting it, perhaps, but for tirelessly pointing out the law office's aggressive practices on behalf of new immigrants. "Listen," Ames said: " *'One State House source recalls that A. Lawrence Lowell has always reserved particular opprobrium for the law firm of Popeo and Gremoli, declaring that it is a travesty of justice and due procedure that this firm continued in operation.'* "

"I understood you did not want that man's name mentioned in this house," his mother said. "Nor do I care to hear it myself. And I think you should be resting, after that terrible fall. You must be more careful in the ice and snow, especially after dark."

"Yes, mother," Ames said.

"And your father thinks it's time you began working with him. It is our civic duty to be useful, after all. Remember, you're to go by the bank this morning, and see about that position. You father went to some trouble to arrange it. Try to act grateful, dear."

"And this: '*Popeo represents the worst of the legal profession. It is a wonder the decent citizens have not risen up against its manifest and continuing improprieties.*' " Ames chortled and took a swill of coffee.

He had done a fine day's work yesterday. And when they next met up, what a delicious time he and Nicky would have. It had all worked out in the end - exactly as Ames said it would. The clock on the mantelpiece chimed eight o'clock.

Ames licked a forefinger and flicked the page. *The Talk of the Hub*, by Tim Owen. His brother Ben seemed a solid enough sort, and easily led. Ben would be stirring things up with Coup DeGrace. Ames would have to check in with Cox and tell him what he'd managed to engineer. He owed it to himself to reap the praise he was due. He had been masterful on short order. Thinking on his feet, as it were, while he sat crumpled under a tree in the Common. He read on, in the mood for the society tidbits that the column offered up:

Who's the Back Bay field flower who's been canoodling with a dyed-in-the-wool Celt? Ask around - the scene is likely to be set to the tune of recorder music. And she's got the same name as her illustrious cousins, but some of them are too busy speaking only to God! Beware - there's a Brutus afoot, with quite a tail to tell...

This was a bit of mischief. No doubt some Blueblood girl had conceived a fancy for a son of the sod, a common workman, with eyes of sky blue, massive biceps, and the gift of blarney. Her family would put a stop to it before she conceived anything else - a little stranger perhaps. Ames, you are the very devil, he thought, and giggled at his own wit.

Psst: From the setting, to the refreshment, to the guest list, the Harvard soiree Tuesday last was the alumni event of the season. Everyone who's anyone Crimson true was -

Ames brow darkened. He threw the paper aside and stood up. "I think I'll rest up for now, mother."

As he passed the front door, he spied a piece of paper lying on the mat. It had been slipped under the door - a lined sheet, torn from a school notebook. Ames picked it up and read:

I will meet you tonight as the darkness falls, where we met first met. Procure with you a bunch of yellow roses so I may discern you from across the street. I promise, tonight you will know the full measure of my feelings for you at last ...

Ames bounded upstairs, the morning winter light just sifting through the tall windows. A shiver of delight ran up and down his spine. He'd be a good boy and go by the bank with Father, and he'd be sure to cadge some cash out of the deal, too. Tonight's revelries would require funds. He headed up the stairs, into the imperial gloom of the third floor, stuffing the letter inside his shirt, next to his skin, as close to his heart as he could get it.

CHAPTER TWENTY-SIX

The church bells in the steeple chimed for a quarter after the hour: 8:15 am. The Abyssinian Baptist Church was devoid of ornamentation, as bare as a garage, and glancing about him, Costa had trouble believing God would establish Himself in a venue so emphatically unadorned. But all the same, a church was safe, neutral ground, and certain to be deserted in the middle of the day. Costa sat in the back pew on the left, Cremesi a rotund shadow hovering over him.

DeGrace was in the pew across the aisle, in half profile to Costa. Directly behind DeGrace, Nigel stood, at stony-eyed attention. DeGrace had in his lap a bank ledger, gold lettering stamped across its cover: The South End Bank and Trust.

"My request is simple," DeGrace said. "I wish only to speak to Prega."

" '*Speak*' to him," Costa said.

"And do what needs to be done," DeGrace said. "By my family. By the loa."

"Get a load of this character," Cremesi said. "Listen, we ain't about to turn one of our own over to your black

129

hands."

DeGrace regarded Costa serenely. "I understand you people have some black hands of your own. And what a not-so-pretty penny *la mano nera* has earned you."

Cremesi bobbed in place. He was smiling beatifically as he smacked his fat fist into his fat opposite palm. "Com'on, boss, just let me -"

Costa looked at Cremesi. Cremesi went silent, and dropped his hands to his sides. His shoulders slumped.

"Mr. DeGrace," Costa said. "you'll excuse my friend here. He is sometimes too anxious on my behalf. I was willing to meet with you because I know you are a serious man, and I will speak to you plainly. I will not hand over Nicolas Prega. I cannot, because we have not ourselves seen or heard from him since the fire. But even if I could, I would not. You understand family loyalty, as I have seen with your unfortunate cousin." Costa shrugged. "But your cousin was out of control. If someone from my crew had not handled him, King David or O'Connor would have done so eventually. As a man of affairs, you know that. And Prega did not act alone. He had an accomplice, Prescott Ames. You have only the judge's word that Nicolas Prega was the ringleader. And that judge is in the pocket of the Bluebloods."

"Thank you for speaking so forthrightly," DeGrace said. "But perhaps the ways of the loa are unfamiliar to you. Baron Samedi is the spirit of the dead. His powers are great. He can, for instance, prevent a death by refusing to dig the grave intended. He can cure any illness."

"Yeah? We'll be the judge of that," Cremesi said.

"It is Baron Samedi who requires I make contact with Nicolas Prega."

"As you wish," said Costa. "If you find Prega, you find him. But you will bear the consequences for any action you take. And I will not deliver him over to you."

Nigel bent forward, stiff as a plank, and held out a pocket watch.

"You'll excuse me," DeGrace said, rising. "I have business elsewhere. I had hoped our meeting might have proved more fruitful. Soon, you may find you feel the same way yourself." With a nod, he departed the church, Nigel following. The gilt on the bank ledger glinted in the half-light.

"How 'bout that," Cremesi said. "*Melanzana* got some big ideas about himself, don't he?"

"King David is his business partner," Costa said, gazing at the door DeGrace had just exited.

"Yeah," Cremesi said.

"I think it's time I paid King David a call."

Cremesi considered, rubbed his thumb along the underside of his chin. "Wouldn't mind hitting a stage show myself." He brightened up. "And down the street, there's Joe and Nemo's. Best franks in town."

CHAPTER TWENTY-SEVEN

In his office at the Harvard Club, Lowell was spending a pleasant morning signing a batch of fresh expulsion orders. With every "t" he crossed and "i" he dotted, he felt the blood of Harvard being purified, drop by drop.

As he reached for the penultimate letter, the telephone on the corner of his desk rang. It was a large, square-bottomed device, with shiny copper fittings, and suspiciously new. It jangled so loudly that the handset rattled. Lowell cast the telephone machine a disdainful frown, and answered.

"Grimley and Graybody calling," a voice said. "Governor Cox for you. I'll put him through, President Lowell."

No doubt the Governor expected Lowell had come to some judgment as to the best course of action in regards to Ames. Lowell was still considering the matter.

"Lowell," Cox said his voice thin, nasal and distant. "I'm calling to offer you a friendly warning."

"Yes?"

"As you have always been so helpful with my own family."

"Indeed."

"That distant cousin of yours. The Unitarian. Most unfortunate, this matter. I feel it keenly myself."

Lowell braced himself for the worst, an eventuality he had prepared himself for since childhood, although he was never precisely clear what "the worst" would be.

"His daughter, it seems, has formed a regrettable alliance," Cox said.

"Oh dear."

"Get a grip on yourself, man."

"Forgive me," Lowell said. "Please, go on."

"You must understand the affair has reached such a stage even the papers have remarked upon it. As you know, my avowed preference is to wait until journalism dies, ascends, and is resurrected as history."

They shared a brief chuckle, although Lowell's was briefer, and considerably more muted.

"However," Cox continued, "the maid left the newspaper open on my desk at the column that your Tim Owen creature puts together. No one is actually named - I believe in newspaper parlance, it is a 'blind' item. But the world around us is not deaf, Lowell, and it is certainly not mute. I'll read it to you: '*Who's the Back Bay field flower*', " he began, and went on, pausing significantly at the phrase "recorder music."

"Most distressing," Lowell said.

"No doubt you'll take action," Cox said.

"Certainly," Lowell said. "I'll confirm first with Tim Owen, that the reference was in fact to -"

"If you think you have that luxury," Cox said. "The facts are only too apparent. And I believe in such circumstances, even journalists refuse to divulge a secret. Their code of honor."

"Like thieves," Lowell said.

"Precisely," Cox said. "An apt comparison. I can hardly be alone in concluding that the reference is to Miss Cabot-Lowell. That in itself does damage - even as we speak. You must act quickly and decisively."

"The Lowell name must not be impeached," Lowell said.

"Never," Cox said.

"This girl must be -"

"Sequestered," Cox suggested, "if only for a brief time."

"Somewhere safe," Lowell said.

"Brookline is a good distance," Cox said. "And Sevenels a lovely homestead."

"Yes," Lowell said. Brookline was several miles away, and Sevenels had many acres surrounding it - plenty of space to clear the girl's head, remove her from imminent danger, and keep her from the opportunity to feed the flames of rumor. "Your assistance in this matter is much appreciated, Governor."

"In light of all the succor you have offered my own family," Cox said. "I considered it not only my duty, but my pleasure."

They exchanged farewells, and hung up.

Lowell took a moment to settle himself. He was stony-faced, and queasy. An Irish workman, full of charm and rye - a glint in his eye, no doubt, a well-developed upper body musculature, a wheedling, airy voice, and that sly ingratiating manner. Just to overhear those people speak sent a faint shiver of disgust through Lowell. They had not become like him, these Irish, though they had every opportunity. They had a superficial similarity, and that made their intransigence all the more disquieting. They arrived speaking English, but dear Lord, what English! Their phrases and intonation took the language of the King James Bible and stood it in its head, sent it doing cartwheels and somersaults. They committed a travesty and a mocking slur upon the King's English with every lilting syllable they uttered. No man would allow his daughter to be pursued by one of them - well, no right-thinking man.

It was woefully apparent that Robert Cabot-Lowell was not of that number. An Irish workman, with a Lowell girl, however distant - the very notion was repugnant, like bathing in polluted waters. He would see to this matter, immediately.

Mrs. Cabot-Lowell had always struck him as altogether more solid than her husband. She was as indomitable and stern as a Roman matron. In her, honor still reigned most high: she was Calpernica, so to speak, to the most unworthy Julius Caesar of Robert Cabot-Lowell. With that good matron's help, Lowell would make the necessary arrangements, and all might be secured. As he put on his coat, his heart contracted. He was almost contrite with gratitude. Governor Cox had warned him. The Governor was an honorable man, and a true friend. It was the Harvard University way. Of course, Governor Cox had gone only to Dartmouth. But Lowell was sufficiently broad-minded to take the limitations of that academic pedigree in his stride. Lowell's own alma mater had fostered such broad-mindedness. No wonder the Harvard Club was a truer home to him than the manse in Brookline ever had been.

CHAPTER TWENTY-EIGHT

DeGrace carried the satchel of bills into the South End Bank and Trust. His face was immobile, betraying nothing of his disquiet. A fair proportion of this deposit was King David currency. DeGrace had reasoned that if the counterfeit currency was paid in as part of a mid-sized deposit, and early in the morning, when the bank had just one teller on duty, it was most likely to go undetected.

Nigel stepped forward on his stiff, lanky legs, and opened the heavy door of the bank. Every customer in the bank was Negro. But the president and the vice president, who worked behind a glass screen, were emphatically white. At his desk, second in command, Josiah Ames sat, chisel-featured, long-faced, and sauterne, peering down at his paperwork. DeGrace recognized him from the courtroom as the father of Prescott Ames. Joseph Napoleon was the only teller on duty. He rolled his red-rimmed eyes, and gave DeGrace a shy smile of greeting.

Shadowed step by step by Nigel, DeGrace went to the counter. He began tallying the bills for deposit, careful to ensure the King David specials were interspersed among

136

the other cash.

King David was brash and intemperate. DeGrace was only a year older, at thirty-two, but DeGrace had begun to cultivate an aggressively sedate style even while still in high school. Since as far back as he could remember, he had felt himself to be the only grown-up in a universe of children. A determinedly bookish student, he wore bone-rimmed spectacles, which his eyesight barely required, and he allowed nothing cheap or flashy to accrue to his person.

King David, by contrast, reveled in daring shades - purple, topaz, and teal, and top-drawer fabrics cut just so. King David "put the swell into elegant," as he told Coup more than once. But Coup eschewed all such display for himself. It would not do to appear cartoonish, or showily elegant. A Negro so attired would be taken as a joker in the first instance, or a pimp in the second; and DeGrace was indeed, as Costa had said, a serious man. He had to give Costa that much.

DeGrace put the first stack of bills to one side. Then he noticed an obvious King David effort. The ink had smeared, no doubt because King David, impatient as a toddler, had wrested the bill from the press too soon. DeGrace slipped that bill in his pocket, and resumed the count. From the first, DeGrace found King David amusing - his high-jinks, physical bravado, and total lack of introspection. Such attributes DeGrace recognized as gifts - small ones, of course, and decidedly not ones DeGrace himself possessed, or aspired to. King David had rolled into the Cotton Club one night three years ago. The music was fine, and the girls, well, they were even finer: "I got to hand it to you - you *schavetes* really know how to live," King David concluded on his first night, and slapped Coup on the back. Brutal and tenderhearted, in short order King David became the mark of every girl on the make.

Within a few encounters, it was clear to DeGrace that King David was half-child, and half-cunning beast: the man was a complete stranger to depression, and reports of suicide, whether long ago, or of a contemporary, plainly baffled him. And his bigotries were so forthright as to be almost innocent. At their first meeting about becoming partners in the Cotton Club, DeGrace admitted he did not care for jazz music, though he did of course see the profit in it. King David looked crestfallen. "I prefer Bach, and Mozart," DeGrace explained. "Beethoven is indeed great, though one is conscious of the effort." "Don't like jazz?" King David said. "Geez." DeGrace looked at him. "I like chitlins, though," DeGrace said. "If that helps." Gazing into the mid-distance, King David thought about it a moment, and, brightening, said, "Yeah - it do."

When King David started passing bad bills in the club, DeGrace caught on from the beginning. He did not take King David seriously enough to confront him over the matter, and nor did it make business sense to upset the solid earning machine the Cotton Club was becoming. Instead, DeGrace used his own accountancy skills to take all the reparation he required.

The bills duly counted and arranged, DeGrace opened up his ledger book. In his tortuously neat hand, he began filling out a deposit slip. Within the bank, a door creaked open. DeGrace glanced up.

It was the murderer himself. He was standing on the other side of the glass wall. Josiah Ames was alongside him, pressing a fatherly hand on Prescott Ames's shoulder, as they stood and spoke to the bank president. Every so often, the father squeezed his son's shoulder, prompting him to give a response, which after a short hesitation he seemed to give. Prescott Ames leaned forward. He shook hands with the bank president. The young man embarrassed his father, DeGrace could see. Josiah Ames was itching to pull strings on the boy's mouth, neck, and limbs, as on a marionette. He would no doubt evaluate Prescott's performance to Prescott in some detail over dinner tonight, and find it wanting in every particular.

DeGrace stepped up to the teller's window. Joseph

Napoleon gave no hint of their recent encounter. In all probability, the ceremony had been so intense Joseph Napoleon had blotted out the memory of it.

"Hello, Mr. DeGrace." Joseph Napoleon's voice was soft and reedy. He took the bills and counted them, one by one. He did not pause or quibble at any of them, just let his mouth fill with air, and let it slowly deflate as he went about his routine task.

As he waited, DeGrace watched Prescott Ames. Ames was now sorting through an enormous pile of mail, making sure each envelope was stamped.

DeGrace slid the deposit slip under the grate. Joseph Napoleon stamped it.

"Thank you, Mr. DeGrace," he said, his voice like wind whistling in the grass.

DeGrace buttoned up his coat, Nigel opened the door, and they went out onto the street. There was a post office diagonally across from the back door of the building. DeGrace figured Ames would emerge from that door. He stationed himself in the shadows of the eaves and waited. A few minutes later, Prescott Ames rounded the corner, a mailbag slung over his shoulder, a sullen pout on his fine features.

"Young mister Ames," DeGrace said, taking a step forward.

Nigel closed in, and blocked Ames's path.

"I'm sorry," Ames said. "I am in a hurry. Earning my keep and -"

"Don't mind Nigel," DeGrace said. "He just makes sure I don't get hurt. In the way that my cousin Andre got hurt."

Ames took a step back.

DeGrace looked at Ames, and tsked. "Quite a hit you've taken. Perhaps I should have seen the other guy, as the joke goes. Who was that, I wonder?"

"Listen," Ames said, "I don't know what Ben Owen told you - what I said, about this scuffle, but I was just -"

"What scuffle would that be?" DeGrace said. "The one in which you smote down my cousin?"

"No. Last night, I -" Ames went silent, his mouth set in dumb insolence.

"Are you afraid of me son? I don't want that. Not just yet."

Nigel breathed deep and close on Ames face. Ames blinked. His long blond lashes fluttered slightly.

"Ben Owen found me beat up on the Common last night. Asked me right off if it was a colored man - if it was your gang. And I said no. I set him straight. Coup DeGrace is a decent upright colored person, I told him. Just the kind my family has devoted itself to serving."

"A decent upright colored person!" DeGrace said. "I am honored. Perhaps you'll wish to honor me further."

"Oh surely. If I can."

"Where can I find Nicolas Prega?"

Ames tightened his lips.

"If I can't locate him," DeGrace said. "You'll suffice, in a pinch. But I won't be entirely satisfied. The loa demands and the loa receives. You see, you are distinctly the lesser of two evils."

"I certainly am," Ames said. "It was Nicky's idea. He can be so treacherous, and -"

"Prega was the ring leader. The judge said so."

"He certainly was," Ames said. "I don't have a violent bone in my body."

"I hope I can say the same of myself. Nigel however is a different matter. As for my friend Mr. Costa -"

"Costa? He'll be on the look-out for Prega," Ames said. "And he'd avenge anything that happens to the boy. Fearsomely clannish, these southern types. As bad as the Irish on that score, in fact. I -"

"You don't say," DeGrace said. He gave Nigel a nod, and Nigel pressed in closer. Ames was swallowed up in Nigel's shadow.

"But I'm certain if Costa knew the truth," Ames said,

"he'd revise his loyalties quick enough."

"What truth?"

"Nicky Prega - he set the fire! In the North End - I tried to stop him but -"

"Set a fire in his own neighborhood. Against his own people. I thought southern types were fearsomely clannish."

" *'His people?'* " Ames said. "Don't you see - Nicky's an anarchist." He shook his head. "I flirted with such theories myself as a student. Who has not? But he -"

"Took it to bed," DeGrace said.

Ames bit his lip, and blushed. "Yes."

DeGrace regarded Ames. "You will suffice. Nigel."

Nigel grasped Ames by the arms.

"You - you promise you won't hurt him?" Ames said. "Nicky, I mean."

DeGrace gave Nigel a signal, and looked at Ames.

"If you do," Ames said, "everyone will know it was you. You're the one with a grudge against him, after all."

"I would do nothing foolish. I wish only to look into the eyes of the creature that so wantonly destroyed my Andre. Satisfy myself that this creature is made as all men are, two hands, ten fingers, one heart - or perhaps fewer, in his case. I wouldn't hurt him any more than I'd hurt you."

Ames shut his eyes. "I know where you can find Nicky."

"Yes?"

"Tonight. The Commonwealth Avenue mall."

"That mall runs several blocks."

"Dartmouth Street - that massive statue, a fellow on an armchair, surrounded by books."

"William Lloyd Garrison. I believe I've heard of him."

Ames opened his eyes. He went on. "Carry a bunch of yellow roses. A private joke. He'll be certain it's me."

"Excellent," DeGrace said. He looked at Nigel, nodded, and Nigel let go.

CHAPTER TWENTY-NINE

Ben walked along Marlborough Street, his head held high. He was on his way to say a proper final farewell to Ellie. He'd done all he could to set things in order at the Den, and now he was free. Ellie was just an old friend, nothing more. But his heart was pounding more than he expected.

A gust of wind kicked up. Ben burrowed his hands deep into his pockets. They felt deeper than before, and the lining was rougher. His fingers sunk lower, and hit a hard cold surface. Ben paused, and drew the item out. It was Owen's little golden harp. Ben looked down at himself, and shook his head. Exhausted from the day before, he'd had woken up late this morning, and slipped on his dad's old coat by mistake, still stout and serviceable after all those years of use.

He considered turning around, going home and changing. He wanted to look presentable, and like he was his own man for this good-bye - when he heard a soft ring of bells. He glanced up. To his left, a tall dark fir tree had been festooned with Christmas ornaments, among them, a little silver bell. The chiming made him take stock, and emboldened him. It was as if his father was beside him, urging him onwards. "Okay, dad," he said to himself. By then, he was in front of Ellie's house. He pushed the creaky iron gate open, marched down the path to Ellie's house, and knocked on the door.

The house was still. Ben looked through the glass panel beside the door. Marc Antony gave him an unwelcoming sidelong glance, and slunk his Labrador self into the greenhouse. There was no sign of Brutus. That was odd. Brutus and Marc Anthony were inseparable.

He knocked again, and this time caught a glimpse of Mrs. Cabot-Lowell in the hall. She sunk back into the shadows. Ben put his face flush to the cold dark glass, and peered in: to the left, in the greenhouse, Ellie's father was in the broken down rocker. The tips of his plaid carpet slippers were in view. He was holding his head in his hands.

Ben rapped on the glass, but Mr. Cabot-Lowell did not stir.

Ben went around the side of the house, down a narrow path littered with clay pots. He tried the kitchen door, and it opened. Cicero, the superannuated spaniel, was trundling around the tiled floor. He did not bark, but gave Ben a look of droopy-eyed, tremulous disapproval.

"And what do to think you're doing?" Mrs. Cabot-Lowell said. She stood on the threshold to the basement. "I am faced with an intruder."

"I'm sorry, Mrs. Cabot-Lowell I hope you don't mind. I just wanted to see Ellie. Before I go back to Phila-"

"You have broken into our home," she said, "via the tradesman entrance."

"Is Ellie -"

"My daughter is not at home."

"Oh. Where is she? I -"

"Safer than she'd be here, I can assure you."

"Safe? Has Ellie been hurt?"

Mrs. Cabot-Lowell regarded him.

"Maybe I could speak to Mr. Cab -"

"Indeed you may not. The poor man has had enough to deal with. I suggest you show him more compassion than you have so far shown decency or common sense, and leave."

"I was hoping to talk to Ellie," Ben said. "Briefly - just to say good-bye."

"I will tell her." Mrs. Cabot-Lowell went to the kitchen door, and opened it. "In your father's day, this city never saw such strife."

A gust of cold wind hit Ben in the chest.

"Before I go, I will see her," Ben said, and he went out.

Mrs. Cabot-Lowell's neck stiffened. She shut the door after him. The latches and bolts on the door rattled as she secured each and every one of them. Ben felt her watching him as he went up the path, and departed her yard.

Where was Ellie? Maybe she'd gone off to the Athenaeum. It was worth a try.

CHAPTER THIRTY

"Okay," King David was saying into the phone, "we got Jerry Fantastico the Plate-spinning Dervish lined up, but that ain't no opening act. I'm looking for something that'll go ka-plang in the eye. I was thinking Viola LaVoile. The original 'puts the wind in your sails' gal. She ain't kidding... Not til Saturday? Who? Naw, no dice. I ain't looking for a cheese and cracker comic."

The sound of flamenco heels clicked down the hallway. At the threshold, Art the stage manager stopped and hovered, diminutive and dapper, his blonde hair oiled back and glistening in the lamplight. He doubled as a Spanish-style troupe dancer ("*El Norte de Boston*"), and the fringe around his hat brim was sent trembling as he pointed a thumb backwards. "A '*Mr. Costa*' wants to see you," he said. He poked his head in closer, and the fringe danced furiously. "Don't look like no hoofer neither."

"Send him in," King David said, and went on talking into the telephone. "The Fantabulous Wong Brothers? They ain't so fantabulous. Especially not the redhead. He's - hey, listen, chum-foo, I got a visitor." He greeted Costa with a wave of his hand. "Not them either. No, they -

listen, call me when you got something worth hearing, okay?"

King David hung up. "So, Al, what brings you to Scollay Square?" He swung his feet up onto the desk, and indicated the chair across from him. Costa's air of old-world formality always made him want to cut loose. "Park it on the Hepplewhite, why don't you?"

Costa sat down. He was not smiling. "O'Connor set that fire."

King David shrugged. "Maybe so. But you've already hit back yourself, and good. A man in blue." He whistled through his teeth. "My compliments, I guess. But a risky move, pal." He picked up the silver-plated cap of his ink well, tossed it in the air, and caught it. "And you can bet O'Connor's got something in store for you guys."

"I am here because we have much in common, you and I," Costa said.

"Yeah?"

"You have your own grievances, Mr. David, as do I."

"King, okay? We're buddies, you and me."

"The first grievance is with Coup DeGrace. While you are partners, of a sort, in the Cotton Club, DeGrace plays comedy with the accounts."

King David threw the ink cap towards the ceiling.

"You are losing money, my friend," Costa said. "To become a laughing stock in any business is no good. In our business, it is fatal."

King David lunged forward, and swiped the ink cap out of mid-air. He slammed it down on the desk. "How the hell do you know what goes on in -?"

"Those who supply the alcohol have a good chance of knowing the inner workings of a nightclub," Costa said. "No more than an irritant, DeGrace's skimming, to a man of your substance and wherewithal. But such trickery suggests he cannot be trusted. And on another front, the Blueblood banks now refuse your currency. Your theater, and all your business ventures, will dry up in no time. We are the only ones you can turn to. The O'Connors are on a rampage. They are already too powerful, and they have settled on an alliance with the Bluebloods as their means to secure yet more power. And there is no Gryffth among us to set matters right."

King David sat up, despite himself. His heels hit the carpet with a soft thump. It was true about the Bluebloods. Just this morning, he'd gone around the corner to the First Patriot Bank with the weekly deposit for the Majestic Theater. The teller had scrutinized each bill, holding it up to the light. Seven bills were duly removed from the tally, with the clear implication the search would be more intensive the next time, and if deemed appropriate, civil authorities would be called. "May I remind you, Mr. David, counterfeiting is a crime," the teller said. He pursed his lips, and called out: "Next in line." Costa was a sharp cookie to know about the crackdown already. Maybe he was in cahoots with the Bluebloods too, or could be it was just an educated guess.

"Stand with us," Costa said. "Or fall on your own."

King David looked at him. He wasn't sure Costa could be trusted. Costa might just be testing his loyalty to DeGrace. And as things stood, Costa was the one on his own. King David gazed at the Sicilian, intently. He concentrated with all his powers. He had not had a drink since first thing this morning, except for that tumbler when he called the stage booker in Jersey. He narrowed his eyes, waiting for the letters *g-a-n-e-f* to take form. He needed only look steadily at a given schmuck, with stone cold sober eyes, say nothing, and if in a moment, he saw the Hebrew letters *g-a-n-e-f* dancing overhead, he know he was dealing with a A-1 *yentzer*. So far, the necessary occasion had seldom coincided with the absolute sobriety required. And this time, not a single letter appeared above the Sicilian's head, not even a glimmer of one. But King David still taste the whiskey on his lips, so he couldn't bet the rent that Costa was on the level either.

"An important decision." Costa gazed evenly back at King David.

King David looked away. "You bet," he said. He was pretty sure Costa was sincere in his offer. But King David and DeGrace had been partners a while. Sure, they'd had the odd dust-up now and then, but nothing they hadn't been able work out. Before he was going to buddy up to anybody else, King David would have to see where things stood with DeGrace.

The telephone rang. "The Dueling Duo-matics bailed," the voice said. The line from Jersey crackled.

"Both of them?" King David said. He swung his feet back up to the desk with a clunk. He ripped a sheet off his desk calendar, wadded it up, and slam-dunked it into the wastebasket across the room. "I got a curtain rising in an hour, payroll to make in three, and this is what you come up with?"

Costa stood up.

"Al," King David said, "Thanks for stopping by. How about I think it over some?"

"I don't ask twice," Costa said.

*   *   *

King David sat on the workbench in the basement of his theater. He was surrounded by sequined 7-foot sea fronds in aqua and fuchsia, props from an undersea spectacular his father had staged years ago. He leaned down to rummage around the large lumpy bundles stowed under the bench.

A small jeweler's box slipped out from the left-hand pocket of his hand-stitched shirt. King David grinned, sat back up, and opened the box - even in the middle of a task, he never hesitated to pull over and delight in his own panache.

He fingered the item inside: a pair of cufflinks fashioned from human molars. It was his lucky amulet -

he'd got the idea from Meyer Wolfhseim a year or so back, when they were training up James Gatz, the sap who renamed himself Gizby or some such, and came to a bad end on Long Island. King David could have told you why too: the Gatz fella did not know who he was - not a problem King David had ever had. He smiled. He pictured himself wearing the cufflinks while he went trolling for babes - they'd be a sure-fire conversation opener at the Cotton Club, and the night wouldn't end with conversation, no sir. But even entertaining such wolfish prospects could not dispel his underlying intensity for the task at hand.

He slipped the cufflinks back, and, taking a deep breath, hauled out a heavy burlap satchel from under the bench. Scrawled across it, in his pop's broad handwriting was the word: KEPPE. Inside was a crude head made from clay. It just needed a little more work. Once the completed head was affixed to the body, his dad's golem would be complete. A scrap of red paper, marked "Emet" (Truth), was in the satchel, ready to be plastered to the golem's forehead, when the time came, to animate the creature. The golem's torso and limbs lay on its back under the stairwell. They were solid as a felled tree, formed of red clay, and so carefully stored that they had never dried out.

If it was coming down to war, King David figured a golem was a good sidekick to have. It couldn't get sick, if Costa tried any funny business. And the golem would survive fire, if O'Connor was planning to pull that stunt again. Only water at a rolling boil could get inside Marty's cracks and cause him to disintegrate. King David wasn't worried. He'd be on easy street, with Marty-boy at his side.

He'd dubbed the golem "Marty" because it was a name he'd always liked, and as a kid, had wished was his. Only the fact there was no King Marty reconciled him to his given name.

King David had first run across the golem parts the day after his father's burial. The golem was evidently his father's last great scheme, never brought to completion. Even now, King David avoided thinking much about his father. The old man had hung on for months, a ragged rasp in his throat. With every breath he struggled to take, the light in his eyes shrunk - his father, who had been strong as an ox, and risen from the rag and bone trade to own the biggest theater in town. Until his last illness, the old man had had a handshake that broke bones, a smile that made tough men want to do him a good turn, and a glower that made them want to do an even better one.

King David had availed himself of Marty once, a season or two ago, as a slam-dunk showstopper. Cashing in on the King Kong craze, King David designed a fetching tableau featuring the golem breaking loose from the columns of his prison. To Yankee-doolize it for the July 4th holiday, King David had the prison guards outfitted as British redcoats. "Ain't exactly historically accurate, is it?" Art said. "History's what you make it, bub," King David replied.

Midway through the stage show, the golem broke free of his ropes, dashed the papier-mâché columns, and tottered across the stage. The crowd roared applause. Some wise guy, front and center, lobbed an apple, and hit the golem square in the nose. "Over here, Big Boy!" the lug shouted. "No Mart - here," King David rejoined. Mighty and lumbering, the golem was teetering at the edge of the stage. King David thought of shouting out "Stop!" but the golem, ever literal-minded, would have fallen of its own crushing weight into the audience. King David leapt from the balcony, and ripped off the scrap of paper from its forehead. The golem fell into several large pieces. The crowd went wild, some booing, some applauding, and King David took a bow. Sure, the repairs to the stage ran steep, and that old beancounter Rhinegold turned blue, but the show had put the Majestic on the map, no doubt about it.

And once he was pieced back together again, old Marty

would keep King David ahead of the game, too.

CHAPTER THIRTY-ONE

In the earth's dark embrace,
Roots sleep through winter, blanketed by the -

Amy Lowell stirred awake. A shaft of light was slanting across her feet, and usually when she awoke, around eleven in the morning, the light in winter fell squarely across her eyes. This hour was later - into the afternoon, she guessed. She could not tell, for she had covered the clock on the mantelpiece with a stout black cloth. The three mirrors in the room were similarly masked, like men about to be executed. Amy had always hated timepieces and mirrors. They were mechanical reminders - no, worse: they were the foot soldiers, armed and unstoppable - of mortality. But still she declined to remove the clock and the mirrors outright: eccentricity requires normality. Amy snuggled into her baronial bed, careful that none of her sixteen down pillows tumbled to the floor, and that the cat curled up at her feet was not disturbed. The cat began to purr.

A watchful muse,
This son of leopards, sun, and sleekness,
Who -

Another poem! Amy reached to the side table, and seized her pince-nez, paper and pen.

The poem that had last night scored the dark secret skies of her mind, and the two poems subsequent just this morning, were nudging her into full wakefulness. A poem was perishable and fleeting, fragile as a dream. Before it was lost forever, it had to be consigned to ink and paper. Amy began to write, with deep looping strokes, and languorous dots and crosses:

Underneath the bed, my old brown shoes are soft with wear and time,

Through the silence of downstairs, the ringing of the telephone sounded. It stopped, midway through the third ring. A light quick footstep sounded, climbing upwards to her room. Amy wrote on:

The feet on which I tread are forever socked and heeled,
or else, so tender, risk wounds and corns and bunions
More lasting are these feet of metre that on the page step smartly and

At the threshold, Ada appeared. Her face was darkly handsome, and etched with worry, and only more beguiling for it. She bit her lip, and wrung her frail slender-fingered hands. "Lawrence has called on the telephone. He says it is rather urgent, Amy dear."

Amy looked down at her page and stopped short of completing the line. Enjambments held a rare and secret pleasure.

"Give me a moment, Ada dear," she said.

She lumbered to her feet, and from the closet, drew out a dressing robe. It was Chinese silk, and patterned like a wisteria grove, in lilac, apple green, and deep French blue. She wrapped the lengths around herself, and loosely tied the sash.

Heavily, with care, like a mountain climber affixed to a rope, Amy descended the main staircase. When she reached the second floor, she was already short of breath. She steadied herself on the rosewood railing, and continued. On the ground floor, she lumbered along the delft blue hallway, gained the telephone, and took up the talking piece.

"Yes, brother," Amy said. She listened a few moments, poetry roiling in her brain. "Oh. A guest, sometime today, or perhaps tomorrow? Of course, if you say... Me? I was writing. Yes, brother, poetry...Yes. I'm still at it." A smile played at her lips. "Good day, brother," she said, and hung up.

"Nettie," Amy called out. Scarcely had the name been uttered than Nettie bounded in, her face as ruddy and fresh as if it had been scrubbed with carbolic soap, her shoes so new and untried they squeaked. "Make up the Ivy Room. A guest will be arriving."

"Very good, Miss Amy," Nettie said, and with a squeak of her shoes, went out.

Amy sat down at her desk, grateful to give her legs a rest. She opened the top drawer. The gun was there, still loaded, atop the last letter she had received from Ezra Pound. In the end, he had proved no true friend. The radiator hissed. Amy hurriedly took out fresh paper and pen, and began to write:

On a wave of humid heat inside, tendrils grow,
and green shoots of vines do reach across the

Ada came in, and stood behind her. Amy went on composing as Ada caressed her neck, and neatened the vagrant locks. Amy was immediately overcome with another image that cried out to be written.

Nimble and quick fingers,
Like tiny footprints in ecstatic dance across my scalp
Which tingles, alive as never been before

Winky the cat stretched out in front of the fire, then spying a scrap of red ribbon, pounced on it with his tiny claws. Almost faint, Amy felt yet another verse coming over her. She reached for a blank sheet of paper.

Poet witch virgin spinster
Provider of milk and fish and warmth -

what am I to you, my feline friend, tiger mine,
miniature and wild, who toys with odd remnants of artisanal
craft?

It was not even dinnertime. Already so much poetry had been written, but there was so much more to be done. As always, the prospect was both daunting and exhilarating. Amy Lowell's fingers itched. Her heart raced. Her blood was singing.

Across the empire of a rough carpet
you do play, bold cat,
on patterns Persian in origin.

CHAPTER THIRTY-TWO

Ellie looked out the bedroom window to the snow-covered meadows and gardens and groves below. The snow glowed pinkish gold in the winter sunset. Her room was high up in the house, warm and well-appointed, with thick coverlets and soft pillows. A sun catcher of Venetian glass in every windowpane gave the light a churchlike feel. They'd been kind, the servants, and Amy Lowell herself. An hour ago, Ellie had pleaded a headache, and said she wished to rest. They promised not to disturb her till morning. "Poor thing," the maid said, "not used to this fresh country air."

"The winter air is fresh but cold, and shakes the bare boughs outside my window," Amy replied. "They tap upon the glass like winter on tip-toes." A look came over her face. She put down her teacup, and took up her pen.

Ellie finished her tea, and went upstairs. She was a prisoner, and she was being kept away from Ben, and the separation had to do with Ben's father's business. She was sure of it.

She had been here just a few hours, but it felt like weeks. The day had gone awry early on. No sooner had

her father left their house for his research at the
Athenaeum ("*Fauna and flora in the Federalist Papers*"), her
mother announced that a visit to the country had been
arranged for her. She already had Ellie's packed valise in
her hands. A car was parked at the curb, motor idling, a
green touring sedan emblazoned on each of the back
doors with a hand armed with three fine darts. The Lowell
family crest, her mother said with a satisfied half-smile.
Before Ellie could protest, her mother hurried her down
the pathway. The car door opened and her mother
elbowed her inside. Brutus gave a yelp. He rushed down
the path, jostling Mrs. Cabot-Lowell, before jumping into
the car. He leaned with all his weight against Ellie.

"Mother really -" Ellie said. "I -"

"You don't know what's right for you dear," Mrs.
Cabot-Lowell said. She took hold of Brutus's collar and
pulled. But the dog was unyielding. He stared straight
ahead. "Come along, Brutus, dear," she said, in a sugary
tone.

Brutus maintained his straight-ahead stare.

"Very well," Mrs. Cabot-Lowell said. "Time is of the
essence." She let go of the collar, slammed the car door
shut, and gave the roof of the car a sharp rap. The driver
pulled away.

The car proceeded down Beacon Street, and headed
west. The traffic was slow on the snowy roadways.
Gradually, the frozen lawns became broader, and the
houses larger. They were set further apart from each other,
and further back from the street. The car turned onto
Heath Street, Ellie noted: the sign was only partially
obscured by a mound of snow. The car slowed, and pulled
into a drive that was broader than the road. They motored
past snow-laden hedges, orchards and meadows. As the
car ascended a small rise, a house came into view. It was
imposing in size, and rambling in style. It was made of
stone, and had three sections, like towers, each one with its
own mansard roof. The front door had a four columned

portico, in the style of a miniature Greek temple.

A few hundred yards from the door, the car drew to a stop, the snow crunching under the wheels. The driver got out, and opened Ellie's door. Brutus jumped out first, his breath wet and warm in the cold dry air. Then Ellie stepped from the car, cautiously, as if she was walking in a dream, or onto a sheet of glass. The driver offered her his arm.

"Sevenels's the name of the place, miss," the driver said. He pushed his cap back with his thumb. "Nice, ain't it? Miss Amy says the first time here, a visitor has got to a stop short of the doorway to take it all in proper like." He picked up Ellie's bag. "Perspective, Miss Amy calls it, and she is awful fond of it. Can't stop talking about it some days. Almost insistent. The way ladies get a bee in their bonnet - beg your pardon, miss. Only more so with our Miss Amy." They went side by side up toward the front path, Brutus circling around them in figure eights. The driver rang the doorbell.

"Now Miss Amy Lowell is a nice lady," the driver said. He chuckled. "So long as she don't find a dirty butter knife or some such. Then she's got a temper that's awful fierce. This way, miss, and hound."

A maid answered the door, frank curiosity in her eyes, her apron askew.

"Evening, Nettie," the driver said.

"Same to you, Sam."

"Here's your visitor, safe and sound." He tipped his hat. "Good day, all." And in a twinkle of an eye, he was back in his car.

"Come along, miss," Nettie said. "Miss Amy's been waiting for you."

Nettie led the way down the hallway, into a large, high-ceilinged room. A lady was at her desk, her monocle in place. Her face was as white and square as a block of lard. She put down her pen, and rose to her feet. She was short and solidly stout. She withdrew the monocle, and came forward. Her eyes were like pale blue fire.

"Hello," she said, in a voice that was so deep it was disconcerting from a person so short. "I am Miss Amy Lowell."

"My name is Ellie Cabot-Lowell," Ellie said. She hung her head low and to one side. She looked up at Amy Lowell with her green eye, then she turned her head and regarded her with the blue eye. The blue worked better. "And this is Brutus."

"Not Cassius, for he has no lean and hungry look," Amy Lowell said. "And this is my feline housemate, Winky."

Brutus was staring down at Winky. With his muzzle, he nudged the cat, and, all four legs tensed, he waited, ready to spring. Winky ignored him, and pounced on a scrap of red yarn. Brutus's ears went flat. He ran to Ellie's side, and sat down.

"Winky has a way with dogs," Amy said. "Never shows a jot of fear, or interest." She returned to her desk, and with a creak of the chair, she sat down again, and went back to writing.

Ellie sat, quiet and bewildered. Brutus stayed by her side, watchful and alert. She was tired - exhausted, really, for no good reason - and her mind felt foggy. Amy Lowell offered her a cup of tea. Ellie accepted. A telephone rang. Nettie appeared at the threshold and said it was for Miss Lowell.

"Oh dear, not again!" Amy rolled to her feet, which were small to be supporting so great a weight.

"Brother," Amy was saying. "Yes, she is. Very welcome. Tell your wife that - ? Wait, let me get a pen - a sad lack for a poet! Now then: Staying at the club, you say...."

Brutus whined. Perhaps he needed to go out. A bit of fresh air would do me good too, Ellie thought, and help clear my head. She took her coat from the hallway, and went to the front door. She opened it, and took a step over the threshold - or rather, she tried to. She could not step out the door. It was as though her feet were made of lead, and in front of her, an invisible and immovable wall had sprung up. She took a breath, and tried again. She was stymied as before. Brutus sat down at her feet, and, whining louder, pawed at her skirts.

"What's that, brother?" Amy's voice went on. "Until Governor Cox has …slower, please …"

Once again, Ellie reached out - but could not extend her hand through the open door. She was trapped. She looked about her, and thought quickly. She partly closed the front door, and went into the library. She took a book from the shelf - *What's O'Clock*, by Amy Lowell. She opened it at random, and ripped out a page.

"Well, it must be important indeed," Amy was saying, "to keep the Governor so late. Hours rummaging through the record offices, you say? Perhaps he is exhausted. Do not let his inaccessibility trouble you. A fatigued mind can run short of courtesy, as a runner grows short of breath."

Ellie grabbed a pen from the desk, and scrawled a message across the torn page. She meant to write: *Ben, I'm in Brookline, at cousin Amy Lowell's. Please come get me, Ellie.*

But the words were coming out differently:

Sevenels in Brookline
At my cousin's manse among the tall firs,
I make to move across the threshold,
To join the snow
And regain the city.
Brookline is the outskirts.
But I find I stay inside,
my will exhausted, my words replenished but…

"Is that all, brother?" Amy Lowell said.

Brutus sidled in closer. Ellie leaned down, opened the biscuit-shaped locket on the dog's collar, and stuffed the missive inside. She snapped the locket shut, and opened the door wide.

"Good-bye, dear brother," Amy Lowell said.

"Go, Brutus," Ellie said. "Find Ben." Brutus shot out into the front yard. Ellie shut the door, and returned her coat to the hallway.

With a slow tread that rattled the windowpanes, Amy Lowell began her approach to the parlor. Ellie had just sat down when Amy trundled in and looked around. "Dear Brutus, is he -?"

"Oh, I just let him out for a bit of air," Ellie said. "He'll come back."

"More loyal than any Brutus ought to be," Amy Lowell said, chuckling as she sat down at her desk.

The maid entered the room, with a china tea set clattering on the tray.

"Nothing like a pot of tea on a cold day, is there, miss?" Nettie said.

Amy Lowell looked up. "I told you to use the Darjeeling, did I not?"

"Yes ma'am."

"And have you?"

"Oh yes," Nettie said. "I -"

"Well, I am certainly glad to hear it," Amy Lowell said. Her pen scratched against the paper.

"Tea, miss?" Nettie said.

"Yes please." Ellie took the cup Nettie offered, and listened to Amy, who spoke in sing-song, as if reciting something she had written. The effect was soporific.

"Distant relations," Amy said. "So curious a phrase. Would close strangers be their counterparts?"

The sun was lowering. The light in the windows was cold and watery. Amy Lowell returned to her poetry, reciting as she wrote:

SUNLIGHT,
Three marigolds,
And a dusky purple poppy-pod --
Out of these I made a -

She reached across her desk for a small red box, and took out a thin black cigar. She lit it, took a puff, and then penned another verse. She recited as she wrote, in a cadence as monotonous as the ticking of a metronome.

Ellie drank her tea, then said she felt a headache coming on, and wished to lie down. And so she had lain in bed ever since, surrounded by thickening shadows.

The stratagem with Brutus had been the last act of conscious spirit she could remember. As the day wore on, and she waited to be rescued, a torpor took hold of her. She'd been trying to memorize the layout of the place. None of the doors were locked, from what she could see. There were no guards or weaponry to keep her from going out the front door - but still, she was held back, by something within and around her.

And now in the bedroom, "resting," the languor in her limbs was undeniable. It brooked no action. With a supreme effort of will, she stood up. She scooped up her shoes, and thought:

I will take the back stairs to the kitchen,
no one will hear my bare footsteps, and as
I pass by the window ledge
that houses a red glass jar - glossy, fine and clear,
the light within it contained and concentrated, a miniature sun
the sole splotch of color in a world gone madly white
I -

What was happening to her? Since entering the confines of Sevenels, her thoughts came in this maddeningly "poetic" form. The steam that rose from her cup of tea, the hang of the curtains, the orange pitcher atop the carved oak chest of drawers - every sight that passed her eyes inspired yet another "poem." It was making her dizzy. She staggered back to the bed, lay down, and shut her eyes.

CHAPTER THIRTY-THREE

In the dusty book-lined confines of his office at Grimley and Graybody, Cox allowed himself a smirk. Lowell was a consummate stooge - so easily led, if you could slow yourself down to his ponderous pace. Cox fingered the *Protocols of the Elders of Merrymount* on the desk before him. Its handwritten pages were brittle with time, vengeance, and moral rectitude. Cox had been perusing a sub-section entitled "The First of the Seventy-first: On the Ancillary and Undeniable Powers of the Blood of the Craven and Condemned": with every drop of blood that fell from the Quill of Justice to the streets of Boson, it seemed, a legion of shades would be summoned, neither dead nor alive, sworn to do the Brahmin overlord's will.

Cox turned to his favorite section of the document. It began with the ceremony of the cold-shouldering. Knowing such a ceremony existed made him feel less alone. There were kindred souls among his people, or at least there had been. The cold-shouldering embodied Cox's preferred social style to a tee: the refusal to return a greeting, the level stare, followed by the look askance. If only Cox could afford to deport himself in so uncompromised a fashion.

Cox's fingertips trembled as they touched, barely, the ancient spidery handwriting of the *Protocols*. The cold-shouldering was but a prelude to the most sacred ceremony of them all: the Sacrifice of the Supreme Brahmin Scapegoat. Cox gazed upon the writing. But he did not need to read it. He knew the order of the sacrifice by heart.

The ceremony began here, at Pemberton Square, in the shadow of both the police commissioner's office and the State House; it ended near Court Street and Cornhill, the epicenter of both Puritan publishing and punishment. Cornhill was a graceful crescent of a street, where Ben Franklin had apprenticed, the Tea Party men had met in secret, and William Lloyd Garrison published his pro-Negro screed the *Liberator*. And at the intersection of Cornhill and Court Street, the colonial prison had once stood. Within its confines, Quakers, witches, and their felonious ilk had been dealt swift and stern justice. The prison had been solidly built, with massive oaken doors backed in iron, barred windows, and gloomy cells, and Cox had often fortified himself in odd moments by gazing at engravings of it.

All these glories of publishing and punishment were in the past - before the waves of vulgar print had swamped the world, and before the hordes of foreigners had decamped and besieged this city on a hill from within, and nearly leveled it. The prison did not stand at present. But when the scapegoat was sacrificed, as according to the dictates of the *Protocols*, that present would change.

Time itself would be undone. On every street, in every building, the present, past, and future would arise as one. The Old Howard was at present a burlesque house. Before that, it had been, in backwards succession, a freak show palace, a legitimate theater, and its first incantation, a Millerite Hall. At the culmination of the ceremony, all those incarnations would burst into being simultaneously inside the present form, like a flame within a flame. With time slipped from its moorings, history itself would be remade. The arrivals of certain undesirables would be forestalled altogether. The ceremony provided a certain means for the Blueblood righteous to regain hegemony.

The Sacrifice had never been enacted, because so far no circumstance had been deemed to require so dire and magnificent a response. *In camera*, Cox himself had broached the possibility during the Boston police strike in 1919, the night the militia stormed Scollay Square and put the rabble to rights. But the fools maintained that the newly finished Custom House Tower rendered the Sacrifice obsolete. Completed just ten years ago, the Custom House Tower was now the tallest building in the city - it had overtaken the Ames Building - and was exempt from all height restrictions. The clock atop the tower was the great eye under which everything in the city transpired. The Custom House Tower set the standard of time in Boston. As there was no escaping time's dominion, and time itself was now under the aegis of the Blueblood master of the tower, the tower's champions maintained that it constituted an impregnable bulwark against the encroaching interlopers.

But Cox knew a clock, however magical, was not enough to hold hegemony. It had hardly done well so far. Every year, the numbers of Irish and Italian, and worse, increased. The neighborhoods grew noisier, and dirtier, and less American. The Sacrifice was the only hope. Its power was beyond compare. Its willful lack of mercy, its denial of all sniveling charity, was invincible. Among lesser peoples, the scapegoat escapes. But the Puritan elders were made of sterner stuff. They knew mercy was a weakness.

The scapegoat had to be a young Blueblood specimen of impeccable pedigree - for had not Cain's meager offerings been rejected? Cox knew that any scapegoat ceremony was, if ever, far in the future. But still, the mere proximity of these near-crumbling pages, which spelled out the intractable and merciless judgments of one's forebears, gave Cox hope and substance. The *Protocols* provided the only emotional cargo Cox had ever deemed worthy to carry inside his hard, compact heart.

With a respectful frown, he put the *Protocols* to one side, reached for the second file, and opened it. This matter was immediate, and more modest, but the procedure was no less exacting. Before him were two property deeds, each handwritten in careful copperplate script that had turned brown with time. To Cox, property deeds constituted the very soul of ownership, free from the vulgar hammering of day laborers, and the incessant clanging of the water pipes. Documents such as these calmed Cox's nerves. They were not published, in the current style of vulgar democracy, but were penned by hand, these deeds, and sequestered in locked safes, away from all noise, light, clamor and tumult. The only sound that attended them was the scratch of a pen, and the barely perceptible breathing of a lawyer.

Print had become too democratic. It had grown clamorous and grubby, comprising a rising tide of spurious opinion and obnoxious broadsides. What little there remained of Puritan seriousness and high purpose was being drowned out by the riffraff and their newspapers, advertisements, and circulars. Print had proved intractable to the powers of transformation - and had become as vilely fecund as the immigrants themselves.

With a deep breath, Cox tidied the two files. He opened the side drawer, and with as gentle a touch as his parched hand could offer, stashed them away. As the drawer clicked shut, there was a knock at his door. Before Cox could answer, Ames sauntered in, his hands in his pockets.

"Something must be afoot, uncle," Ames said. "You've summoned me to the sanctuary of sanctuaries, not the lowly State House."

"Sit down," Cox said.

But Ames already had, in the largest and most

overstuffed chair in the room. His legs were negligently stretched out into the middle of the room. "I've been busy myself," he said, with an insolent grin. His forehead was scratched, and puffiness shadowed his left eye. "I'm ever so keen to fill you in on my progress."

"Indeed," Cox said.

"I'm sure you've heard the hue and cry - that fire in the North End."

"Go on."

"Let's just say there was a fine Anglo hand in it." He held up his own hand and grinned. "And the papers are going after Lowell He's been cast as the consummate rabble-rouser. It is delicious."

"A dangerous proposition, Ames."

"Oh, little Nicky Prega's something of a hothead, uncle. I couldn't stop him. But I've done everything I could to make it work to the detriment of Lowell."

"So you tell me." Cox was frowning.

Ames's grin widened. "And more than that. I've set Ben Owen against Coup DeGrace, most devilishly if I may say. He believes that DeGrace's gang is responsible for my injuries here. I'm fine, Uncle, by the way. Took a little tumble down an icy path is all. Nothing to worry about."

Cox grunted.

"And further, I threw a serious bone of contention between Costa and DeGrace."

"What bone would that be?"

"Little Nicky Prega," Ames said.

Cox scowled. "A snaggle-toothed specimen, that Prega. He strikes me as altogether untrustworthy."

"We have nothing to fear from Nicky. Trust me, uncle. We have made good use of him."

"Somehow I knew you would," Cox said.

Ames, the grin still frozen on his face, coughed, and looked away.

"You are rather sure of yourself, Ames," Cox said. "I wouldn't be."

"I think I did rather well," Ames said.

"Hardly," Cox said. "Young Owen is a thoughtful sort, and a fairly good judge of character. I doubt he'll be acting on the basis of anything you've told him. The young man will require a distraction. Towards that end, I have arranged a frolic for him myself."

Ames raised an eyebrow. "Do tell." He swung his legs over the arm of the chair.

"Sit up properly," Cox said. He waited until Ames complied, then went on. "The enmity between O'Connor and Costa existed well before your singular combustive efforts of today. So far, you have in fact done much to foster certain regrettable alliances among our enemies. Mr. Costa has just approached Jerome David - the Sicilian was spotted leaving the Majestic Theatre, this morning. My lieutenant governor was ….doing some research in Scollay Square, and he made the sighting."

"I've done a bit of 'research' down Scollay-way myself," Ames said. "Planning to do a bit more tonight. Which 'laboratory' - the Tam O'Shanter, or the Golden Dime?"

"Listen and learn, boy. I am about to give you an education that Lowell never could. And see to it you don't bungle my plans with yet more of your hijinks, as appears to be your wont. Your animus against Lowell has got the better of you."

"Uncle," Ames said, "I am hurt." He polished his fingernails against his coat sleeve. "But honored, too, that you would confide in me."

"My attempts to drive a wedge between the Jew and the Negro on the matter of false currency has not been entirely successful. King David and DeGrace have not attacked each other, at least not so far, and indeed have continued running their nightclub. The action scheduled for New Year's Eve may well change things between them, but as of now, they continue in reasonable accord. Thankfully, however, Costa and the Irish are at each other's throats. Costa has already done away with one policeman."

"So far so good," Ames said. "And O'Connor will rise up in revenge."

"Strife is a great boon. Though I'm sure if I gave you time, you'd find some way of bringing the garlic and the potato peoples together as one."

"I could try," Ames said.

"My tactic is to keep Ben Owen distracted, as well as Lowell," Cox said. "How the prospect of settling on a punishment just and true does delight our Lowell. Toward that end, I spoke to Timothy Owen myself."

"The paperboy?" Ames said.

Cox nodded. "I flattered Timothy Owen into placing an item, asked oh so solicitously if he had any bit of harmless information on his brother, the kind that might put a smile on Benjamin's face, and take his mind off the cares and woes, which seemed to weigh heavily upon him. His romantic life might be the charm, I suggested."

"And Timothy bought it? He wasn't on his guard speaking to you, and not Lowell?"

"He seems to have a jealous eye for his brother's position, our Tim. I flattered him merely by deigning to speak to him. He'll divulge nothing of our conversation to anyone. He volunteered as much. He has his honor. He told me so himself." Cox chuckled. "All but sat up and begged."

"Tim Owen, the patsy's patsy."

"Just so. And these are the people Lowell believes might be assimilated unto ourselves." Cox shook his head.

"They are not the worst we are besieged with, uncle."

"True," Cox said. "Our Hibernian friends and their Sicilian counterparts are bad enough, but they scarcely compare with the Hebrews and their Oriental scheming."

"Don't forget the Negros," Ames said.

"Indeed I have not. Some groups, however, present a more pressing threat than others. Consider this: Mayor

Curley is planning to run for governor again."

"I would guess so," Ames said with a shrug. "Politics is so very boring."

"And to raise cash, he is planning to remortgage that house of his. The bank officer tipped me off last month... a good man, Harris Chandler."

"Oh, Harry," Ames said. "I've met him." He flicked a bit of fluff from his sleeve. "One morning, on Commonwealth Avenue."

"So in judicious preparation," Cox continued, "I have obtained the deed to both the Mayor's house, and Alphonse Costa's abode, a far more modest affair, on Hanover Street."

"Over the hardware store," Ames said.

"With the help of Grimley and Graybody, I had planned to effect a certain transformation, closer to the election, so that Curley would find the sale of the house he owned commanded a far more modest price than expected ... the sale would raise Costa's ire too of course. But in light of present circumstances, it seems more provident to arrange the transformation immediately."

"Why so soon?" Ames said.

"The police commissioner went by the North End station today, seeing to the neighborhood after the fire. In a side room, Wilson saw evidence of a contraption - a machination of O'Connor, apparently, some device of sound storage and amplification. He made inquiries. Ostensibly, the device is to enable the parish Christmas choir to be broadcast far and wide, to the Curley daughter still sick in bed."

"How sweet," Ames said.

"I am convinced the device is related to the banshee," Cox said. "It is a conjecture, but my surmise is that O'Connor will use that device to manipulate the banshee's wail tonight, and cause its fatal sound to be visited upon the Costa house. Why else the secrecy surrounding the item's delivery and storage?"

"You have been busy."

"The powers of our race must be concentrated tonight on this one aim: to switch the deed of Curley's house with that of Costa, so that the death O'Connor expects he is visiting upon Costa will be instead be visited upon the good Mayor Curley. Of course, the Irish will blame Costa, but they will also be caught short, bereft of their esteemed, and alarmingly capable, leader. And so their war escalates."

"Fight ye devils," Ames said.

"A strategy of long and proven pedigree." Cox said. "Curley is altogether more clever than is good for him. Intelligence does not become some peoples - as with women, Negros, and certain field dogs, some are best left to the fallow fields of intuition and luck." He stood up, went to the door, and opened it. He peered down the long dark hallway.

At the far end, Farnsworth Grimley, Esq. had emerged from his office. He was progressing up the corridor. The dome of his bald head was pearly, almost translucent in the dim lamplight. The rustling shades - first year associates - scuttled out of his way, like dry leaves in a November gust. Grimley himself was as starched looking as a fresh dollar bill. His progress was serene and ghostly, tight-lipped, silent, and majestic. At the deepest shadow, which was the well of the central staircase, he executed a left turn, and started up to the law library, the domed top of the building. Cox's hand went to his throat. If his bodily humor had been less dry, his eyes would have misted over. The building's dome commanded a view of the Kings Burial ground, the police headquarters, and the head offices of the United Bank of Boston: the dome was the crucible of Boston Blueblood hegemony.

"It is to transpire now," Cox said, in a husky whisper. He melted into the hallway, and maintaining a respectful distance from Grimley, began his own stately, and creeping, ascent to the dome.

Ames took this as his signal to depart. The entire

building had drawn to a hush. The hallway lights were already flickering. Ames went out through the main door of the building, and stood on the front steps, buttoning up his coat. The wind was cold, and the evening had already thickened. On the horizon, the floodlit sign for the John Ward Shoe Company, a gigantic glass slipper, glittered in the near dark. Nicky would no doubt be waiting for him in the shadows of Commonwealth Avenue...they said they wouldn't hurt him. Poor Nicky. He was sweet, and he said the cutest, most devotedly anarchist things. But all the same, he'd been an awful tease. Ames began humming, and skipped down the steps. On Tremont Street, the trolley screeched along ahead of him. He reached the crossing. The street light at the corner had nearly flickered out.

"What the - ?" the man next to him said. He looked overhead and gave his cigar an emphatic chew.

Ames looked into the horizon: the slipper-shaped sign had gone dark. One by one, the lights across the skyline dimmed or went out entirely. Up ahead, the trolley's windows went dark. The trolley whined, slowed, and lurched to a halt halfway around a bend.

"Holy moly," the man said. The end of his cigar glowed red. "Like the world's coming to an end!"

Ames giggled. The transformation was underway!

CHAPTER THIRTY-FOUR

Ben stumbled over a snowdrift, and emerged out onto the road. The dim wattage from the streetlights was more eerie than complete darkness. Shadows slanted around him on all sides, and stood up like knives. He hadn't found Ellie. She was nowhere in the Athenaeum. He had scoured every floor. He even ventured over to Filene's Basement on the off chance she had gone shopping. Girls were supposed to like that sort of thing, but Ellie wasn't like most girls. Then he'd wandered over to the Back Bay again, hoping to encounter her, oh so casually, as she made her way home. But no such luck, and the day was waning.

He regained Commonwealth Avenue. His shoe heels beat an icy tattoo in the bitter chill as he hastened back towards Charles Street and the Den. He heard a chiming, faint but distinct. He glanced around.

Up ahead, a big black Labrador dog was nosing around the base of a statue - John Glover, who rowed Washington across the Delaware, Ben knew, because long ago, his kite had crashed down on the statue's head.

The light was hazy, but the dog was familiar - boisterous and oversized. Was it -?

"Brutus?" Ben called out. He clapped his hands

The dog turned and came bounding towards him. He had a couple of yellow flower petals stuck to his muzzle. He wagged his tail so strongly that the locket on his collar jingled.

"So that's what I was hearing." Ben removed the sprig. "You raid a flowershop, fella?" Brutus nuzzled him. Ben gave him a scratch. "Hey, where's Ellie, boy?"

Brutus growled. He lowered his muzzle and began nipping at his own chest, ridding himself of clumps of matted snow. Ben moved in to help. He pushed aside the biscuit-shaped locket, and noticed an edge of paper sticking out.

Brutus poked his muzzle at Ben, and gave a single sharp bark.

"Just your people's address, Brut. In case you get lost."

Brutus pawed Ben more insistently, and whined.

"Okay, wise guy, I'll show you." Ben knelt down in the snow and opened the locket, expecting to find a slip of paper with the Cabot- Lowell's address neatly printed across it. But what he found was a wadded up scrap of printed paper - from a book, it looked like. He flattened it open. It had been torn from a volume of poetry of some sort.

The Green Bowl
This little bowl is like a mossy pool
In a spring wood…

A handwritten message was scrawled across the typeface:

Sevenels in Brookline
At my cousin's manse among the tall firs…

Ben read the message through. Brutus ran in circles, yipping and wagging his tail, before returning once again to dig at the base of the statue. Why was Ellie in Brookline? Who had brought her there? And was she was in any danger? It was clear she was there against her will. But surely her own mother would not deliver her to any harm.

"Got some business here, mister?" a deep voice said. From behind the statue, a policeman emerged, broad as a desk.

"Oh yes - no," Ben said. His hands wavered in midair. "Just enjoying the snow, officer. Don't get this in Philadelphia."

"Don't say," the officer said. He eyed Ben up. "Owen's kid right? The egghead, not the suck-up."

"Yes," Ben said. "I guess that's a compliment."

The officer grunted. "Too bad all your smarts couldn't save Officer Mulvaney."

"I'm working on it," Ben said.

"Work harder." The policeman was watching Ben with alert blue eyes. Then he turned to face the street and shook his head. "Never saw this trouble when your dear old dad was running things." And with a twist of his billy club, the policeman went back to his beat. He whistled, slow and mournful. His shadow was cast long and crooked down the trees of the mall, as he marched off.

Ben watched him go. When he was satisfied there was enough distance between them, he called out, "Over here, Brut."

The dog paid no attention. Ben whistled, but it made no difference. Brutus went on burrowing into the mound of snow at the foot of the statue.

"Okay, pal," Ben said. "The mountain comes to Mohammed." He trudged over to the statue. A few yellow roses were scattered around the churned-up drifts. Brutus jerked his head up, his muzzle encrusted with snow. He was clutching something between his teeth.

"What you got there, Brute?" Ben leant down and held out an open palm. "Come on, boy, give."

Brutus wagged his tail, and opened his jaws. A scrolled-up notebook dropped into Ben's hand. It was a kid's composition book. The ink was water-damaged, and the pages ruffled. A big splotch of grease darkened its cover. No doubt some schoolchild had lost it on his way home.

Ben slipped the notebook into his coat pocket. Maybe he'd be able to return it, and spare the poor kid some grief.

He'd get a streetcar into Brookline. He hurried over to Beacon Street, Brutus at his heels. A trolley soon pulled up. Ben and Brutus got on. The doors were about to shut, when through the falling darkness, a newspaper hawker hollered: "Read all about it! Mayor's Daughter Dead!"

CHAPTER THIRTY-FIVE

The trolley screeched along the tracks, slowing on the turn. Ben sat in the back of the deserted car. Brutus hunkered down on the floor next to him. They had just passed into Brookline. Ben's heart was racing. O'Connor would not let the death of the Curley girl go unavenged. Gang war was unavoidable.

The trolley lurched forward with a jolt, and the notebook catapulted out of Ben's coat onto the floor. He picked it up. *Cellar Notebooks* was scrawled in a childish hand across the front. He began leafing through it.

The proletariat, forever oppressed, must be forever the instrument of his own liberation.

Strange stuff for a grade-school kid, Ben thought. He flipped ahead a few pages.

Green Shutters is an establishment on Cedar Lane Way where those who play at revolution indulge in corrupt and distracting bourgeois passions of the flesh. The revolutionary imperative requires me to indulge that which I despise.

Ben turned the page.

The fire at Popeo and Gremoli is an example of the honest proletariat misled and exploited by the corrupt thrill-seeking aristocrat.

A tingle ran along Ben's spine. He flipped back to the front. Inside the cover was inscribed: *N. Prega.*

Ben went on reading. His heart felt too big for his chest.

Prescott Ames formulated the idea of planting a bomb. He said the explosion would be contained, and destroy only documents. He said he had an enemy, Lawrence Lowell, 'the professor' he calls him with much contempt, who hated the law firm, and that all harm and blame for the deed would accrue to that enemy alone. And that even if his role or mine were to be detected, the Governor would protect us. Ames is the nephew of the Governor, so affiliated with the apparatus of the state, and therefore is an enemy of the people.

Ben flipped a few pages back.

The evil eye that fell upon the Curley girl was not intended for her. I had been gazing at the policeman at the corner who expressed repeated doubt as to my masculine nature. The deed did nothing to serve the -

"Oh, my," Ben said. Brutus stood up and yipped. The key to peace was in his hands. He'd have to tell O'Connor, and Costa, and all of them - but first, he had to save Ellie. The street lights were flickering. The shadows were thick. Ben could just make out a sign for the Brookline Savings and Loan.

"Come on," Ben said. He drummed his fingers on the trolley seat. Underneath him, the machinery whined and strained.

The car went forward with a jolt. The street went dark. The lights inside the car went out. As the car lurched to a halt, Ben pried the doors open, jumped out, and, with Brutus at his side, landed on his feet in the snowy street.

CHAPTER THIRTY-SIX

A draft came up through the bedroom grate. The glass sun-catchers rattled, and gave a faint chiming sound.

Ellie turned over, and tried to sleep.

But the wind rose, and the chimes grew louder. "Ellie!" a voice said. It was a little deeper than Amy Lowell's, and had a more musical a lilt. "Are you all right?"

She opened her eyes, half-dozing. Brutus rushed up, and pushed his snout up to her face. His nose was black and wet and cold. Was she dreaming?

"Shhh, Brutus," the voice said. The dog lowered his head, and wagged his tail.

She looked up. Ben Owen was hovering at her bedside.

"Oh Ben, I am debilitated." Ellie tried to sit up, but collapsed. "And I - my mother -"

"I know," Ben said. "That's why I came. As soon as Brutus got your message to me. The trolley gave out midway. The lights are dimming - the city's coming apart, Ellie. I got in the house through a side door. Brutus led me straight to you."

"Noble hound," Ellie said.

"Now all we have to do is -

walk out the door of massive oak,
It clicks solid and firm behind us
and quit forever these tended and sleeping yards, of elderberry
and -"

Ben flung his hands out. "All I meant to say was we must - we will -

Depart this edifice,
built as a haven to respite,
a temple to reflection-"

Wincing with the effort, Ellie sat up. "It's been happening to me, too! The simplest utterance becomes

A poem, that has neither rhythm nor rhyme
As a river has not words,
but flows and trills past rocks and -"

She braced herself against the windowsill.

"- runs tinkling through the snowy meadow,
As a magpie plucks at the rushes trembling in the wind and brittle with -"

"Dear Lord," Ben said. "We will return to Boston, and

in the den, with stout wood and iron surrounded
And a mighty fire roaring in the hearth
As the snow falls, as if silence itself was marshaled throughout the city,
I -"

"There it goes again," Ellie said. She gulped. "They have no guards, or guns, and Miss Lowell has been kind -"

"We will leave this place right now," Ben said.

Ellie nodded. She stood up, then wavered a moment, before biting her lip, and gathering her shoes.

"We will return to Boston," she said, "and go

To the den, with stout wood and iron surrounded
And a fire roaring in the hearth
That sustains the marshals of peace
Before they venture back into the snowy city streets, to -

She slumped down, overcome.

Brutus growled deep in his throat.

"The fault, dear Brutus, is not in our stars," Ben said.

Ellie raised her head. "We will go home." She caught her breath, overcome with the effort.

Ben went on: *"But in ourselves, that we are underlings."*

"We will go the Den," Ellie said. "And you will save the city."

"With your help," Ben said. "I'm wise now to their ways."

"What ways?" Ellie said.

"A force more stupefying than any sedative," Ben said, "has incapacitated us within these stout walls. A force more debilitating than any disease."

"Goodness," Ellie said. "What - ?"

"Imagist poetry," Ben said.

Ellie gasped.

"Middling verse is an enchantment of the most dubious and un-Cèltic kind," Ben said.

Ellie's hand went to her throat. No wonder her captors had no need of guards, or drugs, to keep her in their grasp. She had been breathing the very air of imagist poetry, and like a sweet-scented, semi-poisonous vapor, it had made her languorous and indecisive.

"The only antidote known on heaven and earth," Ben said. "is -"

"Brutus?" Ellie said.

"The poetry of a true bard."

From his coat, Ben pulled out his father's small golden harp. He began strumming, low and sweet, and chanted:

"The man that hath no music in himself, Nor is not moved with concord of sweet sounds, is fit for treasons, stratagems and spoils. The motions of his spirit are dull as night. Let no such man be trusted. Mark the music." He paused. *"The Merchant of Venice."*

"You're quoting an Englishman?" Ellie said.

"No," Ben said. "I'm quoting Shakespeare."

Ellie tiptoed to the threshold, looked both ways down the hallway, and emerged from the room. With Ben at her side, she began to descend the staircase.

"Shakespeare was actually Welsh, you know," Ben said.

"My father told me all about it. Through his grandmother. An established, if little-celebrated, fact. Ignored by certain powers that be, my da said."

Ellie and Ben had gained the entrance to the pantry. They peered across it, into the kitchen. The cook was at the table, her back to them as she cut up a chicken.

Ben intoned:

That time of year thou may'st in me behold,
When yellow leaves, or none, or few, do hang
Upon those boughs which shake against the cold
Bare ruined choirs, where late the sweet birds sang.

He plucked the harp strings in melancholy time.

Ellie and Ben tiptoed through the pantry. Brutus followed on light paws.

In a whisper, Ben chanted:

Let me not to the marriage of true minds
Admit impediments. Love is not love
Which alters when it alteration finds,
Or bends with the remover to remove...

They had gained the cold and shadowy back hallway. Ellie snatched her coat from the hook. "I will go out that door," she said.

Ben struck a low-pitched note on the harp. He began to chant:

in my false brother
awakened an evil nature, and my trust,
like a good parent, did beget of him
A falsehood in its contrary as great
As my trust was, which had, indeed, no limit,
A confidence sans bound..

"*The Tempest*," Ellie said.

"That's right," Ben said.

"About two brothers, isn't it," Ellie said. "One's the true prince and a magician." She laughed, and put her hand in front of her mouth. "And the other's -"

"A usurper," Ben said.

With every Shakespearean syllable Ben had uttered,

Ellie felt her consciousness becoming clearer, her will re-invigorated. She lifted the latch, and opened the back door. "I will go out this door

The door that is painted red,
chipped brown with time and -"

No!" Ellie said. She stamped her foot. "We are going out this door. We will take the side pathway to the street."

"Where there's a cab stand," Ben said. And together the three of us will go to the Druids Den." He strummed the harp, and chanted as they slipped out onto the stoop:

He that shall live this day, and see old age,
Will yearly on the vigil feast his neighbors,
And say 'To-morrow is Saint Crispian'

Ellie's lungs were cleansed. Her heart was light. She was no longer sleepy. Already they were halfway down the path. Tail wagging, Brutus led the way.

"The St. Crispin's Day speech was my dad's favorite," Ben said. "He believed it inspired loyalty and valor in all who voiced its words." They entered onto Heath Street. The road was snowy, dark, and deserted. "Shakespeare was taught by a Welshman, you know."

"No!" Ellie said as she loped along.

"Oh, yes. Thomas Jenkins, at Stratford Grammar School."

CHAPTER THIRTY-SEVEN

The party was just getting into full swing. It was such a tasteful get-together, always was, at the Harvard Club. Prohibition was for the little people, Chandler Perkins averred, and none of us here are exactly pygmies. They all laughed, Tim loudest. Then Dixon Gray asked if Tim would mind restacking the chairs in the parlor room. Tim was eager to be of service. He was not a proper member of the club, but was still allowed to attend many of its functions. And in the parlor, he could still hear everything that went on.

"Affability incarnate," Dixon Gray said, turning back to his friends.

"Apropos that business in the North End," Orville Knapp was saying. "I couldn't help but wonder who in Heaven's name might be the patron saint of barbeques."

Tim chuckled. He hoped Orville could hear his appreciation. Orville was quite the cut-up.

"*Winter* barbeques," Bill Leveret said, with a sniff.

"Joan of Arc," Chandler Perkins suggested.

"Amusing," Dixon Gray said, although they were already laughing - some through their noses, others with a short high bark, an odd cackle, and a few outright guffaws. A cork popped, followed by a fizzy hiss, and then the clink of glasses.

Nearly finished at his task, Tim stopped, and looked upon his progress - and by the threshold glimpsed President Lowell, hovering alone in the shadows.

"Good evening, President Lowell," Tim said.

President Lowell was abstracted. He gave Tim a clipped nod, barely looking at him.

"Where is the Governor tonight?" Tim asked.

"Grimley and Graybody have need of him, it appears," President Lowell said. He turned on his heel, and ascended the staircase. Perhaps Tim's question had offended him. Tim couldn't bear for President Lowell to rebuff him. He frowned and set about arranging the last of the chairs.

"The city is in the most awful pickle," Orville Knapp said.

"The Owen boy is not up to the job," Bill Leveret said, and blew his nose.

"A mystery as to why Ben Owen is in Boston at all now, frankly," Dixon Gray said.

"Can the mystery be solved?" Chandler Perkins said.

"Truth to be told, Gryffth Owen himself had been slipping of late," Orville Knapp said. "But this situation is -"

"Unheralded," Bill Leveret said, and sneezed.

"Untenable," Orville Knapp said.

"Undoubtedly," Dixon Gray said.

"No one has a clue as to what the devil that Ben fellow is playing at," Orville sniffed.

"Including the fellow himself, I daresay," Chandler Perkins agreed.

"He appears to be grossly uninformed," Orville said, "as to the most basic workings of this -"

Tim stepped into the hallway, his heart turning over with glee.

"Unfortunate," Dixon Gray said.

Chandler Perkins looked at Dixon Gray, and together they drifted off into the piano room. Most of the other partygoers did too.

"I'm sorry, Tim," Orville said. He stared into his drink a moment. "Those words were not meant for you to hear."

As if there could ever be words not meant for Tim to hear, especially if they were criticism pertaining to his own brother! Ben was in trouble, everybody was saying so - and Tim's heart felt so light, it skipped a beat. He had to find out what Ben was up to. That was what everybody wanted to know. Oh, to help Ben out too of course, and the whole city, by taking over from Ben. Finding out was what Tim did; that, and then tell everybody - certain select everybodies - the everybodies that mattered. It was not merely his job. It was his vocation.

In the next room, Chandler Perkins raised his voice in song, and someone began plunking out the tune on the piano. Orville quitted Tim's side and joined the group in the other room.

Fair Harvard! we join in thy jubilant throng,
And with blessings surrender

Tim marched to the cloakroom, and retrieved his Ulster coat - much like President Lowell's but in a lighter shade of gray. A man had to grow into the shades Lowell favored, in Tim's opinion. Tim revered his betters but he never presumed - that was in large part the secret of his success, he was sure. He put the coat on, and lit out into the night.

Pausing a moment on the cold dark sidewalk, Tim looked up into the windows of Harvard Club. They glowed, warm and golden as amber. Harvard Club was a world apart from the Den. Tim fit in at the Club. Ben never would. Neither would his father have, for that matter. Dixon Gray's father - a surgeon of some considerable renown - had once spotted Gryffth Owen out on the city street, for goodness sake, in a pair of threadbare carpet slippers. A true aristocrat could get away with that. In such a case, the choice of footwear would be a delightful eccentricity, but not in an Owen. Both Ben and Gryffth had proved oblivious to Tim's concern at the time. Even then, their limitations were woefully apparent. Tim's heels clicked along the icy pavement. Dark figures, bundled up against the cold, and bent over to avoid the wind, hurried by. They knocked into him with the bulky shoulders of their coats, and did not even notice the imposition. This was the weather Boston manners were made for!

And Gryffth Owen's own father could not even read. Tim had told President Lowell that, and the President had, gravely hesitant, complimented Tim on his commendable ascent. There was no doubt that President Lowell and Governor Cox were more intelligent and successful than his father had ever been. It was a simple truth, and acknowledging a truth was not disloyal. A sudden sense of his own intellectual honesty warmed him from within as he proceeded across the Back Bay. He walked steadily along Commonwealth Avenue, but not too quickly, so as not to dislodge that goodly sentiment. "Goodly"! - he was becoming a Blueblood already, by deed, and by word.

CHAPTER THIRTY-EIGHT

It really was disgraceful that Ben had let things get to this state, Tim decided. He was marching along the main path in the Common. The sounds of traffic ricocheted off the snow heaped up on either side of Tremont Street. The main illumination was from the car lamps that raked the street as the traffic moved along. The streetlights had gone dangerously dim. The city was going to rack and ruin, Tim thought. Through the ice-slicked tree branches, the windows of the Den came into view, flickering with golden candlelight.

Tim shook his head. So there it was - Ben holed up at home, while neighborhoods went up in flames. The sooner Ben passed on his responsibilities to the brother who actually knew the city and had earned the respect of the Bluebloods, the better. As he turned the last curve in the path, Tim practiced a hurt and accusing look. 'We need to talk, like brothers,' he would say. 'Things aren't going well. There are mutterings everywhere I go. You wanted to follow in dad's footsteps, but it hasn't worked out. At least you have a brother ready and able to step in.'

He turned the key in the door to the Den, and went in.

He blinked.

That Ellie creature was sitting at the kitchen table.

"Oh hello, Timothy - I -" Ellie said. She half-stood up then sat down again. She brushed an errant lock of hair from her eyes. With a slowly gathering thrill, Tim wondered if she had divined yet that she was the subject of his item, the beloved of the dyed in the wool Celt. But she betrayed no hint of being named. "Here I sit, in your Den," she said, and giggled, awkward as a teenager.

"Not mine exactly," Tim said. "Not yet. Where primogeniture holds sway, I'm afraid the younger brother is at a distinct disadvantage." A few feet into the Den, he stomped the snow off his boots, and sauntered into the kitchen.

"Practically a daughter, then," Ellie said.

Tim hadn't thought of it like that, and he wasn't sure he appreciated the comparison. He sat down and gave her a longer glance. Really, if he were writing that blind item at the behest of the Governor now, he would have made merrier with the creature. She was so un-Lowell-like, in mien, posture, and dress.

"I've stopped by to have a word with my brother. Is he -"

"Ben - oh, he went out -" the creature said. She gulped. "He brought me here. Then he went to tell O'Connor that Costa - it seems that. Oh and Brutus wanted to go out too - and then to tell the others, too, that -"

"Do stop sputtering," Tim sat down at the table and looked at her. She was a most unfortunate specimen. "I was just on my way to a dinner dance at the Chandler Harrises. I'm reporting on it. But they would have invited me anyway. Were you on the guest list?"

Ellie shook her head. That strand of hair fell into her eyes again. She was hopeless. Was a lesser Lowell better than none? Perhaps not.

"Oh," Tim said. "No matter. Such lovely get-togethers they have." He looked around. "Dear god, mead! It will be a mercy to put an end to that particular tacky potable." He fiddled with a button on his left cuff. He had observed Lowell do so at the most delicate juncture in negotiations (the seating plan for Class Day exercises, for instance). It was the gesture of a gentleman, worldly and self-contained, with much on his mind, and fine tailoring at his fingertips.

"I'm a bit short on patience tonight," Tim said. He raised an eyebrow and regarded her. "Unusual as that is for a dyed in the wool Celt."

Again, the Ellie creature showed not a flicker of recognition. "Oh, I understand." Of course, she understood nothing. She must have missed his column, because she certainly didn't have the nerve to withstand such a pointed allusion. "I just - well, you see, I was away - visiting - with a cousin -"

"Anyone I know?" Tim said.

She looked up at him, her head to one side, then to the other. "You're Ben's brother so I suppose - it - well, Amy Lowell. In Brookline. I was supposed to stay longer, I guess. But I left early. Ben went there, you see, and my goodness, it -"

"Ben always gets things muddled," Tim said. "I don't see why you would want to come back to this city. Not with the way Ben's running it. Brookline would be positively peaceable by comparison. Sevenels must be lovely in the snow."

"Well, it -"

"There's been no end of trouble here," Tim said. "A fire in the North End."

"Oh -"

"And then the mayor's daughter."

"The Mayor's -"

"She's dead. You haven't heard!" Tim said. He took in his breath sharply, and his eyes opened wide. "Dorothea Curley was sick in bed, and her little brother had fixed her up a game board this afternoon so she could play jacks in bed. She'd said playing jacks was the thing she missed most. She called downstairs - nothing wrong, just asking for a cup of cocoa. And her father made it for her himself, at the gas stove, and carried it up to her. As he was coming up the stairs, he noticed the ball from the jacks set was rolling down the hallway toward him. He began to hurry to her room, calling her name all the while - and by the time he got to her, she was already dead."

Ellie put her hand to her mouth. "Oh dear."

"And the little jacks ball went bouncing down every single step of that staircase, one by one, to the very bottom." His eyes widened and filled with light. "It's just so sad."

"What must they be feeling - her mother and her - oh my." The silly creature looked away a moment.

"This is the city my brother has left for us," Tim said, and sighed. "Why did you leave your cousin's house in such a hurry? And what did Ben think he was doing there?"

"Oh, he -" she bit her lip and fell silent.

"I'm an Owen too, you know," Tim said. "Not that Ben seems to notice very much."

"They think I'm asleep, with a bad headache. They won't notice I'm gone until morning. So they won't be worrying, not a bit. I'll drop word that -"

Tim regarded her. "You should have told them, though, don't you think?"

"Well, I -"

"It's a little rude, isn't it, to just up and leave? Another affair that Ben's mishandled. To treat a Lowell that way - a real one I mean."

"Could I ask that you - please, Tim, don't say anything about what I - it's just that -"

Tim sat up straight. "I won't hold off from telling the truth."

"Ben was -" she said. "You see, I heard that the Governor -"

"Heard what?" Tim said. He gave his most encouraging

smile.

"I - it's - the Governor was all day in the -"

A gust rose through the bare treetops. The branches overhead banged into each other, and the wind began to howl.

"Quite a tempest," Tim said. "I may need to find a teapot to place it in." He laughed at his own joke, a tinkling little laugh that mingled with the winter wind.

"A tempest," the creature said, with a nervous giggle. "So your brother is the prince and magician, and you're the -" She went quiet. She hung her head low, and put her head to one side, then the other. In the end she peered at him, hangdog, out of her left eye, a light silvery green. She was a terrible nervous Nellie. He wondered if the Cabots or the Lowells had ever adopted somewhere along the line. That might explain her.

"The Governor was all day in - what exactly?" Tim said.

"In the - the darkest of moods," Ellie said. "That's all I meant. Lowell called and told his sister as much."

"I can imagine," Tim said. "I don't like dissent within the family, or lies either. And keeping silent is a lie, the most deceitful kind of all." Ellie Cabot-Lowell had been trying to keep a secret, and Tim never liked other people keeping secrets. She'd been an ungrateful guest, to the truest of all Lowells. That was an affront to all who claimed to love this city. And Ben was sweet on this creature. Tim couldn't understand why. Just look at her: her blouse mis-buttoned, her hair unkempt, and that peculiar two-toned gaze. Well, Ben was overdue for some girl trouble, the way he'd been brushing off Tim.

"I'll better be going," Tim said. "Tell Ben that his brother - if he remembers having one - stopped by."

He stood up and buttoned his coat. The first order of business was to go and tell Governor Cox. With an overpowering rush of rectitude, Tim imagined the praise that would soon be heaped upon him, understated praise to be sure, but all the more valued for that. The Governor already respected Tim, and Tim's work - had the Governor not relied on Tim to print up that item about Ben and Ellie?

He set off down Tremont Street, battling the cold wind. On the horizon, the clock on the Custom House Tower rose into view, the eye of time that dominated the city skyline, the Blueblood aegis under which everything transpired. Against the dark sky, the clock face alone still glowed, yellow and inscrutable - practically a Chinaman, Tim thought, delighted at his own wit, *d'après* Orville. He imagined himself visiting that remark upon President Lowell. The President would smile, wryly perhaps, but still a smile. The thought of it all warmed Tim as he hurried along. Soon, he was in Scollay Square. In this section of town the lights still blazed - how typical of Ben's management Tim thought, that the honkytonks were least affected.

A few feet ahead, in a peacock green coat, a woman tottered along. Her hair was as bright as moonlight, and had been marcelled into stiff, uncompromising waves. Her shoes were gilded bronze, and high-heeled, and she had to pick her way through the snow like a stalking animal. A sailor was leaned up against the shop front window, his eyes bright with a chisel-point of light, his hands in his coat pockets. As the woman went past, he gave a long, low wolf whistle. The woman stopped, turned, and put a hand on her hips. She licked her lips, and smiled.

"Nice night for a drink, ain't it?" she said.

"Nice night for a lot of things," the sailor said. The woman snickered. The sailor shoved off from the wall.

Tim shook his head and hurried along. It was ironic that the Grimley and Graybody building directly abutted such a disreputable neighborhood. Scollay Square had an outpost of the Bluebloods in the law office, and the police commissioner's headquarters, but the neighborhood itself was infested with theaters of the most disreputable order, and an unsavory mix of Irish, Italians and Jews, and even Negros. The area had become a hive of greasy spoons, burlesque houses, barber shops, photography studios, and tobacco shops. Just a doorway ahead, the neon sign of the Golden Dime cast a harsh yellow arc onto the sidewalk. The door swung open, and out spilled raucous laughter, the smell of warm grease and stale beer, and a stubble-faced old man in his shirtsleeves. He lurched toward Tim, a withered hand outstretched. Tim picked up his pace.

"Hey," the stubble-faced old man called out, his Adam's apple wobbling, "Don't high-hat me tonight, brother!" Then he hiccupped, and collapsed on a heap of snow.

On the last stretch to the office of Grimley and Graybody, Tim slowed to a stately march. His heels made a slow deliberate tattoo against the icy sidewalk, and to Tim, the sound betokened substance and importance. He maintained that pace as he went up the broad front steps of the Grimley and Graybody building.

Tim pushed open the plate glass doors, heavy with time and tradition, and stout enough to keep out the surrounding riffraff, and entered into the high-ceilinged, marble lobby. It was deathly still, and bathed in amber light. A few steps in, he stamped his boots clear of snow.

A gray-faced minion, his hair and eyes the same ashen tone as his skin, was seated at the reception desk. He looked beyond Tim, at the clumps of snow Tim had just dislodged, melting across the lobby floor. He gave a semblance of a frown. Tim approached, taking on a smile that signaled benign intent.

"Yes?" the minion said.

"I need to speak to Governor Cox, please," Tim said.

"The Governor is not seeing anyone," the shade said.

"Could you please tell him it's me, Tim Owe -"

"Not seeing anyone," the shade repeated, and rising from the desk, turned on a silent heel, and retreated down the hallway. With the sound of new dollar bills rustling, he melted into the depths of the long murky corridor.

Tim stared at the disappearing figure in disbelief. That high-handed minion could not be allowed to deprive the Governor of being the first to know. It would have been nice to be ushered in properly, a dignitary of some importance - but there were other, less direct routes to the Governor's office. The staircase on the left led up to a shadowy mezzanine, Tim remembered, and a side door to the office. That Ellie creature bore the most illustrious Blueblood name - two of them! She absconded, without even the courtesy of a goodbye - and all with Ben's help. The Governor would be aggrieved, and Tim shared his grievance. With that delicious frisson that anticipating another's troubles always gave him, Tim bounded up the stairway.

CHAPTER THIRTY-NINE

Governor Cox sat motionless at his desk. He was not pleased.

The results of his great effort had been disappointing, to say the least. He would go so far as to say they were utterly unacceptable. He crumpled up the newspaper, and threw it to the floor. With a supreme effort of will, he regained control of himself.

The shadowy legal assistants skittered by Cox's office door. They sensed something had not gone to plan, whatever that plan had been. Exhausted by the afternoon's exertions, Farnsworth Grimley had retreated to his inner office, and drawn shut all three sets of doors: the wood, the ivory, and the seldom used, and innermost, doors of gold.

The plan had been to visit the banshee wail, and subsequent death, upon James Michael Curley, not his daughter. This was an unforeseen calamity, akin to the "not of women born" clause, if you like, in *MacBeth*. Cox had failed to be duly specific - an unforgivable fault, he knew, particularly in a lawyer. Too late he realized that when a banshee wails outside a house, foretelling that a member of the household will die that night, it does not guarantee which member. And of course, sick abed, the girl was the weakest constituent. They had outsmarted him without even intending to, those slippery Irish. And this misguided effort to switch the deeds had entirely exhausted the Quill of Justice. It would require complete replenishment before it could once again lift words from a page, and rewrite them. At the moment, even the most paltry codicil would be intractable. The Bluebloods were at a low ebb, and Cox had brought them there. He could not let this stand as his legacy. His reputation must be salvaged, the fortunes of his people restored.

The death of the Curley girl was worse than useless. It would foment retaliation, and an outbreak of hostilities between Costa and O'Connor. Such an outcome would have been most propitious, in any other circumstance. But Curley would work things out. He would know the power failing on the night his daughter died was not mere coincidence, and that would implicate the Bluebloods beyond all question.

Cox ruminated a moment, but he saw no way to frame Lowell as the instigator of this deed, to have him "take the fall," as the vulgate would have it. Unbidden, the image came to him of Lowell as the Brahmin scapegoat, led on a pilgrimage through the streets of Scollay Square. And, Cox thought, if the quill had been powerful enough when dipped in the blood of a Quaker, how much more powerful it would be with the blood of a Brahmin. In which case, the ceremony of the scapegoat would restore the quill to its full luster and potency - and beyond. Cox nearly chuckled at his own fancy, but an undertow of regret and ire and unfinished business tugged at him. With bitterness, he remembered the Welshman's will: how the wizard had thought ahead, and had his testament consigned to vulgar newsprint, beyond the Blueblood's power of transformation. A bitter blow, that, from which Cox had not recovered. His attempt to right wrongs had come to naught. His inadequacy had brought his people low.

The wizard's son was becoming a serious concern. Ben Owen could not be relied upon to see things the Blueblood way. The brother, however, was a more malleable property. Tim Owen had no particular loyalty to his father's legacy. He was already demonstrably Cox's creature, as well as Lowell's. A born stooge, "the patsy's patsy," as Ames put it. It was a fair assessment, and a reasonable turn of phrase.

Cox looked into the winter twilight. Ames had a pawky wit, an even profile, an enviable bloodline. Ames was the Brahmin par excellence. His father was one of the city's leading bankers. He was a distant scion of the family that had built the city's first skyscraper, albeit from a fortune made in shovel-making. Nonetheless, the boy unquestionably exemplified the -

Cox caught his breath He had been grooming Ames for some time, keeping the spoiled degenerate on a string, for reasons he had scarcely articulated even in his own mind. Now the thoughts took form.

He had, he supposed, always envisioned the need would be far in the future, if ever; he had been hedging the boy as a blond and privileged insurance against the rising immigrant tide, and the encroaching darkness that tide brought with it.

But that future was now. For there was one last way, if he dared. Such a deed had never been attempted, and Cox had an abiding sense of what the risks would be. The quill had to be replenished to its former glory, or beyond. The blood of an Ames was more powerful than any Quaker criminal's.

His fingers trembling, Cox opened the drawer, and extracted the *Protocols*. The sight and feel of its dusty pages gave him stern resolve.

Cox's proposal was just. It was fitting. And it was expedient. Ames was a thorough disappointment to both his family and his class. He had long fraternized with such disreputable types that his fate could in truth be ascribed to them: degenerates and radicals, denizens of public baths, and "tearoom" saloons. Really, the boy had brought it on himself. He could at last make himself useful.

There was, however, the ultimate authority. Cox reached for the newspaper. Horoscopes were rank superstition, fit only for jittery serving girls, and limp-wristed dry goods salesmen. The authority Cox was consulting was the very source of Blueblood hegemony: the daily stock market.

All but holding his breath, Cox turned to the business section. The year's final financial quarter was drawing to a close - the "witching hour," so to speak. That was why the banks had "lowered the boom" on King David. The Bluebloods's monies, like their bloodlines, had to be kept especially pure at this juncture. But were the numbers auspicious?

The signs were the best he had ever seen, and his recollections went back to the first administration of Grover Cleveland. The augurs had to be extraordinary to validate a deed this bold. Over two million shares had been traded today. United Steel was up by a hundred points, Standard Oil Company of New Jersey by seventy-five. Such gains were unprecedented. Cox put the paper to one side. The act would have to be done tonight, at midnight, before the markets reopened.

The effect of the sacrifice on the city would be considerable. Once the Quill of Justice left the safe precincts of Grimley and Grimley, magic would begin to unravel throughout the city. The city would likely lose all electric power, not just in pockets here and there, and soon restored - but an out-and-out blackout.

The loss of electric power would be only the beginning. At the sacrifice's completion, at the moment the Brahmin's heart went still, the figures in account books and ledgers across the city would be jumbled up, like noodles in a pot of boiling soup; the same with telephone directories, calculus texts, and cookbooks. No seal or lock could forestall the disruption. The ground would rattle, and buckle, and the graves of Kings Chapel would open: John Cotton, the great Puritan theologian, and John Winthrop, the first Governor, would arise and walk the streets of Boston again.

Cox dared hoped he might be less lonely with such as these alongside him. And, too, with every drop of blood that fell from a Brahmin scapegoat, a contingent of shades would be marshaled to his side - spirits of puritans, summoned from the cold hereafter into the cold here-and-now. Nearly invisible, they would catch the eye the way the movement of a bat in flight does. They were neither dead nor alive, these shades. They were in a twilight state where flesh existed not enough to enjoy its pleasures, but just enough to suffer its decline. And they would form an invisible army ready to sweep through the streets, and subdue all interlopers, and see off all foreign looks and smells and sounds.

And more than that: time itself would be undone. The past and present and future would be as one. All that is, or had been, or was to be, would come to pass in a single moment. In that moment, in the crucible of Scollay Square, time would be unfettered, and history undone.

With certainty he knew, for had not the elders of the *Protocol* so written, that the Ceremony of the Brahmin Scapegoat had other repercussions. The golden dome of the State House would darken, and turn to iron. The gates of Harvard Yard would clang shut, with an untenable quotient of Jews, Negros, and others of like grubbiness milling about in cheap flashy clothing, speaking in coarse accents and vulgar colloquialisms, and indulging in a range of emotions wholly unsuited to a gentleperson. At the thought of such a calamity befalling Lowell's dear Harvard, Cox chuckled. The dangers were great, he knew - but greater still were the possibilities.

This was the way. He had first to secure the deed to the Druid's Den. It was stored next door, in the bowels of the courthouse basement. He would locate the deed himself. No one else could be trusted. He was obliged to undo his misstep regarding the Curley household. Before the night was over, the Druid's Den would belong to him, and his, and the Bluebloods would again reign unchallenged over the city.

A hesitant knock sounded at the seldom used side door. A porter, he assumed, as he called out, "Come in."

The lesser Owen sidled in. His face was flushed.

"Your Excellency," he said. He gave a slight bow.

Cox grunted. He was not in the mood for a toady.

"I have something to tell you," the stooge said. His eyes were gleaming as he approached Cox's desk.

CHAPTER FORTY

The latch on the garage door rattled and clicked. Hands still on the steering wheel, O'Connor gave McClusky a nod. McClusky pointed the barrel of his gun at the door. The hinges creaked open. A Labrador dog rushed in, ears flopping, tail wagging.

"I locked that door up good," McClusky said. "Tight as a drum, I swear I -"

Ben entered the garage, a dusting of snow on his shoulders. Brutus jumped up, and planted his two front paws on the side of the car. His nose was quivering. He regarded O'Connor a moment, then jumped down, and began sniffing the garage floor.

McClusky indicated Ben with a jab of the gun barrel. "Want me to take care of him, boss?"

"Naw," O'Connor said. "Ben's my friend. A friend to everyone."

"Friend to no one then," McClusky said.

O'Connor regarded the older Owen son. "A curious fact, my friend, that lock has kept out the worst of the worst. Yet here it is, yielding to your touch."

"I have my methods," Ben said.

"You are your daddy's boy?"

"I'd like to think so," Ben said. "I need to talk to you. Alone."

McClusky's glare shifted to O'Connor. The gun barrel did not waver.

O'Connor nodded.

"And the mutt?" McClusky said.

"He seems a peaceable hound," O'Connor said.

"So long as he gets his chocolate," Ben said. "Or some bacon. Crazy about that stuff, aren't you, Brutus?"

"A misnomer in terms of treachery, we can only hope," O'Connor said.

"I'm right outside, you need me, boss." McClusky glowered at Ben, and tramped out the garage door. It banged shut after him. Brutus flopped down under the car fender, and chewed on a discarded soap wrapper.

"Fact is, this old car's the only place I find peace in my house," O'Connor said. "Such peace as this city affords anyone tonight. The murder of a child is unforgivable, Ben."

"You didn't set the fire," Ben said. "I know that. I have proof."

"Do you now?" The boy was full of surprises.

"I do. It was Nicolas Prega - but Costa had nothing to do with it. And I know Costa had nothing to do with the death of Dorothea either. I have proof of that, too."

"Oh, it'll be some proof that convin -"

"In black and white." The boy was getting bold, cutting in on the heels of O'Connor's sentences.

"That's grand," O'Connor said. "In black and white, is it? I'll tell that to Mrs. Curley, shall I?" He lowered his brow, and gave the steering wheel a spin. "They deal in death of innocents, the Costa crew. Of lesser beings - even that godforsaken Andre Pierre creature. And don't tell me: Costa had nothing to do with that either. Even though Nicolas Prega's one of his foot soldiers."

"Not entirely he isn't," Ben said. "Prega has ideas of his own - ideas that Costa has no part of. Politics, revolution -

that kind of -"

"A tad convenient."

"The girl's death is awful enough. Don't use it to further your own aims, sully your -"

"A little late for that, son," O'Connor said. "You should have said as much to Costa. I'll not sit back while -"

Ben held up a hand. To his credit, it scarcely wavered. "I'm here to ask you - if only in memory of my father - to hold fire, just for a short while. Come to the Den, for a meeting. Give me that much." The lad's voice began to quaver. "In honor of the saint's day."

"What saint would that be then?"

"St Llewellyn. A peacemaker," Ben said. "Armed with a sword, and -"

"And no doubt a fountain sprung up wherever the good Llewellyn's cane touched the ground, and the water thereof cures all ills."

"As a matter of fact, it did." Ben looked him straight in the eye. "We'll all meet at the den, around ten - make it ten twenty two, as my da favored odd times. And I'll prove to you that Costa had nothing to do with Dorothea Curley."

O'Connor smiled and shrugged. "Revenge is a dish best served cold, though some like it hot, and it's not bad that way either. I can't really say which way I'll be serving it tonight."

"The other gangs will turn against you - all of them."

"Let 'em try," O'Connor said. "There's division enough among them from what I hear."

"I will be among their number," Ben said. He reached into his pocket, drew out a small gold harp, and balanced it on the crook of his arm. He looked at O'Connor, and raised an eyebrow.

"The tough stuff." O'Connor gave the steering wheel a twirl. "Sure. I'll come to your little meeting. But if I'm not convinced, Ben, it's war."

Ben nodded.

O'Connor sighed. "The mayor's not seeing anyone tonight anyway. I went by his house. I was wanting to tell him what went wrong, but he was -"

" '*What went wrong?* " Ben said.

O'Connor was silent.

Ben strummed a single string of the harp. The note was low and clear.

O'Connor eyed the harp warily, then glanced at Ben. "So let's say, for the sake of argument mind, that I was putting a hit on Costa," he said. "Not saying I did, not saying I didn't. But no secret I might want to, least of all to your own good self. I had my reasons. "

"Everybody always does," Ben said. "That's what's so terrible."

"Dorothea was a good reason. Now she's an even better one. In truth, I had the hit in the works a while. Ever since Polcari rolled over that shipment of mine last spring, it's only been a matter of time."

"The wailing of the banshee," Ben said, "gives you great power. To know when the death of a man is imminent, and inescapable. The canary in a coal mine, as they say."

"Do they now," O'Connor said, in a determinedly light tone. His mood had darkened. A canary? What the devil did the lad mean by that? Was Ben hinting that he knew about Hollie and her birdlike form? The sound machine experiment had seemed the perfect smokescreen to cover his possession of a banshee. But had Ben seen through the scheme? The lad needed pressing as to the depth of his knowledge.

"That device I was tinkering with all summer," O'Connor said, with a rueful smirk. "The audio-entrapment machine. Guess I don't have to tell you about it."

"Oh no," Ben said.

"So when exactly did you get wind of my little project?"

"Proj- well, I - a little birdie told me, as the saying goes."

"A saying, is it then?" O'Connor said. Was that another sly dig? "But what's the truth of the matter?"

"My father left a set of notes. Private papers. I've been sifting through them these past few nights."

"Old man Owen - God rest his soul." O'Connor pressed down the clutch and switched gear from first to third. "It was more than a simple recording device of course. It had to be. Standard recording does not keep the sound alive, in any meaningful sense. From its inception, the beauty of my machine was to be that the banshee's wail was not recorded so much as perpetuated, kept alive via a system of echo chambers." His hand described a spiral in the air, then went back to the steering wheel. "One hot night last July, I trapped the wail of the banshee. The night Jimmy Dunne was executed. I stationed myself around the back of his house, on Gustin Street, it was. When the sun went down, the wailing kicked in. It was the eeriest wail I'd ever heard - for Jimmy was not only due to die, Ben, he was condemned to."

Ben nodded, and leaned in. He knew to keep still, and not ask stupid questions.

"I had the device at the ready," O'Connor said. "I got my wail, I presumed, with every property it processes, foretelling death, and fulfilling same. But it was a misfire, Ben. The wail had no potency, none at all. It led me astray grievously. With it, I miscalculated the hit on Polcari. The wail sounded out, like he was goner, for sure. Only he weren't."

"Not that night," Ben said.

O'Connor smiled.

"It's a wonder you'd try the mechanism a second time," Ben said. "I mean against Costa."

O'Connor gave him a lingering sideways look. Wheedling innuendo and sly questioning had also been his dad's favorite method to eke out the truth.

"Risk it, I mean," Ben said. His skinny pale hands flapped around again, like some godforsaken trout on a hook. His voice took on a faint stutter. "Things going wrong again."

"I did what you'd call a modification to the device. An additional echo chamber I was sure it would work this time but -" O'Conner sighed and shrugged. Ben didn't know about Hollie - or was canny enough to hide what he knew. "The first wail I trapped, it was for a man condemned to death - a death ordained by the state. But what was required was evidently a death ordained by a greater power, not legal, or civic, or government - but by God, fortune and fate."

"So you sought a man likely to die," Ben said.

"You're a quick sketch," O'Connor said.

"An elderly person?" Ben said.

O'Connor raised his eyebrows, as if Ben's insight had surprised and impressed him. "Let's say I had a great uncle out in Somerville, so I did," O'Connor said. "And he'd caught a cold at the height of summer, and for a man in late 80s, such an eventuality does not bode well. There was a grove of myrtle around his side porch, so lush that a fella could wait there unseen, a bottle of Ginty's ale at his side, as twilight set in. The crickets got to humming. Their sound was near as thick as the foliage itself. The moon had risen, orange and full, in the soft black August sky..."

And so it had. Hollie had hopped down from deep inside the myrtle grove, twittering, demanding cupcakes, so very sweetly - "you do have them, don't you. Oh. Well, you better get some then dear." O'Connor had never seen a banshee before, but he didn't let on. He'd held a morsel of chocolate to Hollie's tiny red lips, in that face of hers no bigger than a toddler's thumbnail, and she nibbled and chortled, and was his ever after...

"You bided your time in that grove." Ben crossed his arms, and gave an understanding nod. "And trapped the wail foretelling a death ordained by great and unseen powers."

"Tonight, I resorted to the banshee, in its improved state, or so I thought," O'Connor said. He did not mention the hit on Rattigan this August, or the second attempt on Polcari (there had been no need for a third). No need to let Ben know he had succeeded more often than he'd failed. It was not Hollie's fault, tonight's disaster. O'Connor knew she would be getting hungry, and that as soon as he went back into the house, she would be twittering, trebling, and demanding a bit of chocolate. If left too long she would squawk ever louder - even in the garage, Ben might hear her. O'Connor put up his hands, in mock surrender, and planted them again on the steering wheel. His silvery blue gaze was unreadable.

Ben's voice quavered. "You unleashed something tonight you never meant to. Dorothea, I mean. Maybe it'd be a good idea to cast the machine aside, once and for all."

"Smash the infernal thing to pieces," O'Connor said. "I will do that, Ben. Though it shows the glimmer of promise, if tinkered with - who knows - but it won't see another dawn. I hope you'll accept the gesture as a bit of sacrifice on my part. A gesture of goodwill, deserving of your especial consideration at some future date."

"I give all deeds, good, bad, indifferent, their due consideration."

O'Connor gave a sour smile. "Given much thought to banshees before, Ben?"

"Well, I - no," Ben said.

Brutus rolled over on side, and with a clank, his locket hit the floor.

"I hope you won't mind me saying, but the hound has been misnamed," O'Connor said. "Criminally."

"That's for sure," Ben said "He's got a cohort named Marc Antony, and that one's the coldest, leanest hound in town."

"What's in a name?" O'Connor said. "A rose by any other name would smell as sweet."

CHAPTER FORTY-ONE

"My dear young lady," Cox said. He made an effort to smile, despite the sweet smell of mead assaulting his nostrils. The Den reeked of it, and sweet things always disgusted him. "I must ask you again, for the sake of family, for the city."

"I don't know. I -" she wrung her hands. "It's -"

"You seem a sensible enough young lady," Cox said. "If, I daresay, somewhat confused at present. You are convinced, if I understand you correctly, that I have some evil plan in the works. Based on what you overheard at the home of - I believe you said, Miss Amy Lowell?"

The girl presented certain difficulties. He could not afford for her to charge out of the Den and alert others to his undertakings. Timothy the Stooge had been useful, at last, though his bowing and scraping as he imparted what he knew was irritating. The woman was dangerous, but he could turn that danger to his advantage. For surely two scapegoats, of good blood stock, would outdo the one. The pure blood of the Cabots and the Lowells combined would scorch away whatever taint the deviancy of Ames might bring with it. Cox rubbed his hands, then remembered to smile.

"I - yes," Ellie said. She looked at him, head to one side, then the other. The eye that peered at him was an odd shade of green — almost silvery, like green grapes. It would no doubt have proved disconcerting to a person less resolute.

"Come with me then," Cox said. He clasped his long, yellow-fingered hands together. "See the evil I am up to!" He chuckled, in apparent recognition of how silly such a notion was. "Prevent me from doing it, perhaps."

"I'm not sure - I should be - and you are -"

He gave an aggrieved smile. "Miss Cabot-Lowell, my only wish tonight is to locate my wayward nephew, Prescott Ames. The lad has gotten into trouble before. He has developed the lamentable habit of frequenting various establishments - quite disreputable ones. Tonight he has threatened to go drifting through Washington Street, and into Scollay Square, where I fear he will bring yet more disgrace on himself and his family."

She bit her lip, and trembled. She was a ninny, for all that she was a Cabot.

"I believe he is a cousin of yours," Cox said, "distant to be sure."

"Scollay Square is - I have heard it's not so very nice," Ellie said.

"It is certainly no place for a well brought up young lady," Cox said. "Such as yourself - but that would be your great strength - and mine, if you chose to accompany me. Your manifest gentility would shame the lost boy back to his senses."

She looked at him, her chin lowered, as suspicious as a hound dog that knows it, or its master, has done wrong. Sacrificing her would be a service to both the Lowells and the Cabots, not to mention the untold benefits to the city. Cox's heart fluttered at the thought of the historic moment at hand, but his chin remained resolute.

"I am speaking, miss, of the good of the city of Boston." Cox folded his hands, and began intoning:

" *'Chapter II, Executive Power, Section I. The Governor, Article I. There shall be a supreme executive magistrate, who shall be styled, The Governor of the Commonwealth of Massachusetts; and whose title shall be, His Excellency.'* "

Her eye turned glassy. With such blood stock as hers, the law invariably worked a charm: by turns it lulled, by turns it galvanized. Legalese gave a sense of freedom, of security, of outrage, and of righteousness. No other type of language stood a chance against Blueblood legal formulations - none, not blarney, or jazz talk, or Yiddish colloquialisms, or even the language of Dante, which had so woefully degenerated into that of Alphonse Capone. What a fool Amy Lowell was, turning to "imagist poetry" when right under her nose, in her native ken, brewing in her very veins, she had the most potent string of syllabication known to man: legalese.

With a nod, Ellie Cabot-Lowell turned.

" *'Part 1, Title 18,'* " Cox intoned. *"Chapter 127, Section 9. The keeper, superintendent or other officer having charge of a jail shall keep an invoice book, in which ...'* "

On and on he droned, as, her eyes glazed, Ellie Cabot-Lowell began her way towards the door. Cox grasped the Quill of Justice, hidden in his pocket. Then he followed, silent as a shadow, and as close.

CHAPTER FORTY-TWO

Sobriety was bringing King David down. The world was less colorful, the tunes less catchy, and the dames several motes short of an eyeful. This must be what it's like to be a working stiff, he thought, as he headed down the stairs to the basement of the theater. King David had sworn off alcohol for the entire night. The meeting at the Den would come soon enough, and sober as a judge, he would be in command of all his powers.

He sat down at the workbench, and hauled the satchel out from under it. He took out the clay head, brought it over to the light by the stairwell, and looked it over. It was in good shape. The paper was sticking to its forehead like it should. The golem would do his bidding, especially if he stayed sober, and pieced it together right.

In the packed theater overhead, the audience stamped its feet and applauded. The 8 pm show was underway.

The door at the top of the stairs creaked open. Light, quick footsteps clattered down.

Art stopped midway down the staircase and leaned over the banister. He was decked out in a taffy-colored wig, and a helmet with horns on either side. It was Viking Night at the Majestic. "Been looking all over for you! I -

hey, what's that thing?"

"A mummy head," King David said, quickly rolling it under the stairwell with the rest of golem pieces. "Thinking we'll put on an Egyptian revival spectacular. King Tut, all that jazz."

"Sure," Art said. He looked into the mid-distance. His helmet slipped sideways. "Cleopatra. Moses. The parting of the Red Sea."

"Something like that," King David said.

Art reached up, and straightened his helmet by the side horn. "Upstairs, there's a *'President Lowell'* here to see you." He lifted his pinky finger. "And I told him, I says, here I was all this time thinking the President was Calvin Coolidge. Noticed this one soon as he come in. Looking down your nose ain't just an expression. Sat down in the back and watched Eddie the Eagle's routine. Cracked a smile once, but he recovered. In spades. After the show, he asked if I knew where he might find Mr. Jerome David. Says he knows you."

"I'll see him," King David said. What did the old lug have to say for himself? Art clattered up the stairs. King David gave the golem head a little kick, just to be sure it was hidden. From on high, a cough sounded, then footsteps with a slow, deliberate pace, echoed down the stairwell.

Lowell reached the bottom of the stairs and looked around.

"Mr. David, I am a man of my word. I attended your stage show tonight. Given the concern you expressed to me, I felt my presence would serve the interest of fairness."

"So what did you make of it, daddyo?"

"I must say I saw nothing that would warrant disavowing the proceeds thereof. I know of no policy against your theatrical enterprises. And I would vehemently oppose restraints on your legitimate trade and commerce. Indeed I respect your people's abilities in that arena."

"Swell of you," King David said.

"Let us understand each other. I bear your tribe no ill will. It is solely the disproportionate Jewish representation in the Harvard classroom that I oppose."

"And why's that exactly?"

Lowell took a step back. "Since you have asked me - as a group - you will forgive me - the Israelites lack the grace, the swagger, the tall attractive sleekness one has long associated with the Harvard man. Consider: when faced with injustice, the Anglo produced the Magna Carta; the Hebrews, a book of lamentations. An influx of the ostentatious and the abrasive, the nervously disposed and the hollow-chested, will but lower the communal attractiveness of any institution. Even to your own people, in generations to come."

"I look hollow-chested, bub?"

"I speak in broad if uncomfortable truths."

The palooka wasn't pulling any punches about what he thought, King David had to give him that.

"Outside the gates of Harvard," the old coot continued, "I have no quarrel with your people."

"Yeah? I oughta try moving in next door," King David said. "Or marrying your sister."

Lowell coughed. "Your theatrical enterprises, Mr. David, while distasteful to some, are perfectly legal, at the present time at least. They may even be thought to lend a distinctive texture to the city."

"The Majestic's got a lot of texture."

"I should like to see a dramatic performance here someday," the stiff went on. "An American landmark - John Wilkes Booth once appeared here, I believe, as Hamlet."

"It's changed some. I guess you don't think I'm as A-1 American as you."

"But I do. I have always maintained that the flag and indeed this nation belong no more to me and my family,

214

which has been here for lo these many generations, than to the new immigrant who truly becomes American. That belief I do sincerely hold."

"Fat chance me becoming like you, mister," King David said. "When I can't even bank my hard earned cash."

"If true, it seems unjust. I will make inquiries, in the interest of fair play. That is the Anglo Saxon way."

Stern as a Blueblood judge on Election Day, King David fixed Lowell with a steady gaze. "So tell me pal, did you like the show?"

"Ah - yes."

The glimmer of a first letter appeared, "G" *ganef*. It was shaped like a broken bone, and glinted in the half-light. King David grinned. His powers were in full swing. He punched the air with his fist. Old Man Lowell raised his eyebrows slightly, and retreated a half step. King David surprised himself: he was disappointed that old man Lowell had turned out to be a liar after all.

Lowell coughed. "Perhaps '*like*' is the wrong word. Found most edifying, certainly."

The letter shimmered, then disappeared.

King David gave him a quick smile, and went in for the kill. "You in with the banks refusing my legit cash?" Catch him off-guard, that was the ticket.

"Indeed I am not. Nor would I ever advocate refusal of legitimate legal tender earned -" Lowell looked about the basement, his bloodless lips curling slightly - "in a non-illegal, and dare I say, not utterly repugnant fashion."

King David stared at the space above Lowell's head. No way around it, the old lug was telling the truth. If Lowell wasn't in on the squeeze, Cox was, all on his own.

"Sure, let's say maybe I've passed a bum note in my time."

"Solely for the sake of argument, of course."

"Yeah. Once or twice, and not on purpose, either, and now my hard-earned buckeroos, totally legit, are getting the cold shoulder. Maybe your buddy Cox ain't such a square-dealer after all. You got to figure, if all my dough's been given the kibosh, and you don't know nothing about it."

"His trust in me as regards this particular matter might be deemed wanting."

"And in how many other matters, pops? Because you can always trust a liar."

Lowell considered. "To be deceitful, I suppose you may indeed."

CHAPTER FORTY-THREE

Ben looked around at those assembled at the Den. Not everybody had shown for the meeting, but the key players were there. He wished he knew where Ellie had gone. She'd left no note. Maybe she'd gone home to her parents. The mystery troubled him, but he continued with the business at hand. "I am well pleased, as my father would say, that no longer are we enem -"

The door burst open. In a beam of a streetlight, and an arc of swirling snow, King David entered the Den. Lowell was at his side.

"This old lug was hanging out by your door, kid. So -" King David began. "Hey, whaddya know, the gang's all here." With a Havana yellow kidskin-gloved hand, he swatted Coup DeGrace on the shoulder. "Got a proposition for you, Coupster, and it's strictly the business. A stage show spectacular, you and me together." He sat down. "But first things first. Pops and I got a whopper of a story to tell, and it don't bear -"

Ben held up his hand for silence.

King David grinned, pushed back his chair, and splayed his feet out wide.

Ben looked at O'Connor. "Tell him what you just told

us, Jackie."

O'Connor turned, his little cupid's bow mouth twisting. "Al Costa had nothing to do with the sickness and death of little Dorothea Curley."

Ben folded his arms, and looked at Costa.

"O'Connor did not set the fire on Hanover Street," Costa said. "Nor did his people."

"The two have agreed to hold off on all hostilities," Ben said.

"Not everything is rosy," O'Connor said "but it is a bit less prickly. That I will grant you."

"Yowza," King David said. "Season of goodwill, huh! Oh - like I said, pops and I got a little number to lay on you, too. Hit it, Prez."

Lowell coughed and stepped forward. "A certain eventuality has come to light," he said. "Painful as this truth is to confront, delaying it would be even more so. In suc-"

"Enough with the soft soap," King David said. "It turns out the guv's made Lowell here into one ace patsy."

"Unbeknownst to me, this man's legitimate earnings were rejected by the city's financial institutions."

"And how. Bleeding me dry. So's -"

Ben held up his hand. "There's more. Along with Prega, Prescott Ames was responsible for the fire. He made the bomb."

"Young Prescott?" Lowell said.

Ben nodded.

"Did your baby bro' dig this up, kid?" King David said. "Little Timmy Cottontail, hopping down the gossip trail. Not sure I'd believe everything he says. That all you got?"

Ben held the notebook aloft. "Nothing to do with a gossip column. This is the diary of Nicolas Prega. It proves everything I told you."

"*Il mostro* has not been heard of since," Costa said. "The better for him."

"Wouldn't mind taking a gander myself," King David

said, reaching forward.

"The people of the book are ever thus," Lowell intoned from the shadows.

"*Furfante*," Costa muttered. "He will wish he was never born."

"But Nick's a friend of yours, ain't he, Al?" King David said.

"I did not know any of this. *Criminale*."

"What are the odds?" King David said.

"Prescott Ames planned the bomb," O'Connor said. "He knew the chemistry."

"Not as well as he thought," Ben said.

"Young Ames." Lowell shook his head. "It is hard to believe. A history of certain irregularities, to be sure, but I believed them to be largely in the past. With every advantage, of birth and nature - all but one, why would -"

"To make you look bad," Ben said.

"He ain't too fond of you, pops," King David said. "Says so right here."

"Oh!" Lowell's pale hand rose to his pure white shirtfront. He bowed his head. "I trust you will forgive that momentary outburst."

"Let you take the fall, is what young Amesey-boy was planning," King David said. "Read it yourself." He slapped his palms on the table and shrugged. "With the guv at his side."

"All the while in his last days in office, our esteemed Governor swans on undisturbed," O'Connor said. "An unwitting Harvard president to do his dirty work for him."

Lowell raised his nose several inches. "I do have to point out that at this juncture we have only the evidence of a notebook of a degenerate radical. I'm not sure that is entirely sufficient."

"It was good enough for the rest of us," O'Connor said.

"What's the guv up to tonight anyway?" King David said.

"Governor Cox left instructions not to be disturbed, so arduous are his final labors on behalf of the Commonwealth. He's been at Grimley and Graybody all afternoon, in preparation for a legislative session in the morning."

"Taking a break from putting the squeeze on me," King David said.

"No, he's not," DeGrace said.

"You know something I don't but I oughta?" King David said.

"I saw Governor Cox on my way over here. On a street corner." DeGrace smirked. "In Scollay Square."

King David hooted. "Never figured him for that. I could learn to like him after all. On the prowl, huh?"

"Well, he wasn't on his own," DeGrace said. "There was a young lady at his side."

"Our tax dollars at work," O'Connor said.

King David grinned. "Blonde or brunette?"

"I think we have more important things to -" Ben said.

"Dark haired," DeGrace said. "I suppose you'd say. But that's not what I remarked upon."

"No kidding," King David said. "Fill me in."

"The way she held her head - hangdog almost, first to one side, and then the other. Peculiar. Like something was in her eye - a lock of hair perhaps."

"Huh," King David said, losing interest.

"Anything else about her?" Ben said.

"Take it from me kid, you can do better than a hangdog gal," King David said.

"Her coat was odd - purple," DeGrace said. "And considerably longer than the ladies favor these days."

"Lace hanging from the cuffs?" Ben said.

"Now that you mention it, yes. Almost Victorian."

Ben clenched his fists. His jaw went tight, and his heart was chilled. "Ellie," he whispered, without meaning to. Under the bar, Brutus's neck stiffened. He stood up and gave a muffled "woof."

"Enough with the sad sack fashion notes, huh?" King David said. "Listen Coup, I was telling you - I've got an idea for a holiday spectacular, and it's boffo. New Year's at the Majestic'll never be the same. How about you head back with me, check out the set up?" He stood up, and strode to the door. "Now that peace is breaking out all over."

DeGrace considered a moment, then nodded. "A chance to see beyond our own little disagreements," he said. "If these two -" he indicated O'Connor and Costa, "can see eye to eye."

"A spirit of concord is hardly misplaced in this, the season of goodwill," Lowell said.

"You got it, pops," King David said. As he opened the door, a spray of snowflakes flew in. He ushered DeGrace out. "See you in the funny papers." He closed the door behind him.

Ben cleared his throat. "President Lowell, I was wondering if you might help me with something?"

Lowell raised an eyebrow.

"It's an inscription, in Latin," Ben said. He heard a quaver creep into his voice, and his hands began to flutter. With an effort, he kept his hands still. He went around the side of the bar. Brutus got up and followed him, ears prickling. "Around the back. I'm not entirely certain of its meaning - and of course, you are a Harvard man."

CHAPTER FORTY-FOUR

The back hall was so cold that Ben's breath showed in little white puffs. Lowell's breath was invisible.

"The Governor has hold of Ellie," Ben said. "He's leading her around Scollay Square, and I'm worried." He reached into his pocket, and extracted the note. "This was folded up inside the dog's locket. And the dog is Ellie's. Brutus came bounding up to me in the snow, like he was shot out of a cannon."

Lowell examined the note.

"A plea for help," Ben said. "Scrawled out across a page of doggerel. That's how I found her and brought her here."

"For reasons, I confess, not clear to me. She was surely safe in Brookline. But it does not follow that she is necessarily in danger now."

Ben shook his head. "Cox is -" He punched his clenched fists together. "I couldn't let the others know, not just yet."

"Peace is ever fragile," Lowell said. He raised an eyebrow, frowned, and handed the note back. "That 'doggerel' as you put it is my sister's lifework. And I am sure that Miss Cabot-Lowell's people would never allow her to

222

wander adrift into such a place as Scollay Square."

"Coup DeGrace painted a quite a picture. It's Ellie he saw. I'm sure of it."

"There are other girls with purple coats," Lowell said. "And a fair number of those coats may well be trimmed with lace."

"Hanging down from the cuffs," Ben said. "Head hanging to one side, then the other. It's her."

"I believe you mean to say '*she*'," said Lowell. He looked at Ben and squared his shoulders. "Let us assume for argument's sake that she is adrift in Scollay Square. What is the danger? She is in the presence of Governor Cox, after all. I maintain your fears are misplaced as regards him. Whatever else, he is a gentlemen, and an officer of the court. His intentions toward Miss Cabot-Lowell are -"

"I'm going out there," Ben said, putting on his coat. "If the well-being of Ellie, and of this city, means anything to you, you'll come with me."

Before Lowell could answer, Ben was already out the backdoor, Brutus at his side.

CHAPTER FORTY-FIVE

As the backdoor swung shut. Costa's glass of mead jumped. He reached forward and held it steady.

The *irlandese* glanced at him. "Nobody here except you and me."

Costa nodded, but said nothing. A truce was one thing; attempts at sustained comradery, another.

"The nerve of that Governor," O'Connor said. "And Prega and Ames - setting us good souls against each other."

"Leading us to do deeds we would not have otherwise contemplated," Costa said.

"Way I see it, Mulvaney's death belongs to them that set the fire. So that's another thing they got to pay for."

"We are, in a sense, brothers in vengeance," Costa said.

"Like that crazy play old Owen kept pushing at us," O'Connor said. " '*We band of brothers.*' Wishful thinking on his part, weren't it?"

Costa smiled. "Drink up. Remember, it's for free."

O'Connor drained the last of his glass. He held it to the light and drank once more, just to make sure. "I'm not cheap, mind."

"Oh no," Costa said.

"It's just that I can't stand waste."

"Of course," Costa glanced around the Den. "Strange to be here without an Owen present. It is perhaps to be wondered, if our powers would be diminished in such circumstance?"

"Or amplified," O'Connor toyed with his glass. "Maybe Ben Owen wants to see what we try, you and me, when we're left to our own devices?" He looked up at Costa. "Test the durability of our truce."

"They did leave in a rush," Costa said. "King David and DeGrace, with talk of a theatrical enterprise. A likely story."

"And here I was, thinking the same, though I'd hate to be called a suspicious sort."

"And the *inglese* just now departed with the Owen boy," Costa said.

"Ben Owen needed help with a Latin inscription?"

"Is not the Owen boy a scholar himself?"

"So he is. Like I say, I'm hoping you won't find it suspicious of me, but I find my good self wondering if -"

"You and I are not being set up," Costa said. "Would young Owen dare to -"

O'Connor stood up. "More likely he's somebody's patsy, like the sainted old Lowell." He buttoned his coat. "Come on."

Costa nodded and got to his feet. He positioned his fedora at a suitable angle. "Where to?"

"To Scollay Square, where it seems Ben's lady of the old-fashioned style is taking a stroll."

CHAPTER FORTY-SIX

"Come along, Ames," Cox said. They were heading down Brattle Street, on the last stretch of the pilgrimage, just a block away from Court Street and Cornhill. They were passing the site of what had been the first meetinghouse. With a joyous shudder at the prospect of all that was soon to change, Cox shepherded his scapegoats along. In the doorway of a pawnshop, a disreputable type was loitering. He clutched a brown paper bag in his hands. He raised the bag to his mouth, and gulped.

Ames sniffed the air, and looked around, his nose quivering. Cox gave him a shove, and Ames staggered forward into a shin-deep drift of snow, and stopped. "Uncle," he said. "I do wish you to know how very truly I esteem you!" He slumped back against Cox, who, with a bent elbow, deflected him. Ames swayed in the opposite direction, into a streetlamp. He put his arm around the post, and grinned companionably up at it. "I meant to say, Uncle - my, you are imperially slim these days. And your face, a positive beacon of -" He hiccupped. "There's a most welcoming est- establish -" His face collapsed into a soppy smile.

The boy was of good blood stock. All evidence to the

contrary, there could be no denying that fact.

"It was awful," Ellie said. "That place we found Mr. Ames - it -"

"A very fine - estab - estabal - place," Ames said. "Where they know how to treat a man."

Cox clamped a hand onto Ames's shoulder, and pried the creature loose from the streetlight. With the same grip, he propelled Ames forward. The boy stumbled into a snow bank, took an unsteady step, and then proceeded. The girl followed along, picking her way, as ungainly as ever, a lock of hair in her eyes. This is what the mighty families of Boston had come to - but still, their blood could be reaped and put to civic use.

"Back there," Ellie said, "outside that casino establishment, they were saying hello to you, as pleasantly as can be, and you looked right through them - as if -"

"The cold shoulder," Cox said. He had forgotten what a thrill it was, even to witness, or indeed be the brunt of! It was a pure assertion of self - of privilege, and standards, of indifference and Puritan backbone, and the power of almighty cold. And none could stand against such cold.

"I just felt it was awful, to treat someone as -" Ellie said.

Cox's jaw tightened. The creature was in danger of asserting herself, and worst of all, emoting. He intoned, in a low, humming drone: " '*Part the Second, The frame of Government, Article III. The general court shall forever have full power and...*' "

The light in Ellie's eyes wavered. She hung her head low, and staggered forward a few steps, falling into line on Cox's right, Ames on his left.

Cox continued as he led them onto Tremont Street: " '*....or other courts, to be held in the name of the commonwealth, for the hearing, trying, and determining of all manner of crimes...*' "

A gale of laughter and the smell of roasting nuts assaulted them. On one of the marquees, a gigantic electric star revolved, and cast its bluish light over the street below.

Next door, in a diner window, an electric pink shamrock flashed on and off. A catcall rang out. A woman's voice resounded shrilly into the night: "You ain't the only one what thinks so!"

Cox grimaced: the realm of cheap entertainment and cheaper female companionship was nigh. He whisked his two scapegoats along. Just ahead, over the darkened rooftops, the Steaming Kettle, affixed high on a storefront, was sending puffs of vapor into the winter night, and obliterating any snowflakes in its ken. He watched a moment, finding that particular spectacle cleansing to the soul. Cox glanced over his shoulder at the Custom House Tower - 11:39 already. Tremont Street was noisy with music, laughter and traffic, and ablaze with tawdry lights - but still Cox's heart rose. For at last Cornhill had curved into view - the Puritan center of the old Puritan city. This was the street of bookshops, publishing, and presses. Cox caught his breath as he thought of all the words that had been enshrined into print there, before print had fallen to the hordes: Benjamin Franklin, Increase Mather and his "Heavens Alarm to the world"; William Lloyd Garrison's anti-slavery screed The Liberator. ("By all means, be free, Negros," Cox's heart proclaimed, as he led his doomed duo down along the snowy street, "but be free elsewhere."). Alongside his exhilaration, Cox felt a sense of completion, for the Quill of Justice traced its origin back to a basement office in Cornhill.

Governor John Endicott signed the death warrant of the Quaker Mary Dyer with this quill. Himself a practitioner of certain secret and darkish arts, but only to better serve the Puritan state, the Governor had drawn a dram of Mary Dyer's blood, unseen and unsuspected. Then, again in secret, he repaired to Cornhill, where his cousin was an engraver of ill-repute. Chanting the words to the writ of Mary Dyer's execution, John Endicott dipped the quill into Mary Dyer's blood: and so was born the Quill of Justice. It was created from Puritan righteousness, and purveyed the same. It knew not mercy, but only justice - terrible, untempered and unregenerate. And tonight, in the very basement where the quill had come into being, civic wordage and the purest of blue blood would converge to form a maelstrom of righteousness as never seen before. Cox had caused the quill to all but run dry, but he would shortly redeem his error a thousand fold. The quill would write with the blood not of criminals, Quakers, and witches - but of Boston's finest families, the bluest of blue. And the Den itself would at last be deeded over to the Blueblood persuasion, and rightful hegemony reestablished.

Cox allowed himself a grim chuckle. There was a "live by the sword, die by sword" neatness to the equation: publishing may have diminished the quill's scope, but these old publishing sites would be the place of the quill's reinvigoration.

Beside him, the Cabot-Lowell girl stumbled into a mound of snow. She faltered, and nearly slipped. A few flakes of snow drifted onto her lashes, and with a trembling hand, she tried to brush them away. She stood uselessly, her head hanging low. A gaggle of hooligans swept by, hooting at her as they passed. Ames was still careering along the side of the road. He was singing too, in a sweet pure tenor. The words to the Harvard song leaked out onto the frigid air. They were scented with alcohol.

The girl began to take a step, then hesitated again.

"Oh, come along," Cox said. He held out a bony wrist. She did not move. He interjected what he supposed was warmth into his voice. "My dear Miss Cabot-Lowell."

Not looking up, she reached out and took hold of his hand.

Cox's other hand was in his pocket. The tip of the quill was razor-sharp. It could easily score a milk-white neck, or two. His fingers grazed the lining of his pocket - and he felt a long rip across the silky lining. A tiny shard of feather, dun-colored and lifeless looking, drifted out from the hem of his coat. Cox watched the shard fall with grim satisfaction: at least, there could be no doubt the quill was sharp enough to do the deed required.

"Oh Uncle," Ames said and swayed towards him, "I am so very tired!"

But Cox was still staring at the ground. The bit of feather had shriveled to nothing, and where it landed, the word "pursuant" appeared. It was stamped into the snow, about the length of a red brick, in neat, cursive script. Cox had been unaware that his pocket was torn, or that the quill could shed its parts, or further, that the shards carried any effect - and the unforeseen always displeased him. Ames hiccupped, and began listing toward him. Cox shoved him back, as a headlight from a passing car beamed full onto the spot. And in the steady light, the solitary word had already faded away as if it had never been.

CHAPTER FORTY-SEVEN

Brutus yipped, nose to the ground, and scampered on ahead.

"No doubt we shall soon enough happen upon our trio," Lowell said. "Just where do you imagine they are headed?"

Ben turned to answer. They were walking along Tremont Street, near the corner of Kings Burial Ground. "I'd say -" Ben began, when an unexpected movement inside the graveyard caught his eye. He stopped, and looked over the iron fence posts.

Through the bluish shadow, Ben made out an arched headstone near the center of the yard. It was half-sunk into the ground, with an angel of death carved across the arched top. The wings of the carved angel unfurled, and fluttered. Ben gripped the railings. He stared into the graveyard. The carving had moved as if alive. Some power deeply rooted in the history of the city must have given way, and the traditional balance was in flux, and under threat. Magic had been released from its accustomed moorings this night. And it had to do with Cox, Ben was certain.

"Did you see that?" Ben said. Brutus sidled in beside

him, and poked his snow-crusted muzzle between the railings. The dog whined, ears flat to his head, and turned away.

"See what, precisely?" Lowell said, drawing up.

Ben pointed. "That headstone there - Elizabeth Pain."

Lowell lifted his nose and peered into the burial yard. From the behind the crooked gravestone, a pigeon rose. With a heavy flap of its wings and a faint squawk, the bird ascended into the dark and snowy sky, and disappeared.

"Merely a pigeon roosting, it would seem," Lowell said. "Your imagination is proving a bit over-active, I fear. A Celtic tendency you'd do well to curb. I trust we'll find much the same as regards your dark suspicions of Governor Cox. They are at present completely unfounded. I assure you he is a gentleman."

High up in the dark city sky, the clock in the Custom House Tower began to chime the quarter hour: 11:45. The bells quickened Ben's mind and steeled his resolve. Without stopping to think out the why of it, he said, "A gentleman - was Governor Cox the same year as you at Harvard?" He kept his eyes round.

"Not at all," Lowell said.

"A year or two before you then?"

"As it happens, the Governor is a Dartmouth man."

"Oh!" Ben flinched, just enough. The clock in the tower finished chiming.

Lowell started off again, frowning a bit now, with an abstracted air.

Ben set off after him. He knew what he had just seen in the burial ground, and what it meant. The very air felt different to him - colder, freer, and fraught with a wayward power. Some underpinning deep beneath the city had shifted, as ominous as the first tremors of an earthquake. He was passing a lamppost festooned with a garland of red ribbons. The silver bell tied to each ribbon gave a tiny, merry tinkle - and Ben felt that somewhere his father was nodding in sagacious approval.

" *'The center cannot hold,'* " Ben said, as he caught up beside Lowell.

"My sister often speaks in such riddles," Lowell said. The snow crunched under his feet. "A lamentable habit."

Ben struggled to keep up. The falling snow stung his brow and chin. Brutus made a long, loping shadow alongside him. "William Butler Yeats wrote that - a Celt -"

"I feared as much," Lowell said. "Poetry would appear endemic to some peoples."

"Like your sister."

Lowell glanced down at Ben, his eyebrow raised. He said nothing. They were at the corner of Tremont and Court, on the edge of Scollay Square. Above them, a brightly lit marquee blazed, with an electric sign affixed to it, bluish tinged, and in the shape of a star. The star revolved over and over, casting light, and shadow, like a giant illuminated pinwheel. The street was busy, and echoed with the sounds of traffic and laughter and stray bits of tune.

Ben listened: behind those sounds, commonplace and expected, was another - several others. The musical notes were not just stray bits from a radio, or a jukebox. The snow was falling, at a slant, and each flake was descending with the sound of a musical note to it: one flat, another sharp; this one drawn out, and that one as clipped as a plucked string. Brutus looked around. He rushed at one snowflake, and then at another. He yipped and wagged his tail.

Ben heard the falling snow even as they crossed the street and dodged a stream of traffic.

"Listen," he said as they gained the curb.

Lowell turned and looked down at him. "Yes?"

And just then, the snow swirling around them went silent. The sound drained out of the snowflakes, like a phonograph slowing and coming to a stop. Ben looked into the sky, and wondered what had changed. But he did not doubt what he had heard, any more than he did what he had seen in Kings Burial Ground. "The center cannot hold" - all things were possible this night, for good or ill. He had to find Ellie.

"If I may ask," Lowell said, "just how do you propose we locate our quarry? At the moment we appear to be haplessly wandering."

"Like Hansel and Gretel," Ben said.

"They had at least had the benefit of a trail of bread crumbs, if I recall correctly."

And he and Lowell were on a trail, too, Ben thought - one on which magic had broken loose from its bounds. On one street corner, magic was bound up and securely anchored as when his father had been running the city; on the next, the magic was unleashed, and wayward. There *was* a path of some sort.

Of course! Ben stopped and slapped his forehead.

"Young man?" Lowell said.

The magic was unraveling along the path Cox had taken. And if they followed the signs of wayward magic, they would surely be led to Cox - and to Ellie. Ben looked around, seeking hints of wayward magic, and a clue as to which direction to take.

The buildings on this stretch of Tremont were tall, and cast imposing shadows. The short stretch of street ahead was in total darkness. Neither the lights of the revolving sign, nor from passing cars, impinged on it. On the stoop of a tobacco shop therein, a man was standing. He took out a cigar. With a rasp and a snap, he struck a match, and a flame flared up. And in that flash of light, Ben saw something lying on the ground, by the man's feet: the word "litigant" was etched into the snow, written in a neat, copperplate hand. The man took a deep slow puff, and the cigar glowed a steady red. The word began to shrivel up as if touched by a flame.

"Do you see?" Ben said, pointing. But just as he spoke, the word disappeared without a trace.

"I hope this is not one of those infuriatingly figurative

questions poets are so fond of," Lowell said. "Let us complete our circuit of the Square. So that your fears of Governor Cox may at last be put to rest." He moved off, and proceeded at a fair clip.

Ben started after him. "The thread of magic that stitches this city together is being picked at." He struggled over the mounds of snow trying to keep pace. "It's unraveling, and in Cox's wake."

"Governor Cox," Lowell said, glancing down but not slowing.

"He's tearing through these streets - like a pair of scissors through a length of silk."

"Most whimsical, I'm sure," Lowell said. "Say it simply, man." He had reached the intersection of Tremont and Court, and was waiting for the traffic to clear.

Ben looked up at him. "Anarchy."

Lowell frowned. "I witnessed an occurrence of such in 1919, the police strike. I see no evidence of such mayhem tonight."

Ben was about to answer, when the star-shaped sign beamed full over them. Across the busy street, at the entrance of a side alley, the tall spare shape of O'Connor, and the squatter one of Costa, his fedora at its characteristic angle, were sharply and momentarily spot-lit. The light revolved away, and the alley was again shrouded in dark.

"Hello there," O'Connor called out. "Knowing a good shortcut or two has always come in handy, so I've found."

"Thus we encounter our good friends," Costa's voice rejoined. "Who left us both behind."

And, side by side, O'Connor and Costa emerged from the dark alley into the well-lit thoroughfare. They waded into the traffic, dodging a sedan, and approached Ben and Lowell.

CHAPTER FORTY-EIGHT

"Sky's the limit, Coup. Anything's possible." King David was perched on the edge of his desk. He punched the air with one fist, then the other. Around them, the cramped ground floor office of the Majestic shook with the hoots and hollers of the audience on the other side of the wall. The receipt box on the edge of the shelf was sent jittering. King David reached up and steadied it.

DeGrace nodded. He'd had that feeling all evening long, that anything was possible. It had come over him before he'd arrived here. But it did not please him. While waiting in his hallway for his drive to the Den tonight, DeGrace had been gazing out at the sidewalk. An old man came limping by, weighed over with a heavy sack of groceries. The man's shadow cut a dark jagged line into the light. But the shadow was not that of an old man. It danced along, in a young man's quick step, the back straight, the arms swinging side to side, and fingers snapping to some secret rhythm. But surely the city was under better control than this eventuality would suggest. The sight had to be a trick of the light - a matter of perspective, and light reflecting off the snow, DeGrace told himself. He took off his spectacles, and rubbed his eyes. He looked again, and sure enough, a younger fellow was entering into view, steaming along the sidewalk, all but dancing along. The car pulled up to the curb. As DeGrace proceeded down the sidewalk toward it, a pure white cat crossed his path- never a good sign. It traced a circle thrice, meowed, and vanished into thin air. The snow, of course, could explain that, DeGrace reminded himself. This city had its magic under control, operating according to time-honored protocols. But nonetheless, DeGrace was uneasy, and out of sorts, as though he was walking on spilt sugar. And here in the Majestic with King David, for all that he'd taken due precautions, the unsettlement was unabated.

"Zombies'll make a swell show, all kinds of tricks no mortal can do. Undaunted by fire, or sword cuts, or anything like that. We can't open the Cotton Club for New Year's, thanks to the boys in blue, so I got to thinking, why not use the Majestic, and stage a New Year's Eve spectacular like no other."

On the other side of the wall, the audience erupted into applause and foot stomping. With one hand, King David kept the receipt box in place. "Got lemons, make lemonade, capiche?"

DeGrace nodded.

"Struck me as a great way to recoup - ha." King David's face collapsed in pleasure at his own pun. He reached over and bopped DeGrace on the shoulder. DeGrace absorbed the impact, but his spectacles were knocked askew. With the tip of his ring finger, he pushed them back into place.

The audience stamped their feet. The shelves of the office shook, and the receipt box crashed to the floor.

"A sound proposition," DeGrace said. "All things considered."

Another clamor arose - not through the wall, but below, from the basement. The sound was like the thunder of a bowling ball rolling down the alley. It ended with a

237

crash and a thud.

"Wanted to get you in on the act, see," King David said. "So your New Year's ain't a total washout, financially speaking. On account of we are partners."

"And I supply the musical performers," DeGrace said.

"That too."

Beneath the floorboards, there was another thud, then a third.

DeGrace looked at King David. "A previous act, perhaps? One that met with disfavor?"

King David cackled. "Good one, Coupster."

The thudding was growing louder and more frequent, like an eruption. King David stood up. He swiped a hand through his hair - a gesture DeGrace did not associate with King David, stylish and self-confident to a fault. DeGrace gave King David a quizzical glance.

"Just the old furnace is acting up," King David said. "Always does, in a cold snap. So how's about you head on home and talk to your -"

Just outside the office door, there was a single thump so jarring that the mirror fell off the wall. A scream sounded out, then the pounding of running feet. DeGrace reached for his gun, and aimed it at King David. Maybe King David had been setting him up this whole time, although DeGrace, until this moment, had not suspected anything. But tonight, all things were seeming possible.

King David glanced at DeGrace. "Cut the comedy, Coup." He stared at the door.

The door was flung open, so roughly it was nearly torn from its hinges. A figure wider and taller than the frame blocked the light from the hallway. It cast a gigantic shadow into the office.

"Marty!" King David said. "Knock it off." The figure ripped the door from its hinges, and flung it the floor. "Stop! Do nothing, that's what I mean."

Marty went motionless. King David turned to DeGrace with a rueful grin. "Sometimes, I wish he'd just get lost, you know what I mean?"

"You shouldn't have said that," DeGrace said. He put away his gun.

"Huh?" King David turned around, and caught a glimpse of Marty's broad back, as the golem lumbered out the door, into the wintry streets.

CHAPTER FORTY-NINE

Raucous music sounded from every bar. The squalor of Scollay Square was only too apparent, but the incongruity between his surroundings and his own self gave Tim Owen a contentment that glowed warmer with every step he took. He was on a mission. President Lowell was abroad in this Square right now.

Taking it upon himself to inform the Governor's deputy, Tim had gone to the Harvard Club in search of President Lowell, only to find that the President had left. No one knew where he was headed. Claiming he'd left a glove in the President's office, Tim was granted entrance, where he examined the blotter on the President's desk, and read, in what he knew to be the President's painstaking script, the address of the Majestic Theatre, with the notation: curtain, *8:00 pm, just ½ hour duration (thankfully)*. Dear God, Tim had thought. If he exercised discretion over this most surprising of finds, President Lowell would esteem him that much more. It was glorious to be in the know, almost intoxicating. Tim hurried down the stairs, onto the streets, in the direction of the Square, anxious to catch the president in this unlikely setting.

He'd quickly reached the depths of Scollay Square.

Several doors down, the Christmas lights inside Bucky's Tattoo Parlor gleamed against the shop front window. A sailor was sprawled out on a chair. His eyes were shut, and he winced as the needle was applied, the last touch to a red rose tattoo taking shape on his forearm.

Tim stopped and watched a moment. Before his eyes, the tattooed rose withered, and bloomed. No, what nonsense - the vision was just a trick of the light, and his own nervous exhilaration. The tattoo artist stood up and looked at Tim. He jabbed the needle into the air, and Tim felt a sharp prickle across his forearm. With a start, Tim moved along. It was just his imagination, what he thought he'd felt and seen just now. There was no magic loose on the street. Or, rather, there shouldn't be. It had always been confined to its high priests, so to speak. That was the arrangement that had kept the city in order. But Ben was such a bad leader, perhaps that order itself was dissolving. Really, Ben had no business trying to run this city. His inadequacy had been obvious from the first, and was becoming ever more so. The sooner Tim took over the Druid's Den, the better.

He walked under the glare of a marquee, sidestepped a braying panhandler, and rounded the next corner. Above him, the Steaming Kettle puffed into the winter night, and just beyond it, Cornhill curved into view. A shop sign clanked on its rusty hinges, and all down the crescent-shaped alley, the darkened window fronts glittered. From the depths of the shadows, a metallic rattle echoed, and then with a clink, something fell onto the icy pavement.

Tim peered down the alley. About halfway down, a tall, shadowy figure was picking something up from the pavement - a set of keys, Tim guessed, from the metal glinting in the dark. The figure half-turned. The profile was aquiline. The figure's stance was self-possessed, almost haughty. Tim caught his breath. It was Governor Cox!

The governor had a companion - a tall figure hovered at his shoulder, listing slightly - perhaps President Lowell?

To catch them both in this section of town was more than Tim could have hoped. How he longed to exercise discretion on their behalf, and demonstrate he was worthy of their friendship.

"Governor Cox," Tim called out. "Your Excellency."

The Governor turned and faced him. He did not return Tim's greeting.

CHAPTER FIFTY

In the middle of Tremont Street, the lights blazing and the traffic streaming, Ben Owen was still jabbering about the need for cooperation and shared responsibility. Dear Lord, O'Connor thought: old man Owen had delivered a similar line of guff every so often, but he didn't flap his hands around so much.

O'Connor tightened his lips, and rolled his eyes skywards. A flock of birds was alighting from the rooftop of Slim Jim's Friendly Pawnshop - a dozen of them, each one so bright and true a color that it seared O'Connor's heart just to look upon them in that winter night. They were emerald green, scarlet, sapphire blue, and imperial yellow. They were no bigger than sparrows, and flew in a perfect v-formation. They were not a species O'Connor recognized, and what with Hollie in his stewardship, he had come to know a lot of them. He narrowed and peered upwards. They were flying in pairs. Each bird seemed to have just one wing, and one eye, but united, they did soar. O'Connor raised his arm, and pointed. "Look -"

" - agree on that much, I hope," the Owen kid was saying. He turned to O'Connor.

A snowflake landed in O'Connor's eye.

"I must ask myself," Costa said, "for how long?"

"If I may," old man Lowell began, "I…"

O'Connor opened his eyes, still pointing upwards.

There were no magnificently-colored birds flying in pairs. There were no birds at all. The sky was empty. Snow fell in a slant against the winter night. It must have been an illusion, some kind of downtown mirage - a cloud passing over an electric sign a few rooftops over maybe. Still, O'Connor felt disconcerted, and ill at ease, as though someone were getting the better of him in a bargain.

His feet were numb. He stamped them against the snowy pavement. On impact, there rose a short-lived squawk, like a musical note, a squashed-up musical note. O'Connor looked up at Costa, Lowell, the Owen's kid, each in turn. None of them gave the slightest hint they'd heard it. Costa was looking increasingly dubious. The Owen kid said something about "comity." The kid was flailing his hands out again, and O'Connor was obliged to take a step backwards.

Costa shook his head. "You cannot placate us so easily, my young friend."

"Or set us up either," O'Connor said. "Leaving me and Al, in the Den to face the good Lord knows what."

"I've already told you, that was no set-up," the kid said. "The *good Lord knows what* is out here, on these very streets, tonight. Where Governor Cox walks. He's got Ellie with him."

O'Connor crossed his arms. He was already impatient for more seasoned sparring partners, Lowell or Coup, or even King David.

"Ellie?" Costa shrugged. "With such I am not familiar."

"A distant relative of mine," Lowell said. "Ellie Cabot-Lowell, to be exact."

"The Governor is involved with all this strife," the kid said. "He's the one - we've got to - don't you see?"

"The notebook made clear as much," Costa said. "*Infamita*. And the Governor his patron."

"If I may," Lowell said. "The Governor's role in the North End fire is still merely putative, Mr. Costa. There is only the word of an avowed degenerate and agitator, and evident renegade, to credit the supposition. Aside from that, however, I will admit the Governor seems to have been pursuing certain of his own aims, with which I am unfamiliar at present. I doubt his aims are as nefarious as Ben supposes, but nonetheless his secrecy in regards to me is somewhat disconcerting."

"And to one who strives to be concerted above all else," O'Connor said.

"Listen to me," young Owen said. For once his hands were still. "Magic has broken loose - block by block, street by street, site by site - wherever the Governor has happened by."

Lowell sniffed. "Hypothesis, not proven."

"It's - uncanny, what's going on tonight." Ben's eyes were round and white, and in the glare of a passing car, his face was as pale as the moonlit snow. "The center cannot hold."

O'Connor raised his eyebrows. The phrase had a surprising ring to it.

"You notice anything, amiss or awry, on your way here?" the kid said. "Things happening that couldn't be, shouldn't be?"

Costa shrugged. "No," he said.

O'Connor was about to answer, the same as Costa, when he felt a stir and rustle at his chest. A faint twitter rose. He glanced inside his coat front.

At the bottom of his shirt pocket, Hollie was scrunched up, a piffle-weight stowaway. Her queen of hearts face was turned upwards. She opened her eyes, blinked twice, and then chirped. She ruffled her top feathers, and fluttered her wings. "Cupcakes dear," she trilled. "You'd better get some. Several dozen. Don't you think?"

O'Connor reached into his pocket, where he had a bar of milk chocolate. He broke a sliver off, and dropped the morsel inside his coat. Hollie chortled. He drew his coat tighter. No one else could hear Hollie, except maybe Brutus, as her high-pitched trill did not carry far. Sure enough, the hound padded over, his ears standing up, his head cocked to one side. He lowered his head and growled.

Ben reached down, and pulled the hound away by the collar. "Take it easy fella."

Hollie had been hiding in his pocket all this time; and she'd kept still. O'Connor could guess when she'd made her move. Late this afternoon, he'd gone down to the basement to feed her a plate of shortbread cookie crumbs. Hollie was eyeing the plate dubiously as he unlatched the cage door. "Leftovers, dear?" she said. She fluttered against the silver bars in a graceful arc - and then Rosemary had called down the stairs to him, the news about the mayor's daughter. Distracted, he must have left the cage open, leaving Hollie free to fly out, and hide inside his coat. She had been there this whole time, carried throughout the length of the city, unknown to her bearer. And until just now, she'd kept quiet. Both eventualities were unprecedented, of a piece with little Ben Owen taking command. Maybe the kid was right: something was afoot tonight.

"See what I mean?" Ben said. "Something's abroad in these streets." He indicated beyond O'Connor with his chin.

O'Connor turned and looked back. A distant but recurring thud sounded out. The buildings on the far edges shook slightly, and the ground beneath his feet shuddered.

CHAPTER FIFTY-ONE

"I did so hope it was you, Governor," Tim said, He gave a merry wave. It was a treat to be encountering the Governor like this, on Cornhill - the frisson of culture in the midst of the shabby confines of Scollay Square. If Tim was not mistaken, Cornhill was the street where Ben Franklin himself had apprenticed. And to think, Tim's own grandfather couldn't even read. He had never told the Governor that story.

"Governor," Tim said, "I have an anecdote about my family, delicious in its irony."

The Governor took a step forward, and the figure lurking at his side came into view. It was not President Lowell, Tim saw, with a pang of disappointment, but a fair-haired young man, somewhat the worse for wear. He was leaning against the wall, listing even more precipitously. And cowering in the shadows was Ellie Cabot-Lowell - that simp. Her head was hanging down, in that peculiar and unattractive way she had, one eye visible, and glinting in the dark, like some woebegone sea-creature lurking by the rocks in the ocean depths.

The Governor turned away from Tim. He raised this arm high, and swiftly brought it down. A silvery glint caught the light.

"Ouch!" the fair-haired young man said. "Uncle, that does smart!"

Around the Governor and his companions, the falling snow began to whirl around. The wind had quickened, and the alley nearly twittered with its motion. Tim felt left out, at the other end of the alley, as he watched His Excellency enjoy a private snowfall. He sallied forth a few steps.

"A veritable wind tunnel, isn't it," Tim said.

"Timothy Owen." Governor Cox turned around again. "How very unexpected."

"And welcome, I hope," Tim said. "Always glad to be of service."

"You will be, I'm sure." The Governor smiled. Then his gaze shifted, to the street behind Tim. In the near distance, a dog yipped. Ellie's head jerked up. She brushed a strand of hair from her eyes, and took a faltering step away from the Governor.

The Governor began to recite: " *'Section 1. Article II. No bill or resolve of the senate or house of representatives shall become a law, and have force as such, until it shall have been laid before the governor for his revisal; and if he, on -* ' "

The silly fool slunk back, as well she might. The governor was magisterial. He was intoning legal formulations - so cadenced, in a voice that was stern and yet mellifluous. He glanced over Tim's head, into the street beyond.

Frowning, Tim turned to see what constituted the distraction. The road was lined with a row of squat brick tenements. The outermost of them appeared to tremble. It reminded Tim of the tenements of the North End, this afternoon, when they'd been engulfed with flame, and appeared to sway in the waves of heat. With a rumble and a rush, snow slid from a peaked roof, and hit the sidewalk with a thud.

"Another fire!" Tim said. His eyes were round with hope and anticipated sensation, as he turned to the Governor. "My heavens, what won't those Irish get up to?"

A thud echoed off the pavement and the banks of snow. Windows, near and distant, rattled.

"Perhaps you've called in the national guard, Govenor."

Governor Cox extended his hand. "Your arrival is indeed provident," he said. "Come, dear Tim, join my merry band."

And ducking his head with delight, making an effort not to hurry - haste was so very obvious - Tim sauntered towards him.

CHAPTER FIFTY-TWO

"Now Coupster, how about you beat it?" King David said. "I got more sway with Marty, you don't mind my saying, on my own." He winked.

DeGrace did not wink back. He and King David had followed the golem to Scollay Square, and he vowed he would be leaving with him. Ever since that unsettling play of shadows, and the vanishing white cat, this night had been fraught with uncertainties. DeGrace shook his head. "We're partners, are we not, through the thick and thin." And not losing a beat, he proceeded along Tremont Street.

"Wonder if Marty ain't heading for the waterfront, to Fan'eul Hall," King David said. He kicked a mound of snow in front of him, demolishing it. "Demand his rights, at the cradle of liberty."

"A slave trading fortune built that hall."

"Always with the downbeat, Coupster." King David laid a firm hand on DeGrace's shoulder, and propelled him along.

"There are times I wonder if our city must suffer," DeGrace said, "to redeem its collective sin of slavery."

"Got to admit, I never thought of it that way," King David said. There was an alleyway on their left. King

David slowed, peered down it, then resumed his progress. "But then I ain't no Baptist." Just ahead, puffs of steam rose from the eaves into the night. The copper kettle affixed to the roof came into view through the falling snow.

"More a strict Calvinist doctrine, actually," DeGrace said. He glanced behind him. A tall, lean figure was weaving through the crowds, back straight, head held back, eyes dead. The creature wore a long dark winter coat, but the coat was open, the shirtfront showing starchy and white, and at the collar, a bright red bowtie. Nigel had always been an able tracker, an estimable shadow. DeGrace had arranged this measure early tonight, as a precaution. Nigel even had his own valet now - he had amply earned such distinction.

A thud sounded out on some nearby street. King David grimaced.

"There has been no clamor, no screams, on these city streets," DeGrace said. "Your creature Marty is likely taking a clandestine passage through the city, via shadowy byways rather than the broad thoroughfares."

"Sure looks like it," King David said. He swiveled his head, and scanned the crossroads just behind them. "Marty!" he called out, and still looking in that direction, strode around the corner of Tremont Street and Court - straight into an imposing, granite-like figure.

"Watch it, bub. I got - oh, Prez!" King David said.

Lowell did not budge, merely raised his nose, turned and gazed at King David.

"Never expected to see you here," King David continued. "And looky here, Coupster - the gang's all in. Little party you forgot to tell us about. Me, I got a theater to run, just around the corner. What's your excuse, being in this neck of the woods?"

"One might ask the same of Mr. DeGrace," Lowell said.

"Coupster's in on my act," King David said. He laid a

companionable mitt on DeGrace's shoulder. "Partners, Coup and me, see, in all enterprises theatrical." King David turned, and eyed up Ben Owen. Smiling with one side of his mouth, he took a step towards the boy and prodded a forefinger into his chest. "What brings you here, Bensy?"

Before Ben could answer, a fresh wind bore down on them, from a new direction, arctic in its cold. DeGrace stamped his feet. Brutus raised his muzzle. His nose was quivering. He yipped, and pulled at Ben's sleeve.

"To my certain knowledge," O'Connor said, "the only thing that could get this hound so agitated, is a bar of Hershey's chocolate."

Ben leaned down and put a hand on Brutus's collar. "Fella," he said. "Take it easy."

King David laughed. "Had my hands full tonight myself, keeping a lid on things."

"You and me both." DeGrace glanced behind him. In the near distance, Nigel was weaving his way through the crowd.

"Marty," King David called out. He turned to take in 360 degrees of the square.

" '*Marty?* '" Lowell raised an eyebrow.

"An employee," DeGrace said. "Willing if unskilled." He turned on his heel too, and took in the traffic, the marquee lights, the passing crowds, the shop fronts and shadowy stoops. Finally his gaze returned to the giant kettle overhead.

"That's a good boy, Brutus," the Owen boy said. He was well-meaning, DeGrace allowed, but so callow. "You just -"

A scream pierced the skyline.

Brutus barked. He made a constrained leap into the air, and then broke free from Ben's grasp altogether. Plowing up snow on both sides, he scampered to the curved entrance of Cornhill, and disappeared into its shadows.

"Ellie!" Ben said. "Brutus knows where she is."

"With our buddy the Gov," King David said. "I've been itching to meet up with that one myself." And not waiting for anyone else, he strode off after Brutus.

CHAPTER FIFTY-THREE

Cox released another droplet of Ames's blood. It fell dark and glittering from the silvery point of the quill into the snow mounded up at his feet. The cold bluish air stirred, and with a whoosh, a fifth, and final, contingent of shades was conjured up. The alleyway was swarming now with velvety, deep blue shadows. The eye did not see them exactly - no more than it catches a flutter of a moth's wing on a summer night. But their swoops and whirls and flights charged the air, and their presence was palpable.

"Dear Lord," the Owen stooge said, as he drew up beside Cox. He made a gesture as though swatting away flies. "Fleas or some such - in this perishing cold! Another example of the city falling to shreds." He gave Cox an understanding smile. "My brother isn't suited to be master of the Den, I'm afraid."

Cox looked at him, stony-eyed. Then he remembered to chuckle in agreement. The patsy was providing an unexpected bit of security for this last, most dangerous phase of the ceremony, and Cox had seized on the opportunity. The Cabot-Lowell female had clearly recognized the dog that barked in the night. Was it her dog, out and about with someone looking for her? Cox could guess who: Benjamin Owen. If it came to it, Cox would give Benjamin Owen a choice: save the Cabot-Lowell vessel, or his brother Tim. Tim would throw a spanner in Ben's works. The boy was already well practiced in the art, Cox could guess, and all too eager to perfect it.

Cox looked up, and consulted the Custom House Tower clock: seven minutes to midnight. It was time to begin the ascension, and commence the sacrifice of the supreme Brahmins.

"Tim," Cox said. "I wonder if you might do me a favor."

"Surely."

"Come up with me, to the roof. This sadly diminished property -" Cox looked about himself, and shook his head. "I have hopes, you see, of establishing it as an historic landmark."

"How wonderful!"

"Bring Ames with you, could you. He's been a little unsteady in his feet, but bit by bit improving."

"Out celebrating, was he?"

"Something like that," Cox said. "Ames family support will be crucial, I daresay, to my endeavor here."

"Ah, show him the vantage point this roof affords."

"Exactly," Cox said, and his smile stretched thinner. Dear God, would this creature keep still, and simply do what he was told?

"We might see as far as Faneuil Hall, with its grasshopper weathervane - its history is extraordinary, isn't it?" Tim gave a knowing chortle. He was insufferability incarnate, Cox thought. "I wrote an item about it last year," the fool continued. "Perhaps you read it."

"Perhaps not," Cox said. It never did to give an eager stooge too much at once. Denial of approval was required to keep his appetite whetted.

Tim looked at his feet a moment. "Well, perhaps you'll read my next item then." He planted a firm grip on Ames's elbow.

Cox laid a hand on the arm of the Cabot-Lowell vessel. It offered no resistance. The building had a spiral fire escape that led from the street to the flat-topped roof. Tim and the male scapegoat began to scale the icy metal steps. A flat clang resounded with every rung, until they reached the flat rooftop, and their footsteps crunched softly on the gravel. Cox and the Cabot-Lowell creature followed.

"This certainly affords a wonderful view!" the Owen toady said, as he looked around wide-eyed at blackness and blank brick walls. Cox grunted - the ascent was not complete. This rooftop was low, and sheltered from the wind. The adjoining roof was a story higher, and provided the vantage point Cox required. A second fire escape, like a ladder at a slant, connected the higher roof to the lower.

This time Cox led the way, and the lesser Owen followed in his wake. The ascent was steep, but Cox quickly reached the top. His scapegoats and the stooge were not far behind.

Cox stood tall on the high roof, and took a deep breath. The cold air was bracing, and so pure it nearly hurt his lungs. The pain was a good sign: Cox had just gained the highest point of Cornhill, and the sacrifice was at hand.

The rooftop was raked with wind. From the north, wind blew in from the seafront, smelling of salt and diesel and fish; from the west, warm vaporous clouds from the Steaming Kettle drifted in. In the eastern horizon, the Custom House Tower rose, its amber implacable clock face visible through a veil of falling snow. At the stroke of midnight, Cox would take the quill, and turn his attention to the male scapegoat, then to the Cabot-Lowell vessel. With the quill replenished as never before, he would be empowered to make history anew.

Ames was slumped against the chimney, his eyes half closed, his face droopy with a sleepy drunken smile. The Cabot-Lowell creature was huddled up next to him in the shadows, her teeth chattering, her head hanging low.

"Now Timothy, could I ask you to cast your glance towards Faneuil Hall?"

"Certainly." The stooge stepped lightly across the roof, and gazed out, feet planted in a mound of snow, his upper body leaning forward.

"Legend has it that a worthy Blueblood can see its frontage from here most clearly," Cox went on, "while plebeian eyes cannot."

"The princess and the pea," Tim said.

"So I ask you to count the bricks on the front façade. I hope thereby to demonstrate the incomparable prospect this roof affords, to the right sort." Faneuil Hall was hardly visible at all from this vantage point, but the stooge would be all too eager to please. And devoting all his attention to the task, he would be distracted from anything else.

"What a most telling detail - the number of bricks," the stooge said. He made a visor with his hand, and faced the sea.

"Can you see Faneuil Hall?" Cox held the quill out, its sharp metal nib glinting in the moonlight.

"Oh yes, very clearly." And with no prompting began: "One, two, three…"

It was forever the tradeoff: useful idiots, to be useful, had also to be truly idiotic. Cox turned, the quill tip glinting in the moonlight, and approached the supreme Brahmin scapegoat number one.

"Uncle," the creature said. "How big your eyes are."

Cox raised his hand, and positioned the quill at the scapegoat's throat. The creature giggled and ducked his head. "The feather does so tickle!"

Cox cupped his fingers under the scapegoat's chin - and from the alley below, a high-pitched yip sounded.

The Cabot-Lowell creature sat up with a jolt. "Brutus," she said, in a whispering quaver.

" '*Article 4, Code 19,*' " Cox intoned. The Cabot-Lowell vessel collapsed back into the snow. Cox peered over the eaves. The canine was rushing down the alleyway now, its breath rising in moist gray curls. And behind it, footsteps rang out.

"Where is she, Brut? Where's Ellie?" It was Benjamin Owen.

"Twenty-four," the stooge counted. "Twenty-five."

And Benjamin Owen was not alone. At his side was Lowell, dark, tall and stalwartly stupid - so stolid as to constitute a monument to his own stupidity. They were trailed, nearly flanked, by the swarthy Sicilian bootlegger on one hand, and the Irish munitions dealer on the other - exactly the elements Cox would be expunging from the city's history. Both primitive and Papist, the Irish and the Italian altogether lacked the sturdy independence of mind and freedom from orthodoxy that a Protestant republic required. Two more cohorts were close behind - equally and distinctively repugnant. The Hebrew counterfeiter strode along arrogantly. Physical self-confidence was rare in his people, and it did not become him. He bore himself not with grace, Cox thought, but more a bullying swagger that was half-mechanical, and half-bestial. Even the manner of his dress was distasteful. The flashy, over-designed coat, and the vulgar, no doubt over-priced accruements were almost Asiatic in their dubious luxury. Last of all, came the Negro speakeasy operator. The lenses of his spectacles made blank discs in the darkness. DeGrace was a Negro who would yet appear respectable. He had washed all traces of the field hand from his person, Cox noted: he sedulously aped correct grammar, and adopted understated attire. Cox found the attempt repugnant in its presumption. All of them below, the foreign and unassimilated, would be corrupting his city on a hill no more. He looked at the Custom House Tower clock. 11:55. The hour drew near.

Cox raised his right index finger high into the air. Out of the night, swarms of shades emerged, ribbons of darkness that spun around his finger, and settled there like thread around a spool. A high-pitched twitter rose. Below, the dog yapped again.

"O mighty shades of the puritan elders, impede the interlopers's progress, and let my fearsomely righteous deed be done!" Cox pointed directly to the alleyway below.

Like a thousand skeins falling from a coil, the shades unraveled towards the ground. They swirled in the alley, making its darkness darker. They swarmed around the interlopers. The air was thick, as if with murmurs, shadows, and accusatory innuendo. The Owen heir, Cox observed with glee, could barely move. He staggered forward a step or two, and then faltered. Cox stepped away from the eaves.

"Oh Uncle," the primary scapegoat said. "I am so tired."

"Thirty-one, thirty-two," the stooge went on.

CHAPTER FIFTY-FOUR

Ben was aghast. Ellie was so near - but advancing up this last stretch of alley was proving impossible. It was like wading through a sea of invisible and treacherous weeds that entangled his limbs, and tightened their grip with every move he made. He could hardly breathe, and a high-pitched moaning filled his ears.

Up ahead, barely visible through the falling snow and the thick swirling shadows, Brutus let loose with a bark. The bark was cut short and ended in a whimper.

"Brutus!" Ben called out.

" *'Cry: Havoc! and let slip the dogs of war,'* " Lowell said. "Or more sorrowfully I fear: *'Argos passed into the darkness of death.'* A worthy hound is Brutus, to your Odysseus."

King David, Coup DeGrace and O'Connor were all in the dead center of the alley, stalled, their coats and faces plucked at, as if with a thousand invisible hands.

Costa was leaned up close against the low brick wall. He managed to take a step forward. He took off his hat, and held his head at one angle, then another. All the while he glared, as though answering an impudent interrogator.

"I cannot see them, my friend - whatever they are, but I promise this - they can see me, and feel the power of my

260

gaze - and thus I render *maloccio* unto them."

In one corner, and then another, the high-pitched moaning diminished. It was replaced with shrieking, then silence. Bit by bit, the air felt lighter. Ben braced himself and tried to take a step forward. He could almost move again.

"Now if I had but been wearing my thinking cap," O'Connor said, "I'm thinking that a gust of wind, controlled and contained as is within my ken, might carry these troublesome beings away."

"That's an idea," Ben said.

Costa held his hat in front of his chest. "It may be possible, now that I have weakened them."

"Hit it, Jackie-boy," King David said.

O'Connor raised his hands to shoulder-height, his palms facing outwards. As he stretched his fingers wide, a wind rose, whistling, through the alley. The sound of dry leaves scuttling filled the air. A cloud, whittering, dark, and amorphous, was swept upwards, silhouetted briefly against the amber face of the Custom House Tower clock, then against the moon, then was whisked out of sight entirely.

King David rushed forward. He punched O'Connor on the arm. "Hey, buddy!"

"Almost midnight," Lowell observed. He inclined his head like a church elder in prayer: " '*Tis now the very witching time of night/When churchyards yawn and hell itself breathes out/Contagion to this world.*' "

Ben nodded. "When Cox's plans are most likely to hatch. If we had even a few more minutes, could make all the difference."

O'Connor smiled. He looked weary. "If the winds at my disposal were to, say, push back the hands of time on that great clock face? That would be a boon, so it would."

King David punched him on the shoulder. "You ain't kidding."

"Never been attempted," O'Connor said. "And my powers are a bit drained at the moment, after the dispersal of those -"

"You've got to try," Ben said, a catch in his voice. "For Ellie, and -"

O'Connor nodded. "Just let me catch my breath."

Costa put his hat back on.

King David glanced at him. He frowned, reached over, and re-angled the brim. "Much better, kid. Nice chaveau, don't mind me saying."

"Chapeau," DeGrace said.

"Indeed," said Lowell.

"Yeah," King David said. "That too."

"I thank you, my friend," Costa said.

Ben led them down the alley once again.

CHAPTER FIFTY-FIVE

"And these Interlopers have driven a Trade of Commissioning from their Confederate Spirits," Cox intoned. He was nearing the end of the final incantation from the *Protocols*. He spoke quietly and quickly, but not a syllable was rushed or slurred. "They do conspire to do all sorts of Mischiefs to the Righteous Bluebloods, and to Root out the Blueblood Hegemony from this City, and set up instead of it a more gross Diabolism than ever the Commonwealth has seen before."

The footsteps in the alley had resumed. They echoed against the brickwork. He heard voices - oh, what butchery of the language of Puritanism and freedom, nasal and slurred, lilting and clipped.

The Puritan shades had delayed the approach of these infernal barbarians, but evidently had not prevented it. Some damnable combination of garlic-stinking, poteen-fueled, Israelite and negroid sorcery must have "conspired to do all sorts of Mischiefs," as the Elders of Merrymount had put it, and seen off his army of shades, sprung from the bluest of all bloods.

Below, the dog barked. This time, the Cabot-Lowell female barely stirred. The Civil Code and the Protocols had subdued her, once and for all. Cox grasped the quill, and poised it once again at the throat of the supreme scapegoat. Under the milk-white skin, blue veins were faintly visible. The scapegoat lolled its head to one side, foppish hair ruffling in the wind. "Uncle, how assiduously you do attend to me!"

Cox looked at the Custom House Tower. The hands of the clock were within a few seconds of meeting at midnight. Cox took a last breath, ready to strike.

But the clock hands did not move.

No chimes sounded.

As Cox looked on, incredulous, the wind strengthened. It rose, whistling, and howled so fierce and unrelenting he had to step back from the roof's edge, and drag the supreme scapegoat with him. Aghast, he watched the hands on the Custom House Tower clock. They were spinning backwards, slow at first, then faster - pushed by a great wind, to 11:59, then 11:58. The hands stopped at 11:56.

Cox's hands crumpled. He cursed not his luck, for that was the way of lesser peoples, but his very self. How often had he aimed for perfection, and failed? He was forever making up for some fault of his own: the lack of foresight that allowed Gryffth Owen to consign his will to print; the quill he himself had so grievously depleted; this scapegoat ceremony, arranged precisely for midnight so as to be most potent - and now? Thwarted, again, and perhaps forever disgraced.

The clang of footsteps on metal stairs echoed upwards. Cox glanced down at the adjoining building. The older Owen boy came into view. He was scaling his way up the spiral stairs.

Cox caught his breath. Around him, the cold wind whipped. He was reminded of a painting in the State House office: Governor John Winthrop alone on a windswept premonitory overlooking Boston Harbor. The shared bleakness of that scene and his own present situation gave Cox a curious warmth. A sense of resolve began to percolate through him. Certainly the chimes of midnight were the most propitious moment for the sacrifice. *The Protocols of the Elders of Merrymount* were categoric on that point.

But was not a narrow perfectionism the hobgoblin of precious minds, most typically French? This was no time for preening hauteur. Had he not secured two Brahmins for the sacrifice, rather the one? And did not one of those scapegoats contain a double quotient of Blueblood? Cox raised his nose. The rest of him followed, face and shoulders.

Already, he could envision the city below him re-made as it always should have been, with no showmen, slaves, or shamans to befoul its citizenry. And might not this slovenly wind play into Cox's hands? For they had, unknowingly perhaps, begun to pick at the very fabric of time themselves. When time unraveled, history is made anew.

The crest of Ben's head appeared. He was climbing the fire escape that joined the two roofs. Just a few more rungs, and he would be alongside Cox on the high roof. A metallic clang announced every step he took.

Cox streaked over to the edge of the roof. He put his hand at the back of the stooge's neck. The stooge glanced at him. "Governor?" he said, and went on counting. "One hundred sixty-four -"

"Benjamin, should you wish to save anyone," Cox called out, "I suggest you refrain from taking another step."

The footsteps halted.

"Where is she?" the Owen boy shouted. "Ellie!"

The Cabot-Lowell creature stirred, and murmured.

"One hundred seventy, one hundred seventy- one," the stooge continued.

"She's under my care," Cox said. "And will be tended to as befits her station and family bloodlines. It's Timothy

you should concern yourself with, don't you think? He is
your brother, after all. A tragedy if something awful befell
him. Doubly so if you could have prevented it."

"One hundred seventy-nine - oh, the Governor's
joking, of course," the stooge said. "His Excellency
respects me. One hundred eighty, one -"

"What is life without loyalty, Ben?" Cox said. "And the
first loyalty's all about blood, isn't it?"

"Loyalty's about belief," Ben said.

"For that you'd betray your own flesh and blood?" Cox
suppressed a chuckle. Tribalism was rampant among the
unassimilated races. They had never truly allied themselves
to civil society, and never could.

"*La famiglia,*" Costa's voice intoned.

Cox glanced down. The ragtag band of primitives,
down to a dog, and that dullard Lowell, had followed the
Owen boy's lead up the spiral staircase, and gained the
lower rooftop.

"Who could ever trust you," Cox said, "if you fail to
save your own."

"Had a brother once myself," the Hebrew said, in his
nasal quick fire. "Poor kid. Died awful young."

"For sure, it's blood that keeps us warm-hearted, makes
us human," the Hibernian said faintly, in his oh-so-
whimsical lilt. "Saves us from becoming like the good
Governor here."

"There are priorities," DeGrace said. "In both scale of
value, and in point of time."

"And thanks to our buddy O'Connor here," King
David said, "we got ourselves a little bit more time."

"Indeed," Lowell said.

Owen sighed. A curl of breath rose into the frosty
night. The top of his head dipped below the eaves.

"Save your brother," Cox said. "He is the one in
immediate danger."

"What about Ellie?" Owen said.

"My dear young man, is she not the flower of two

esteemed bloodlines?" Cox said. "What harm would I possibly wish on her? She is here as a first guest of the Commonwealth, I assure you."

"And my brother?"

Cox cackled. "A guest of sorts, although some guests are more expendable than others. Some, I may say, are interlopers, and may be disposed of as such, one way or another."

" '*Interlopers!*' Oh, quite the kidder, our Governor!" the stooge said. "One hundred -"

Owen said nothing. But Cox recognized the quality of the silence. Owen's resolve had weakened. Doubt had taken hold.

"I have invited Miss Cabot-Lowell to this important site," Cox said. He gave the stooge a sharp prod. "Explain it to your brother."

"This address is an historical landmark in the making," the toady said. "The Governor has divulged details only to those deemed worthy. The Governor invited me up here." The "me" was slightly scented, Cox noted. He felt a fresh surge of contempt for this lamentable fool. "One hundred ninety-seven, one -"

Cox tightened his grip on the stooge's collar.

"Lord save us from all anxieties," the Irishman said, no doubt blessing himself.

"*Santo espriti,*" the Sicilian murmured.

"Amen," the Negro said.

"Yowza," the Hebrew exclaimed.

The Owen boy sighed. He was giving in. He had no stoutness of soul. Then Cox heard the clang of metal. "I'm coming up there myself," the Owen boy called out. "Hold on, Tim."

"Ben, don't be stupid. The governor respects me," Tim said, as Cox pushed him off the roof.

CHAPTER FIFTY-SIX

Heavy as a bollard, Tim hit Ben squarely in the chest, and knocked him off the fire escape. They crashed together into a deep mound of snow, and lay there, winded, Tim on top. With a sniff, Tim got up and brushed off his sleeves. "I must have slipped."

"Cox," Ben gasped. "Ellie!" He was dazed, and could barely sit up. "We have to rescue Ellie. She -"

"The Governor assured me that Lowell-Cabot girl is a guest of the Commonwealth."

"As was your own good self," O'Connor said. "And a fair lot of good it's done you so far."

"If Ben had not interfered," Tim said, "I would have completed a task of considerable historical importance. The Governor assigned me to -"

A thud sounded from the alley. A clay pot on the edge of the roof teetered, fell to the icy pavement, and smashed. In the corner of the roof, Brutus barked.

"It's okay, fella," Ben said in a thin, hopeful voice. He was certain it was not. He managed to stagger to his feet, and glanced down into the alleyway. The entrance to Tremont Street was blocked off. A gigantic figure was hovering, lumbering in from one of the side streets, and closing up the entrance to the alley. The figure was roughly hewn, man-like, not misshapen so much as non-shapen. It took heavy, hobbling steps forward. Plastered to its forehead was a leaf? - no, a bright scrap of red paper, Ben discerned, with some word or number scrawled on it.

"Marty!" King David called out. "Over here, Marts. We just got lucky, folks."

Whatever "Marty" was, King David evidently wasn't afraid of him. Ben turned back to the fire escape, a quaver creeping into his voice. "I have to get Ellie." He put his hands on the ladder, and began to climb again. But with a loud rusty creak, the fire escape swung sideways, tipping him back onto the roof. He looked closely at the ladder. One of the brackets had given way under the combined weight of him and his brother, leaving the fire escape dangling loosely from the wall.

"Maintenance standards throughout the city have dropped precipitously of late," Cox called out, with a cackle.

A heavy metallic clank echoed from below.

King David leaned over the eaves. "That's the way, Marty."

"But Ellie! She's still - I've got to - "

"Hold your horses, kid. Marty'll take care of it. Does whatever I tell him, see. Just let me handle him. Marty's a slow learner."

Marty was ascending the spiral stairs, a solid thud ringing out with every lumbering step.

"That creature has no business here," Tim said. "I doubt the Governor approved his presence. Did he?"

"Your friend Marty better get a move on," O'Connor said. "The winds I summoned are near exhausted." He shook his head. "They'll soon give way, the hands of time will spin forward, and the clock will strike midnight. Our enemy the Governor -"

"Marty," King David called down, "shake a - aw, I mean, move faster."

"The Governor is hardly my enemy," Tim said. "I hope you haven't made him yours, Ben. But I suspect it's too late for that."

In the midst of his turmoil, Ben's spirits lifted: O'Connor had said "our."

O'Connor winced. He held his hands up higher, and, fingers tensed, made one last great effort. But to no avail.

Released from the restraining wind, the hands of the clock spun forward with pent-up alacrity to midnight. The first chime of the clock sounded. It was a melancholy deep chime that resounded through the city streets, and echoed off the iron gray sky.

" '*The iron tongue of midnight,*' " Lowell said.

"Ellie!" Ben called out. He was desperate. Then he glimpsed a flash of red, the paper fixed to Marty's forehead. The creature was only a few rungs below the lower rooftop.

"Marts, come on," King David urged. "Just a couple of steps."

The second chime began, dolorous and deep.

"What's that scrap of paper say anyway?" O'Connor asked.

"Word's '*emet*' " King David said. "That much I can tell you."

"Means 'truth,' " DeGrace said.

O'Connor and King David looked at him.

"The study of scripture is a hobby of mine," DeGrace said.

"Okay, Marty, just one more rung," King David said.

"Mr. DeGrace," Lowell said, "you are akin to the good Boston matron Mrs. Cabot, who learned Hebrew in order to be able to greet her Creator in his own tongue."

O'Connor's lips twitched. "The good Mrs. Cabot must get mistook for a DeGrace all the time."

"So Marty, you decided to join us," King David said. "Folks, this here is what you call a golem. Over here, Marty."

Ben held his breath. The golem had just gained the lower roof. On King David's command, it raised its left foot and planted it down. The building shuddered, and the windows along the alleyway rattled. Then the creature raised its right foot, and planted it in front of the left.

"Baby's first step," DeGrace said.

"And how," King David said. "Okay, close enough, Marty." He pointed at the higher roof. "There's a stranger up there, see, and he ought to be here."

"Ellie!" Ben said. "We have to get Ell-"

"I suggest we attend to the known danger first," DeGrace said. "That in itself will ensure the girl's safety."

"Get Cox to where we can keep an eye on him," Costa said.

"Of whatever variety," O'Connor said.

"The Governor has authority over this site, Ben," Tim said. "He explained the entire situation to me."

"The pasty-faced old coot, Mart," King David said. "Bring him down here, pronto."

And the golem lurched forward, like King Kong. It reached up with a mighty arm-like appendage, and with one sweep, knocked Cox off the higher roof onto the lower. The Governor dragged a pale young man along with him, like a toy on string. They landed with a thud in a deep snowdrift.

"Your Excellency," Tim said. "I must apologize for my brother, and his disgraceful treatment of you. And of myself. Do you know he -"

Brutus faced Tim, and bared his fangs.

"You've got to do something about this dog, Ben," Tim said. "It appears to be rabid."

"Prescott Ames," Lowell said. "His throat - is it bleeding?" He turned around, and Ben saw Lowell was white around the mouth. "Dear God, just what has the Governor been up to?"

Cox had crooked his arm around Prescott's Ames' neck. He held a steely-tipped quill to the young man's throat. "Stay back," he hissed.

CHAPTER FIFTY-SEVEN

"Ellie!" Ben cried out. "What you have done to Ellie, you monster? We've got to -"

"Keep your shirt on, pal," King David said. "She's up there, safe and sound. Marts, bring the girl down - but this time, easy does it, capich?"

Marty's left arm jolted upwards, through the clouds of steam from the giant kettle, and slammed onto the roof.

"Easy," King David said.

The gravel on the rooftop crunched under Marty's massive hand.

"Careful!" Ben said.

"Enough with the mitts, Marts," King David said. The gravel stopped crunching. "See? Mart listens good."

But Marty's arms had stopped moving altogether.

"Is it, has he -" Costa began.

"The steam, from the kettle," DeGrace said.

"Cooked the clay," King David said.

The left forearm fell off first. It crashed in a single piece to the pavement. Then it rolled across the alley, and landed with a thump against the brick wall. Then the right arm began to crumble. A crack opened at the shoulder, and clay fragments rained down like hailstone to the pavement.

Cox drew back, into a shadow. His arm was still crooked around Ames's neck. Ames snored loudly. His shock of blond hair rose and fell with the sound.

Brutus barked. Tim took a step back, but Cox took no notice.

Lowell stepped forward. "Governor, you are in violation of the laws of the Commonwealth, and of decency. I must demand that you surrender yourself to the courts immediately."

Tim frowned. "The Governor is the Governor."

The clock chimed.

"That's six," O'Connor said.

Cox began to chant in low drone: " '*Section 1. The state purchasing agent shall supervise the state printing and all publications by the commonwealth shall be printed under his direction…*' "

Lowell backed off, his hand to his brow. He had slipped into a slight stupor, Ben thought.

" '*provided,*' " Cox went on, " '*that the foregoing provisions shall not apply to topographic maps issued by state departments…*' "

The law was soporific in its cadences. Ben felt himself half falling under its sway.

Brutus gave a yip. "Now wait a minute," Ben began. But a tide of black swept over him. He was bone-crushingly sleepy.

" '*All publications by the commonwealth shall be distributed under the direction of the state secretary unless otherwise provided, unless…*' " Cox went on.

Ben's legs went weak, and his shoulders slumped as though under a great weight.

CHAPTER FIFTY-EIGHT

Costa stared at the Owen boy. The young man was not so completely undone as the *inglese* Lowell, but he was pale, and sweating. His shoulders were bowed, like an ox under a yoke. The hound whined, and lay down at his feet.

"My friend," Costa said. "Are we not united against both these *malvagios*? He who hid the instigator of the fire - and the instigator himself."

With an effort Costa could feel, Lowell stepped forward. "The weight…" Lowell said, and winced. After a moment he continued in a strained whisper: "…of law. The confluence of Owen's people and mine is indeed -"

"Lamentable," DeGrace said.

"The source of all justice," Lowell said, "is law."

"Slavery was legal," DeGrace said.

"So it was," O'Connor said "And famine, or them that allowed it, was never served a summons either."

Ben's hands made the merest flutter before they flopped down helplessly to his side. "There are laws higher than what's codified."

Cox's voice rose and fell, intoning passages of personal property law, the administration of estates, and punishments and proceedings.

Costa glared at him. He would render *malaccio*. He squared his shoulders and summoned all his power. But a mote in his eye distracted him. His shoulders twitched. This chanting was almost liturgical - *sacreligio*! But he could not deny the incantation had gained some hold over him.

"Okay, pal," King David said. "Leave it to the pro." His hands made fists, and he raised them high as his chest. He swung a punch. Midway to his target, his fists stopped. They dropped to his sides. He looked at his hands, disbelieving. "Must've, I dunno, got a cramp in this cold."

"Scatter his words to the winds," O'Connor said. He raised his hands above his head. But it was as if he were working against some great invisible constraint.

"Nigel," DeGrace whispered. He raised his head, as if preparing to roar out the name. But his voice had no strength. No sound emerged, only the whitish curl of his breath in the cold.

The wind came howling through the alley, and another chime just began to sound, leaden and foreboding, across the winter sky.

"Nine," O'Connor said.

Il governatore went on, chanting. In his hand, a bit of metal glinted, and a sweep of feather stirred the air.

"So that's the way the cookie crumbles," King David said. "This working together biz was some fun while it lasted, huh?"

"The law," Lowell said, in a hoarse whisper. "It binds us all." He was leaning against the wall, but he lifted his head, and gave them each a look in turn. The *inglese* smiled. "All of us - each - Americans."

"Ben, you really have made a mess of things," Tim Owen said. "You should apologize. Don't you think?"

And Cox's voice rose, smooth and clear, a dire chant pertaining to statutory rules, easements, and preemptive rights.

Ben turned, his head roiling in despair.

"You may as well give up, Ben," Tim said. "And begin

by telling the Governor you're sorry."

"No recourse," Lowell said. His eyelids drooped. "The law."

"Look!" Ben said. He was looking upwards, and pointing to the roof.

Costa turned. He saw only trails of steam from the giant kettle.

Lowell, taller, craned his neck. " *'But soft, what light through yonder window breaks?'* "

CHAPTER FIFTY-NINE

Ellie was hovering on the edge of the high roof, clouds of mist from the Steaming Kettle surrounding her. The full moon was beaming down on her like a spotlight.

" '*We, therefore, the people of Massachusetts,*' " Cox declaimed. His gaze was on Ellie. Ben could feel it himself - cold, objective, and unrelenting. " '*Acknowledging, with grateful hearts, the goodness of the great Legislator of the universe, in affording us, in the course of His providence, an opportunity, deliberately and peaceably, without fraud, violence or surprise…*' "

"Oh dear," Lowell said in a hushed voice. "The preamble to the Constitution of the Commonwealth."

"Yeah?" King David said.

"The quintessence of the law," Lowell explained.

Another chime struck. A puffy streak of cloud passed over the moon.

"The tenth," O'Connor said.

Ellie turned, and faced down at them all. She looked directly at Cox, and in a pure high tone, she made her voice heard. It quavered at first, but it soon gained in strength as it went on:

"*I, thus neglecting worldly ends, all dedicated
To closeness and the bettering of my mind*

With that which, but by being so retired -"

"*The Tempest*," Ben said. His heart soared to look at her, and hear her. "Describing Prospero the Duke."

"Sounds like a description of you," DeGrace said.

"Mr. Teacher Man," King David said. "Coup's got a point."

"Moreover, Prospero is a magician, and the rightful ruler," Lowell said. "And he has a brother who is treacherous and disloyal."

"It's just a play," Tim said. "Hardly Shakespeare's best either."

Meanwhile Cox droned on: '*Article I. All men are born free and equal, and have certain natural, essential, and unalienable rights; among which may be reckoned the right of enjoying and defending their lives and liberties; and so in ...*' "

And, at the same time, not deterred, Ellie intoned:

"..........*in my false brother*

Awaked an evil nature. And my trust,

As my trust was, which had indeed no limit."

Tim tsked. "She doesn't have any brothers!" He looked at Lowell and shook his head. "Amateur dramatics - when the Governor is trying to tell us important things. Things that matter."

" '*Dost thou hear?*' " Ellie declaimed.

"Can you believe this, President Lowell?" Tim said.

Lowell rejoined, " '*Your tale, sir, would cure deafness.*' "

"Call and response," DeGrace said. "It is the way of all great congregations."

"Brings the people together," O'Connor said.

"In comity," Lowell said.

"*Eucharisto*," Costa said.

"Sure thing," King David said. "Like a jazz combo, when they jam."

"I am familiar with the concept," DeGrace said.

Cox's incantation continued, unperturbed, and unhurried, a confident persistent murmur: " '*The people of this commonwealth have the sole and exclusive right of governing themselves, as a free, sovereign, and independent state...' "*

Ellie declared:

"Not marble, nor the gilded monuments
Of princes, shall outlive this powerful rhyme."

She did not put a syllable out of place as she began to descend the fire escape. Ben watched, his hands clenched, his heart pounding. Only a single bolt now secured the ladder to the wall, but Ellie weighed much less than Ben or his brother. The fire escape swung side to side under her feet, but less violently than when Ben had attempted it. With every step she took, her voice held steady. It was like the beam of a small candle in the dark - "so shines a good deed in a naughty world," Ben thought - Portia, *"The Merchant in Venice,"* Shakespeare, who, he knew, for had not his father told him several times, was in fact Welsh, and had been schooled by Welshmen, too ...

"But you shall shine more bright in these contents
Than unswept stone besmear'd with sluttish time."

His Ellie - for that was how he thought of her now, decanted poetry onto the winter night.

A chime sounded. "The eleventh," O'Connor said, as Ellie stepped off the last step of the fire escape, and gained the lower rooftop.

"From this day to the ending of the world,
But we in it shall be remembered"

Declaiming still, and trailing clouds of steam, she approached Cox. The light was dim, the moon still covered with cloud. Brutus, wagging his tail, left Ben's side and leapt in circles around her. But Ellie was not distracted. She hung her head first to one side, then straight on, and then to other side - was the eye that could see only evil needed to keep Cox in focus, Ben asked himself. His father told him that years ago, but he had disdained such notions, for he had earned a masters degree, with honors, and had no truck with such old country beliefs. Now he was less sure.

Cox's chin held firm. His voice was steady, his eyes

focused like a duelist taking aim. " '*And the people of this commonwealth have also a right to, and do, invest their legislature with authority to enjoin upon …*' "

Ellie was now in the shadow of the inert hulk that was Marty's face. She did not miss a beat.

We few, we happy few, we band of brothers;

Cox went on: " '*Article 4 -*' no, I mean to say: Article 5: '*All power residing originally in the people…*' "

"I actually am Ben's brother," Tim said. He sighed. "Though you wouldn't know it from how he treats me."

"For he to-day that sheds his blood with me
Shall be my brother; be he ne'er so vile,"

" '*and being derived from them,*' " Cox went on. He hesitated. He raised a yellow hand, and it stirred the cold air momentarily, stiff as a paddle. The light in his eyes had changed, Ben noticed, slipped to a chisel point, like a chip in a slab of slate. "But they are flawed: '*people.*' " Cox said. "With Adam's fall we sinned all. I cannot fail again, not now. I will save this city and redeem the days. I must - if I…." Cox shut his papery-thin eyelids and clenched his fists. He recommenced: " '*vested with authority, whether legislative, executive, or judicial…*' "

Ellie took another step, and nearly slipped. She was beginning to tire. Her chin shook. Her shoulders were stooping. Her head was hanging lower, and with an effort Ben could feel, she raised it, angled it slightly, so that her green eye was again focused on Cox.

"This day shall…gentle his condition;"

" '*their substitutes and agents, and are at all times account-accountable to them.*' " Cox's voice was strained, as if his throat had dried out and he was about to cough, but still he carried on.

Ellie's voice was wavering now.

"And gentlemen in England now-a-bed
Shall think … think them…"

Cox pressed forward: " '*Government is instituted for the common good; for the protection, safety, prosperity and happiness of the people; and not for….' "*

"*Shall think….think ….,*" Ellie said. "Oh dear."

" '*family, or class of men,*' " Cox said. " '*Therefore the people alone have an incontestable, unalienable, and indefeasible right…*' "

"*Shall think themselves accurs'd,*" Ben said.

"to institute …." Cox paused, flustered.

"*they were not here,*" O'Connor declaimed.

"A government!" Cox said. "That's what is instituted…but why not instead a covenant, with all worthy Puritan powers light and dark? Why not a - oh but where was I - '*And to reform*' - no, flush out at will the foul influx this city has sustained. They do not do to be here. They are not of us, nor of this place, and I am he who - the word of law is everything, it must be -"

"*And hold their manhoods cheap,*" Lowell recited.

"*whiles any speaks,*" DeGrace proclaimed.

A gasp escaped from Cox. He collapsed but Ben could not look at him, not yet. His eyes were on his companions at arms.

"*That fought,*" King David said. He looked at Costa. "Hit it, Al.'

"*With us,*" said Costa.

And all of them - Ben, Ellie, O'Connor, DeGrace, Costa, Lowell, and King David, rejoined as one: "*Upon Saint Crispin's day.*"

With this, Ellie took a last, gliding step. She stood now at Ben's side. Exhausted, breathing like a little bird that has flown through a storm, but her eyes were shining. Ben reached for her hand. Her glove had a rip across its front, and he pressed his own palm directly against hers.

The final chime of midnight sounded. But neither the hour nor its proclamation held any terrors.

Cox was curled up in the snow. He muttered a few incoherent syllables. His long yellow fingers twitched. Beside him, Ames snored. Cox rocked back and forth. "Villians!" he cried out.

They had spilled their shared breath together on this

winter night, and with it, had dispelled Cox's scheme, whatever it had been.

"The Governor, I am afraid, has misunderstood the nature of law," Lowell said. He cleared his throat. "What gives law its power is not ink or paper."

"Same as with poetry," Ben said.

"Not posturing senators, or bullets, or swaggering policemen."

"Not laureates, or braying professors," Ben said.

"What gives law its power is the belief of men," concluded Lowell.

Ben nodded.

"And the girlies, too," King David said. "Can't forget them girlies."

"No sir, we can't," Ben said.

"The second person God created," DeGrace said solemnly.

Costa looked at Ellie. He swept off his chocolate-colored Borsalino hat, and holding it over his heart, bowed deep. "*Ma donna de Shakespeare!*"

Ellie looked down and smiled. A lock of hair fell into her eyes.

Something sliver and glinting rolled free from Cox's twitching fingers, and landed at Ben's feet. It was an old-fashioned quill pen. But inside its feathered top, there swirled a maelstrom of words. A few spun so fast they were pitched from the plume altogether, and landed, scattered over the snow, about a foot long and formed in perfect copperplate script: "property," read one: "liabilities," and "proceedings."

"Look," Ben said, and pointed to the words. The cloud over the moon lifted. Under the full beam of moonlight, the words shriveled up, and disappeared, scorched to nothingness.

"An old fashioned pen," O'Connor said.

"Figures," King David said. "Old codger like him. College chum of yours, Prez?"

Lowell shook his head. His lips made a thin gray line. "The Governor is, let us not forget, a Dartmouth man."

With the click of his nails against the ice, Brutus ran to the quill pen. He gave it a sniff, then picked it up in his mouth, and carried it away. A bit of feather drifted away as he trundled across the roof. He scrambled down the spiral fire escape, and landed in the alley. They watched from the rooftop as Brutus began digging in the snow.

Under his front paws, a gutter was soon exposed. Brutus dropped the quill in the snow, and nudged it forwards with his muzzle. With a splash that echoed down the alley, the quill fell into the depths of the sewer. Then Brutus stood back, looked up at them all, and gave a full-throated yip.

Cox stirred. A high-pitched, despairing whine escaped him.

"You really have done it this time, Ben," Tim said. "You and that cur. Not to mention that silly little girl. President Lowell, I hope the Governor can forgive me for Ben's behavior. A man does not choose his own relatives."

"Ain't that the truth, Bensy," King David said.

"There's one relative a person does choose." Ben looked at Ellie. "And that's what makes it the most important one of all."

EPILOGUE

The smell of sun-warmed blossoms was heavy in the air, and a gentle breeze stirred the yellow-green foliage on willow trees. Only the first of March - St Daffyd's Day, the patron saint of Wales - but spring had come early this year.

From an oak tree, a robin called, and from a beech across the gravel path, another robin answered. Lowell strode past the statue of George Washington, the tails of his frock coat dancing behind him, the Public Garden before him.

"So many blossoms," Lowell said, to whoever might hear. "They're blooming early this year." He had always enjoyed making playful reference to Louis XVI in the Tuileries.

The lagoon in the center of the park gleamed flat and calm. A swan boat was docked at the near edge. On the waterfront, a band of musicians was setting up. They stood out against the pastel green of the grass, severely elegant in black and white. The metal instruments glittered in the mid-morning sun. The other guests were already gathered at a fair remove, up a slight incline from the water.

Lowell progressed toward them, down the very center of the path. Stolid and unperturbed was he, and felt himself as much: a steel ship loaded with stone monoliths. He took his place under the low-bending boughs of an old chestnut tree, and coughed, by way of greeting.

"- and the salesgirl," King David was saying. "She was a peach, with the sweetest little - oh hey, there, Prez!" With a restraint Lowell welcomed although did not entirely trust, King David refrained from punching Lowell on the shoulder. "Happy day, huh!"

Lowell nodded. "Indeed." With half-lowered eyelids, he noted King David's get-up: the tie was a raucous pattern of purple and an improbably bright green. The suit was made of fawn-colored linen - a subdued enough shade, but no gentleman wears linen before Memorial Day.

"We were just discussing what to get the couple who has everything," O'Connor said.

"Good morning, President Lowell," a voice called out. A hand raised in greeting, Timothy Owen was heading towards him, rounding the last curve of the path.

King David nudged DeGrace. "Looky what the cat dragged in."

"A rat," Costa said.

Timothy Owen stopped and stood alongside Lowell. He had a notebook in his hand and he flipped it open.

"More a mouse," O'Connor said.

"Or a worm," DeGrace said, "and he looks to be still digging."

"Got to get details right, Timmy-boy," King David said. "Now them ribbons in the flowers - yellow, or peach?"

"I'd say off-apricot, I would," O'Connor said.

Tim Owen frowned. He fussed with his notebook. Then he sidled closer to Lowell. "I've been meaning to ask you, President Lowell, how is Governor Cox? One hears so many stories. And you have been difficult to track down of late." He licked his pale lips, and waited.

"The ex-Governor is still under the best of care," Lowell said. He looked into the horizon. "The dean of

Harvard's medical school is overseeing his treatment. Now, if you'll excuse me -"

"My brother's wedding," Tim said. "You're an honored guest." He sighed. "And I'm here as a reporter." He wandered off towards the lakefront. He stopped midway, peered around, and took a few notes.

"Gifts," O'Connor said. "It weren't easy, this one, at all."

"I been saying a long time, gifts make the man," King David said. "I searched high and low, scoured every upscale shop there is. In the end, I had the gizmo made up special, and shipped over." He extracted a gold cigarette case from his jacket, and popped the lid open. "From Damascus." He took out a small cigar, lit it and took a puff. "Since you asked - a highboy cabinet. Holds books and gizmos druidical and whatnot. Loaded with marquetry work."

"Oh," DeGrace said. "I thought perhaps you might have had Marty make -"

"Mr. Marty-pants is still in the shop," King David said. "But I got to tell you, this highboy's pure class. It's got words, see, figured in gold, all across the front." He paused, took another puff, and exhaled. A leisurely plume of smoke rose in a widening curl. " '*Mene, Mene, Tekel, Upharsin.*' "

"The handwriting on the wall," DeGrace said.

"Indeed," Lowell said. "The Book of Daniel."

"Book five, verse 25," DeGrace said.

Lowell had no rejoinder. This Negro would bear watching.

"But it ain't just your run of the mill writing on the wall. No sirree. This one is, the first time it's in the presence of a liar's speech, the writing fades away. Just the once - a truth-sniffer's gift. When I saw it, course, I had to have it. Snazzy, but no overkill."

"Your natural understatement asserted itself," Lowell said.

"Mrs. Costa and I also gave the matter considerable thought," Costa said. "A gift of ourselves that did not overface the young couple. My wife assembled it herself: an ancient pot, that she planted with several herbs and flowers from our own back garden."

"A bit…economical," O'Connor said. "If you don't mind my saying."

"And if even O'Connor here finds a gift chintzy," King David.

"Hold on to your hat," DeGrace said.

Costa drew himself up, and swiped the air with a disdainful palm. "If I may continue. The pot survived Pompeii. Each plant will bloom only once, and will burst not into flower, but into tune. And each tune contains a charm that will cure one particular ailment. A broken leg, a head cold, a punctured lung, what have you."

"To the couple's good health," DeGrace said.

Costa bowed.

"Nice touch," King David said.

"My own offering came to me as easily as a bird from the tree," O'Connor said.

"And no doubt as …economically," DeGrace said.

"*Grazi*," Costa said.

"A tiny hooded raven," O'Connor continued. "Who has a cry so high and so piercing that it can see off the wail of the banshee - but only the once. After that, the bird is rendered mute."

"To their long life," Costa said. "The happy couple."

A twitter, like a high-pitched call of a bird sounded, so close it seemed to emanate from within O'Connor's person. "Wedding cake!" it seemed to say. O'Connor turned away.

"That's using your noodle," King David said. "Gifty bird can set up shop in that Taj Mahal cage I sent old man Owen a while back."

"Gryffth Owen! God rest his soul," O'Connor said. He bowed his head.

Costa blessed himself.

After a pause, DeGrace said, "I wrote a musical composition."

King David raised his eyebrows. "Don't tell me - the Zombie Rag?"

DeGrace shook his head. "Classical. A piece inspired by the loa Papa Legba - the great elocutioner, you see. It's mathematical in its precision and use of pitch. I've titled it, '*St Crispin's Day Sonata*.' "

"No kidding," King David said. "Won't find that playing on every street corner."

"It compels certain creatures within earshot of it to do Ben's will, for as long as the tune is playing. But the tune can be played only once - the notes self-destruct the moment they are realized, and the tune can never be recaptured."

"Whoza!" King David said. "We are a team of swell gift givers."

Lowell coughed.

"Oh, right," King David said. "How's about you, Prez?"

"A portfolio of stock options." Lowell straightened the stem of his boutonniere. "I brought them by the Den last week."

"Always one for the personal touch," O'Connor said.

"It seemed the most sensible option. I -"

Behind him, applause burst out. "Hizzoner!" someone shouted. O'Connor swept past Lowell, his arm outstretched.

Courtly, immaculately groomed and appropriately attired - Lowell had to admit it - Mayor Curley had arrived. He began making his way through the park. He was smiling, and here and there, he paused to shake hands. He kissed a proffered baby, and then joked briefly with a bug-eyed young man. The common touch, as Kipling said - there was an ease to Curley that Lowell almost envied, even as he despised it. Mayor Curley managed to avoid the oppressive air of bestowing himself, although the event was in a sense taking place under his auspices. The Mayor had given express permission for the wedding to take place in the Pubic Garden. Such permission was unprecedented - a circumstance which was never a recommendation to Lowell, as it so often seemed to be for others.

King David nudged Lowell with an elbow. "Some shindig, huh."

"A most pleasant occasion, certainly."

Coup DeGrace gave the bandmaster a cue, and the musicians struck up a tune.

"Jazz," Lowell said, and shuddered. He turned away and looked towards the water.

The swan boat gave a slight stir. Ben Owen was standing on deck now, and beside him a minister, struggling to straighten his collar.

The tune had become recognizable: the Wedding March from *Lohengrin*, but the musicians were playing it in a minor key, and with a syncopated, unseemly rhythm. The Germanic tune was taking on a distinctly Jewish and Negro inflection. Peace was paying many dividends, but Lowell could not count this musical innovation among them.

From the opposite end of the lake, a second swan boat was launched. It glided out into the middle of the water, the paddlewheel scarcely disrupting the glass-like surface, and circled around the small center island. On deck stood a woman in a long white dress, lace trailing from her cuffs. She wore a long lace veil, and her head was hanging first to one side, then to the other. Hugh Cabot-Lowell, in a pearl gray afternoon suit, stood beside her. At the prow of the swan boat, Brutus the Labrador, was stationed at attention, stalwart watchdog and masthead.

The sound of weeping rose. Lowell scanned the edges of the lake. In a dark brown dress, Mrs. Cabot-Lowell was doubled over, dabbing at her eyes. She was more emotional than is required of the mother of the bride;

indeed, she was almost wailing, Lowell was pained to admit, in a positively Mediterranean fashion. She had no excuse, not of upbringing, nor of race. He had sadly misjudged her strength of character.

The second swan boat glided on.

"Look who's pedaling the boat," Costa whispered.

Lowell craned forward, and as the back of the boat came into view, he caught sight of a figure almost as fair as the swan boat itself. The Ames degenerate was at the wheel, peddling at a serene and regular pace. His eyes held a dead flat calm. Lowell has not seen him since that December night when his fate had been sealed. No great loss, Lowell had conceded, and Ben Owen seemed taken aback at how swift and unperturbed Lowell's acceptance of the proposed settlement was. At least the Ames creature was now engaged in legitimate and useful labor – though in his state, Ames scarcely had a choice. He had been deprived of his will, and perhaps too of his degeneracy. Lowell could but hope.

"And there - *il mostro's* most worthy master," Costa said. He pointed to the bridge. The unfortunate Prega creature, a red ribbon straggling off his wrist, moved mechanically from bouquet to bouquet along the stonework, tidying up the yellow daffodils and purple irises. Off to the side, a tall thin black man, his red bow tie in stark contrast to his white shirt and jet black suit, directed Prega, pointing from spot to spot with a silver topped cane.

"Prega is Nigel's valet," Costa said, "and Prega's valet is Ames."

"Ames to placate Al," King David said. "And Prega to placate them that ain't Al."

"An arrangement that served the best interests of justice," Lowell said.

"Parity," DeGrace said.

"Comity," Costa said. "Amici."

"Oh, it helped towards good-feeling all right,"

O'Connor said. "Not to mention good business."

"No doubt about it, business is booming." King David grinned. "Something to be said for this peace jazz, I got to admit."

"Policing the peace is paying dividends that knocking heads couldn't match," O'Connor said.

The second boat glided to rest beside the first. The water lapped gently against the dock.

"And speaking of business," O'Connor said, "We should arrange a meeting of our own good selves, before we convene with the new governor."

"Oh that Alvey!" King David said.

Lowell coughed. "Governor Alvan Fuller, I believe you mean. The car salesman." A Dartmouth man had been bad enough. Out of the frying pan, into the - dear Lord, worst of all, such people as car salesmen had the evident effect of fostering cliché, even in the haven of one's own mind. They were an insidious and corroding influence. "Frying pan" - oh lamentable day!

"Do you, Benjamin Owen…"

Lowell concentrated. "We have been left to negotiate between Scylla of Dartmouth, and Charybdis of motor vehicle sales," he thought to himself. There - that was the expression of a superior self. Classical references were invisible bulwarks that held the barbarians at bay.

On the boat, a small object gleamed gold in the sun.

"With this ring I thee wed…"

This January, Ben Owen had suggested to him, on the day of Alvan Fuller's inaugural in fact, that perhaps it was time to look beyond university label, and see instead the man. Lowell looked merely aghast, and let the remark pass. He had much to learn, the Owen boy. Still, the boy did have potential, as Lowell noted in his diary: young Owen might yet rise above the degree from, where was it - the University of Pennsylvania?

"I now declare you man and wife."

The couple kissed, and at that moment, bells rang out

from every belfry in the city. The sky resounded with clamor. Ben Owen turned, looked into the sky, and smiled, and the gathering on the lakefront applauded. The nearest figure to the edge of the lagoon - a lanky old man, his hair oil gleaming in the sun, and his formal collar stiff, and obviously unused, put his hand on the shoulder of the ancient doll of a woman next to him. Likely some family retainers, Lowell thought: a telling mark of a man is how he treats his inferiors, and how those inferiors esteem him in turn. Ben Owen indeed had promise.

"Maggie," the man in the stiff collar said, "Never thought I'd see the day."

An Airedale yipped. The man at its side, a short-legged, peculiar sort with his cap pulled down low over his eyes, gave the leash a tug. "Eloise, keep still." His patrician accent and the clear tone to his voice took Lowell aback.

Coup DeGrace gave the musicians a nod, and they switched into a discordant, syncopated tune.

"Dig it, pops," King David said, snapping his fingers and swinging his arms from side to side.

To avoid being jostled, Lowell stepped back - and felt a sharp prod in his side. He turned and looked.

The offender was a length of piping. It protruded from the satchel that was slung across a Chinaman's shoulder. He was a day laborer, this Chinaman, dressed in dark blue and gray, drab but for a flash of silver embroidery on his right cuff. He bowed his head, nodded, and gave a quick smile, as if to say, sorry. He had no command of English, Lowell could see. Lowell nodded, unsmiling, and watched the laborer move on.

No doubt he was living in the area around Harrison Avenue, where all too many Oriental laundries and eateries had sprung up. Once or twice, Lowell had passed through the neighborhood. It was clamorous and filthy. The signs on the business fronts were all in Chinese, and the sounds of their speech were so foreign as to be almost bestial. The streets smelled of sandalwood and spice and dark mysterious things Lowell had neither the inclination nor the experience to identify. The neighborhood teemed almost entirely with men. No wives had been permitted entry to the United States. And thus, thankfully, no progeny would be spawned within this republic, no hatching of foreigners who lacked all tradition of freedom or democracy. Lowell looked at Costa, O'Connor, DeGrace and David - the city had enough to contend with already on that front.

Lowell watched the laborer pick his way through the Public Garden at a quick lope, the heavy bag causing his spare frame to list slightly to one side. He headed towards the gate that opened out onto Boylston Street. And there, it seemed to Lowell, and he was not a creature of fancy, that the laborer leapt into the air, and somersaulted in slow motion, his satchel still remaining close to his person in defiance of laws of gravity, and nothing – not even the length of pipe - spilt to the ground. In an instant, the workman landed on his feet on the sidewalk, nimble as a cat. Lowell blinked. The sight was no doubt a trick of light, or perhaps the stress of today's momentous event. Still, he was never more glad of the law, passed just last year, ensuring that no alien Orientals would ever be citizens of this great land. "So very foreign," Lowell said. "Those Asiatics."

"Ain't it the truth" King David said. He lit himself a cigar, and offered the gold pocket case around.

"Thank you, no," Lowell said.

O'Connor pointed toward the waterfront. "The new bride and groom need greeting."

"Perhaps they should speak to their family first," Lowell said. By the lagoon, Mrs. Cabot-Lowell blew her nose, and erupted into a fresh gale of wailing.

"And then we'll all greet the couple as one," DeGrace said.

"Wouldn't have said that last year," King David said.

"The comity among our neighborhoods has been much

furthered," DeGrace said.

"Sounding more like Lowell every day," King David said. "It worries me, pal."

Lowell coughed. "If I may, it seems we found we shared a bedrock of common principals. Ideals. Law."

"And how," King David said. He turned on his heel to watch a girl in a knee-length skirt pass by.

*   *   *

Sam Wu, the laborer with the embroidered cuff, had just returned to his room in the boarding house. In the park, he had passed a wedding, and though not an invited guest, he was now compelled to send a gift: it was bad luck to glimpse a bride on her wedding day and neglect to send proper regards. And in the months he had been in this city, there had been no weddings to celebrate. There were almost no women or children in this neighborhood: just men working, and living alone. It was a neighborhood of men without wives, children, or country.

Most worked at digging roads, or laying train tracks, and knew only sweat and toil. Oh, for a sorcerer of the type Sam Wu had grown up among - who created mountains out of a handful of mud, who needed only to draw a line in the ground to create a river and direct its course. The work of the road crews would be so much easier then. But what sorcery could bring them wives, and undo the invisible cordon that lawyers and officials had wrapped around them tight? That was why Sam Wu was here.

He had a lineage few suspected, but many soon would come to fear. His mother had been the most notorious soul stealer in Shanghai. She had tricked the souls out of many mortals in her day: a one-armed general greedy for a last victory, a beggar child delirious with hunger, a royal concubine ambitious that her only son should live. She had amassed an arsenal of these souls, and such was her power that she could animate at will figures of clay, or paper, or glass. A rival marketeer in souls denounced her, and the emperor had her burned as a witch. Only Sam Wu knew where her stash of souls was hidden, or that there was a stash at all.

He sat down at his table. The left leg was broken, and kept steady with a washrag wrapped around the base. Before him was an atlas of Boston. He turned to the page with the Public Garden. He opened the drawer and took out his materials: a calligraphy brush fashioned from his own baby hair; a pot of black ink that was shaped like a tear drop and was no bigger than his thumbnail; and a sheet of paper that was so fine and sheer, it was like a flat surface of light. He opened the pot, took up the brush, and with a twirl of its slender bamboo handle, filled it with ink. With swift sure brushstrokes, he drew a flock of birds, dozens of them, wings outstretched in flight, and all in pairs. They were as unremarkable as sparrows, but for this: each bird had only one eye and one wing. One bird required another to complement and complete it. The two were thus inseparable, and so represented husband and wife. He had conjured birds this way once before, a snowy night last winter, and since then, he had gained in skill and speed.

Sam Wu laid the drawing over the map. On the fourth finger of his right hand, he wore a heavy gold ring, scored with symbols. He passed the ring over the drawings of the birds. All the while, he breathed gently over the page, and, finally, he rapped the ring sharply against the center of the sheet three times.

*   *   *

At that moment in the Public Garden, the sky resounded with a metal thud, as if the sky had been struck by a huge metal mallet, once, twice, three times. Lowell looked up. From out of nowhere, it seemed, a flock of birds arose, twittering, into the sunlight. They were small and glinted in the light like gold. They rose in pairs towards the sun.

O'Connor scrutinized the sky. "Not a bird I've seen before in this town," he said.

"Dreadfully vulgar," a twittering small voice inside his coat said. O'Connor coughed to cover the sound of her, and executed a circle on his heel, still scanning the horizon. "Cake!" the voice said. "There will be wedding cake, won't there dear?"

Lowell glanced at him. O'Connor coughed again.

"Hey, Coup," King David said. "Never knew you was such a great showman on the sly. My razzamatazz must be rubbing off on you."

"Not my doing, I'm afraid. I wonder if it is the handiwork of our friend Al Costa," DeGrace said. "Such a romantic touch surely belongs to a son of Italy."

Costa shook his head.

O'Connor looked at Lowell, his eyes narrowing, although his smile was still in place. "I'm wondering if the good Mr. President Lowell here arranged a -"

Lowell looked stolidly back. "Arranged a -?"

"No," O'Connor said. "Forget it."

"A gift from the heavens, then," DeGrace said.

"An unknown donor - a generous aviary keeper perhaps," Lowell said. "Adept with some sleight of hand."

"Well, sure is a snazzy touch," King David said.

"Perhaps you'll bear it in mind when you take the plunge yourself, Mr. David," Lowell said.

King David laughed. "Don't count on it, pal."

The music started up: a waltz, Lowell was relieved to hear, with no dubious musical innovation imposed.

O'Connor strolled over to his wife, and reached out a hand to her. Costa regrouped with his, and then DeGrace followed suit. They were outfitted in various degrees of inappropriateness, Lowell thought. Mrs. Costa had insisted on wearing black. Evidently, Mrs. DeGrace had heroically struggled against the Negro love of show and pageantry, so subdued was her dress; but the effort was all too obvious. And Mrs. O'Connor was entirely too fresh and unsullied looking for his liking - she was the wife of a gang leader, after all. Still, their overall mien and deportment could have been considerably more dismaying. Mrs. Lowell, stern and stiff-necked, with a jaw that clicked and a loud toneless voice, came to mind. Lowell crossed his arms. "Mrs. Lowell is occupied with her gardening club today," he announced to no one in particular.

"I never ask a dame to come with me to a wedding," King David said. "They get ideas, and I ain't talking a waltz."

O'Connor tried a smile, but he felt an uneasy twinge at his heart as he glanced up in the sky. The birds were still glinting in the light, twittering, and rising in a mass. It was as if a cloud was passing over the sun. He glanced at the lagoon. Ben and Ellie Owen, hand in hand, were coming up the small rise. His heart lifted, but a foreboding still tugged at him.

"Hey, Bensy-boy," King David called out. He trotted down the rise to meet them, almost spilling down the hill in his haste, as overhead, the last of the mysterious birds disappeared into the vast unanswering sky, with cries that were like a distant screaming.

AFTERWORD

If you enjoyed this book, you might be interested in *Fly By Night*.

FLY BY NIGHT

BY

E.N. MCMAHON

It's 1930s Hollywood, and Nick de Blegny is a vampire on a mission. This town just doesn't get it. Jean Racine, now he really knew how to tell a story. What the movies need is more Phèdre.

So what if the studios are giving Nick the bum's rush? He has his minion; he has his genius - and exploitation movies are crying out for a creative type who knows how to save a buck or three. Who needs actors, when this burg is chockful of stock footage, just waiting to be snapped up and put to good use?

No - the only good thing about actors is their celebrity - and Nicky D, the man who invented celebrity culture back when he was still warm - knows how to turn a pretty profit: by selling extra-special blood to the more discerning vampires.

Everything's coming up roses - so long as he can stay ahead of gangsters - both warm-blooded and vampiric - and keep from being once again rudely interrupted by the local gendarmes...

Meet Nick de Blegny: self-styled genius; acknowledged father of PR; and the greatest physician, adventurer, huckster, and vampire that 17th-century France ever produced. As he'll be the first to tell you.

ABOUT THE AUTHOR

E N McMahon has a Master's degree from the London School of Economics, and a PhD in French literature from Duke University. She has worked as a reporter, television researcher, bagel maker (briefly), and (even more briefly) in encyclopaedia sales. She divides her time between England and America.